THE UNEXPECTED CONNECTION

ALSO BY
CATHERINE GUPTA

THE MANOR SHE LEFT BEHIND

The Unexpected Connection

The chance of a lifetime,
a dream rewritten.

CATHERINE GUPTA

The Unexpected Connection
©2024, Catherine Gupta. All rights reserved.
Published by Quiet Nook, Durham, North Carolina

ISBN 979-8-9886521-2-0 (paperback)
ISBN 979-8-9886521-3-7 (eBook)

The primary setting of this book is a fictional Willowston, North Carolina, and all names, incidents, and dialogue have been invented. When real places, products, and public figures are mentioned in the story, they are used fictionally and without any claim of endorsement or affiliation. Any resemblance between the characters in the novel and real people is strictly a coincidence.

Publication managed by AuthorImprints.com

*To anyone struggling. May you find your
way home to peace, love, and joy.*

· CHAPTER ONE ·

Libby tossed the mail on the counter and made her way over to the tea kettle. At the age of thirty-four, she had settled into a routine closer to that of an eighty-year-old rather than someone in their thirties. But after months of rotating day shifts and night shifts at the hospital, Libby needed her tea, neck warmer, and fuzzy socks first thing when she walked in the door, even if it was the middle of summer in her small town in western New York.

The small house Libby had purchased was her favorite place on earth. Nestled at the far end of a quiet street, the house was barely visible from the road. Tall, vibrant green trees hugged the property, which led Libby's friends to name it "the treehouse." When her parents visited before Libby had bought the property, all her dad could see were liabilities. Tree roots invading the foundation, endless leaves cluttering the roof, and a constant threat to her life with a tree just waiting to land on the house. But all Libby saw was peace, and after years of therapy, she had learned to trust herself over her anxious father.

After Libby finished her tea—lemon ginger with a big spoonful of honey—she pulled out the chair at the counter and started to sort through the mail. For the minimal clothes shopping Libby allowed herself, she always marveled at the countless catalogs that were always in her mailbox. Whatever mailing list she had gotten on was surely wasting their time sending them. Libby shuffled through the pages, laughing at the $500 cardigans promising to be family heirlooms.

At the bottom of the pile, Libby noticed an out-of-place envelope. It was a deep navy with a stylish plaid pattern across the middle and calligraphy-level writing with her address but no return address.

These marketers are really upping their game. Libby pondered as she carefully opened the envelope, not wanting to disturb the elegant exterior. A dozen ideas floated through her mind on how she could re-use the expensive paper.

As soon as she took out the letter inside, equally stylish and expensive, Libby realized this was not a marketing ploy. It was a letter from a fan. More specifically, the son of a fan.

Libby had published her first novel a year ago. It was an expression of love, of a mother-and-daughter bond, inspired by the love Libby had for her mother. It was a charming, cozy-mystery story about a mother and daughter that went away for a girls' weekend in a small lake town, only to end up working together to solve a decades-old cold-case murder. Libby had fallen in love with the characters as she wrote the story, sometimes feeling closer to them than many people in her reality. Writing the book became an escape from her everyday life and challenged her mentally to weave a complex but approachable mystery. To Libby's delight as she scanned the letter, she saw words like "inspired," "brilliant," "blissful," and "charming." A smile spread across her face as she put the letter down to compose herself.

Countless hours spent writing the novel, time often shoved between nursing shifts and social commitments, resulted in a book Libby was ridiculously proud of. Despite the lack of sleep, she had found the moments when she was writing to be a magical experience and oddly therapeutic. After the book was released, the magic of the writing experience faded. The sales barely covered the cost of self-publishing, and some of the comments online were enough to send Libby back to the low self-confidence she had in middle school. Despite the fact there were overwhelmingly more positive comments than negative, those negative comments ran endlessly through her mind: "unimaginative," "wasteful," "pointless." In another life, Libby dreamed of writing as her career. Apparently, this dream was as original as a bikini selfie on a beach in Cancun during spring break.

Libby gently tapped her thumb and pointer finger together, a habit she'd had since childhood, to return her attention back to the present moment rather than the wild rollercoaster her mind always seemed hell-bent on riding. The letter was from the son of, his words, "Libby's most enthusiastic fan, bordering on obsessed." At first, Libby couldn't decide if it was sweet or creepy that the son was writing rather than his mother, but she decided to finish reading the letter before making her decision. Suddenly, Libby threw the letter like a giant bug had landed on it.

This can't be real.

Not only had the sender written a letter on behalf of his mother, but he was pretending to be a major rap artist that had emerged in the past year.

Libby wasn't on any social media, but she also didn't live under a rock. Lake Sterling was in his midtwenties and had released an album that brought him widespread popularity. From what Libby had heard, his songs were decent, but rap had never been her first choice of music genre.

Immediately finding her phone, Libby called her best friend Jane who, unlike Libby, was a big fan of rap music and would obviously agree that this was not real.

After filling Jane in on the letter, Libby was shocked to hear her best friend's typically very rational response be the opposite of what she'd anticipated.

"How do you know it's not real?"

"Seriously? Is this some sort of prank you're a part of? Of course it's not real! The book barely sold, and there's no way a famous rap artist was one of the readers."

"It sounds to me like he wasn't, but his mom was. It's possible, that's all I'm saying. I typically prefer old-school hip-hop, but his stuff is decent. And as a bonus, he's cute. I mean, he's a child at the fresh age of twenty-six, but still."

Jane had a habit of referring to anyone more than a couple of years younger than her as a child. She worked for a big-city law firm that was known for representing up-and-coming businesses, typically run by younger entrepreneurs. Her frustration with her clientele may have contributed to this habit.

"This is absolutely ridiculous. I'm giving up on you and calling Mom."

"Fair enough, but I say you consider his offer."

The offer Jane was referring to was the last line of the letter.

Give me a call on my personal cell if you're interested in hearing my thoughts on your book and a proposal.

Libby looked to her succulents sitting on the counter and said, "You agree this is ridiculous, right?"

Catching the irony of seeking validation from her house plants, Libby dialed her mom's number.

After walking her mom through the letter, a google search of Lake Sterling, and attempting to explain some interesting lyrics one wouldn't typically discuss with their mom, Libby waited in silence for her mom's thoughts.

"I think it's absolutely real. My daughter is the most talented writer on the planet, and why wouldn't a rapper's mother find her to be of utmost perfection?"

"Uh, I think you're exaggerating some of the comments in the letter, but seriously? Jane thinks it could be real too."

"Of course she does, honey. Jane is a very smart woman and often has the same thinking as your mother."

Libby chuckled to herself, replaying the endless times Jane had the exact opposite opinion of her mother but was able to strategically appear otherwise while simultaneously getting her mom to change her side.

"I need to clear my head. Between you and Jane and this letter, I think the world may have fallen off its axis."

"See? What a cute line that is! You should write that down and put it in your next book. How is that coming along?"

"It's no closer to finishing than it was yesterday when you asked. I love you, Mom. Call you tomorrow."

After hanging up, Libby put her head in her hands. If she was honest with herself, she realized that every part of her hoped it was real. Lately her life had become repetitive, lacking more excitement than she wanted to admit. Her days revolved around her nursing schedule, tending to her succulents, and reminiscing about her lost hope of becoming a successful writer. More than anything, she missed the sense of community that seemed to have escaped her present existence. With no interest in social media and her college days well behind her, Libby felt like the world had moved on to a reality she never understood. She was grateful for her relationships with her parents, Jane, and on-again, off-again boyfriend Thomas (currently off-again), but there were times she wanted more.

To distract herself, Libby poured a glass of red wine and put all her energy into an advanced dinner recipe; at least, that's how the cookbook had labeled it. Libby had set herself a goal to try cooking one new recipe a week to build her confidence and love of cooking. Cooking had never come naturally to her, so it required every ounce of her attention, a quality Libby both appreciated and despised.

Ah, apple and goat cheese flatbread. How hard could this possibly be?

Libby had a new sense of confidence as she started prepping the ingredients, most likely attributed to the wine she'd consumed. A few minutes into cutting, Libby found herself putting Lake's latest album on. The emotional depth of the lyrics caught her off guard and the beat was all-consuming, continuously drawing her attention away from cooking. The supposed forty-five-minute recipe took double that time, but by the end of the process, Libby had a very crispy (severely burnt) flatbread and her decision. She would be calling the number in the letter. Worst case, she briefly engages with a creepy yet creative individual. Best case, she gets a story for a lifetime.

*   *   *

The next morning, Libby woke to the familiar sound of birds as they busied themselves outside her window. She'd always enjoyed the variety of bird sounds that accompanied the early morning at the treehouse but had to admit there were a few birds that weren't so much singing as screaming. This morning seemed to be featuring the screamers more than the singers.

Not allowing the shrieking sounds to spoil her mood, Libby went to the bathroom to start her morning ritual. Her skincare and grooming routine varied dramatically from day to day, depending on her job. Thomas, the not-so-much Prince Charming, often commented on her appearance, going as far as to say she had her pretty days and her ugly days, which typically aligned with her nursing schedule and health status. As horrified as Libby was at his offensive commentary initially, she'd become too comfortable and reliant on Thomas for his attention. The strong, bold, and confident woman that existed in her was greatly overshadowed by the insecure, full of self-doubt woman who of course had a louder voice in her head. Libby wished she could take the microphone away from that side of her mind, or at least turn the sound down.

Grateful that her next shift wasn't for two more days, Libby allowed the luxurious face mask to melt into her skin while she took her twenty deep breaths. Four breaths in, she heard a loud knock on the door. Her body tensed at the noise, not appreciating the early-morning interruption. Checking her front door camera, the single ladies' modern, safe way of answering one's door, Libby was surprised to see a delivery man dropping off what looked to be multiple bouquets of flowers. She walked to the door, simultaneously excited and alarmed. When she opened it, she was met with at least a dozen flower arrangements.

Before she knew it, she had slammed the door closed and grabbed her nearest weapon. Of course, she had very little in her home that resembled a weapon, so the umbrella she held tightly made her feel more like Mary Poppins than Wonder Woman.

Libby took a few breaths, trying to remember what her therapist had told her to do when she felt threatened. Her college career had included challenging chemistry courses, a lot of time spent in the library, fun-filled nights out, and the not-so-normal experience of having a stalker. His name was Drew and he had serious issues. Unfortunately for Libby, she had extended too much kindness before recognizing the signs. She shuddered, remembering the countless interactions that sent waves of fear throughout her body. His favorite way to show his affection for Libby was flowers, thus the trigger. Drew had harassed Libby for a full year before he had moved away, having found someone new to harass. He even had the gall to send Libby an email explaining that he had grown tired of her and needed more from a relationship.

A few minutes after the initial shock of seeing the new delivery, Libby felt the wave of safety return to her body, and she went back outside to face the trigger also known as colorful flowers.

Scanning the bouquets, her eyes stopped on the one to her left. It was beautiful like the others, but this one had the exact flowers she had mentioned in a scene of her book. Next to the vase she noticed a card: not your typical white rectangle propped up by a plastic rod, but a shimmering silver envelope with her name written in bold black letters. Libby sat on her porch steps and opened the card.

My mom is as patient as a bunch of toddlers at an ice cream shop. Thought I'd emphasize how much it would mean to us to hear from you and discuss next steps. Also, I finished your book last night and it's not half bad. Not my typical read but thought it was entertaining and I appreciated the humor you infused into the story. If Mom asks, I read it six months ago and thought it was literary gold, the best thing I've ever read and should use it as lyrics for my next album. Look forward to hearing from you.

Libby found herself smiling at the note. This Lake or not-Lake person was quite entertaining. She sent off a text to her mom and Jane with a picture of the card and flowers. Less than ten seconds later, her phone was ringing.

"Why have you not called him yet?" Her mom's tone was surprisingly stern for the early-morning hour.

"Seriously, Mom. I just received the card yesterday. I wanted to put some thought into it. What's the rush?"

"The rush is this poor woman who loved your novel is having to wait to hear if she will ever get a sequel. It's torture; have some compassion. As you know, I can relate to wanting to read more from the world's best author."

Before Libby could respond that the mention of a sequel was nowhere in the letter, she heard her dad's voice.

"Oh Betty, quit encouraging this. Libby is a nurse and should be focused on that career. Authors are a dime a dozen; that's the last thing the world needs more of."

Libby rolled her eyes, hearing her dad's ever-present disapproval for her spending any time on her writing.

"Good morning to you as well, Dad."

Before her dad could continue on his tirade, which almost always ended in asking about her continuing-education requirements for nursing, her mother piped in.

"Now John, Libby is incredibly talented and spreads so much joy with her writing."

"Yeah, keep it as a hobby, like your plant stuff. Now what's the status of those continuing-education requirements?" John replied.

Ah, right on cue.

"Right where they need to be, Dad." Libby responded calmly, instead of giving voice to the sassier thoughts that drifted through her mind.

"Eh," John replied.

Libby heard her father walk away, most likely back to his computer to continue his latest online course on history, religion, or the brain. The man never understood relaxing or the art of entertainment. If you weren't learning or producing anything, you were wasting your time, in the mind of John Autumn.

Libby heard Betty sigh. In an attempt to smooth things over, Betty said, "I'm sorry, dear. Your dad loves you; he just doesn't understand the remarkable impact fiction books can have on one's soul or the concept of joy in life." She shouted the last part, to make sure John could hear it.

She continued in a whisper so quiet, Libby had to turn the volume up and strain to hear.

"Plus, he lost his pickleball game last night to Simpson, and you know how that puts him in a mood."

Libby replied, "It still hurts when he's dismissive of my writing, Mom. Even after all this time. I know he loves me; I just wish he tried to understand me, too. Anyways, could you try not to use speaker phone when we're talking? He's always wanting to illuminate me with his wisdom."

"Of course, dear. You know he's like a panther, creeping up silently before he goes in for the mood kill."

"I heard that," John shouted, from a distance.

Libby smiled, appreciating her mother for her ability to turn a tough interaction into a positive one within a minute.

"I've decided I am going to call this person, just so you know. But I don't want you to get your hopes up. It's most likely not Lake Sterling. Tell the panther I love him."

"Wonderful. If you get a chance, I'd love some of those flowers. The place needs some color to cover up your dad's cranky mood."

"Right here, Betty. I am still right here," John once again shouted.

Libby chuckled and said, "You got it. I'll bring an arrangement over later today. I love you."

"Me more!" her mom shouted, before hanging up the phone.

Her mom had found herself hilarious a few years back when she ended the call by saying she loved Libby more. Since then, it'd become a game to see who could end the call first, saying they loved the other. But if Libby was honest, she often let her mom win, never growing tired of hearing her say how much she loved her and the accompanying giggle followed by a click on her phone.

Having caught a glance of her skincare-mask-covered face in the hallway mirror, Libby made her way back to the bathroom to remove the mask and finish her bathroom routine.

Walking back out to her bedroom, Libby smiled, seeing her phone ringing with a call from Jane. The two had always joked how perfect the timing of their calls could be, like they had intuited the exact moment a phone call would be best received.

"Are you okay?" Jane's voice was filled with concern. Unlike her parents, Jane had known all the details of Drew's stalking and understood why flowers were particularly disturbing.

"I am, thank you for checking. And before you ask, I'm planning on calling this guy today."

"If you want me to be on the line to give you an extra layer of security, I'm more than happy to do that. I've been listening to his music more and have a perfect ear for his voice at this point."

Libby smiled at the protectiveness in Jane's voice.

"I'll be just fine. I listened to his songs and was thinking the same thing. We will know by today if this is coming from Lake or a non-Lake."

"Still cracks me up that he's named after a body of water. I mean, you know I love a waterfront view, but it wouldn't have been my first choice. Of course, I also know you appreciate a waterfront view. I believe you've said lakes are your preference. Based on my search, he's as good a view as any lake might offer . . ."

"Okay, I'm hanging up now. I'll text you later."

Libby shook her head as she put down the phone and changed into her clothes. Settling into light-weight-cream sweater and buttery soft dark denim shorts, Libby outlined her plans for the day. She reveled in her days off that allowed her to calm her nervous system, not waiting for the next patient to code, not getting yelled at by frustrated family members. She had the technical skills and genuinely liked helping people, but the environment of the hospital, combined with the constant human suffering and negative attitude of the majority of patients, families, and management, affected her in ways she didn't see in her colleagues. Some days it felt like she was missing the crucial ingredient in her career as a nurse that would allow her to succeed without draining her soul.

Libby sat at the counter, enjoying her first steaming cup of coffee as she wrote her daily list. *Repot plants, clean front porch, buy groceries, drop off flowers at*

Mom's, and call Lake/non-Lake (TBD). She laughed to herself at the insanity of the last item. Knowing it would be a struggle to focus on her other tasks, Libby decided to call Lake first. As she dialed the number, she felt a pang in her heart telling her this would be important; good or bad was yet to be decided.

CHAPTER TWO

Libby half-expected the number to be disconnected or, at the very least, go directly to voicemail. Instead, after one ring, she heard his voice.

"I really thought it was going to be the mailman that did it." The distinctive sound of Lake Sterling's voice came through the phone.

Libby was stunned into silence. It was him, the famous Lake Sterling, talking to her on the phone. She tapped her thumb and finger together to bring herself back to the moment. An uncomfortable amount of time had passed, but she was at a loss how to respond.

"It is you, right? Libby Autumn? I can't imagine why anyone else with this area code would be calling me."

"Yep," Libby choked out.

"You thought this whole thing was fake, didn't you? I get that a lot when I meet a fan, unexpected. No one ever believes it's me. Of course, a random man dresses up as me in Times Square, runs around naked, and the whole world is convinced it was me. Now back to my thought on the mailman. Was there a point you were going to have him be the killer?"

Libby relaxed, listening to Lake ramble on. The question on her book had eased her nerves.

"I didn't decide who the killer was going to be until I wrote half the book. The mailman was very much in the running, but I decided he was a bit dim for the complexity of the murder."

"Huh. Is that how people typically write these mysteries? Figuring it out as they go?" Lake replied, sounding intensely curious.

"I don't think so. I've seen some very complex outlines, but I found it more fun to let the story form itself."

"Good on you. I like different. Now, the question my mom is desperate to know. Are you writing another book? We assumed it was part of a series."

"I am. Sort of. It's been a bit hard to find the motivation, honestly."

"Are we talking writers block? Or like boredom with writing? One-and-done-type stuff? Or you're too busy with the husband and kids?"

Libby smiled, enjoying the sincerity in Lake's voice as well as the not-so-subtle comment on her relationship status.

"Not exactly. I put a lot of time and love into this book. I had hoped that others would see my passion and fall in love with it and possibly allow me to do this full-time. The reality was, after a year of the book being out, I barely covered my self-publishing costs. My dad thinks I'm wasting my time writing and should stay focused on my career as a nurse. Of course, my soul is depleted every time I finish a shift, so . . ."

Catching herself sharing significantly more than she had meant to, Libby cleared her throat.

"Wow, sorry. That came pouring out. It's in progress," she responded, hoping Lake would forget her awkward rambling.

"Passions are tough. You feel them so deeply and yet no one around you can fully grasp it. When you're doing them, it's like the world finally makes sense. This flow and ease that happens without the painful effort that most things require. I get it. Appreciate your sharing. This is incredibly helpful information and exactly what we were hoping for."

"Sure," Libby said, trying to figure out which part of what she said was the information they were hoping for.

"Alright, so are you available on the 24th to be in Philadelphia? We're hoping to meet with you in person to discuss our proposal."

Libby once again found herself tensing and caught off guard.

"I'm sorry, but what proposal?" she found herself saying, as a million thoughts raced in her mind.

"Best shared in person. So does that date work for you? My assistant Viv will get your travel arrangements set up so you can focus on retaining your soul through your next nursing shifts."

The way he weaved humor and thoughtfulness pulled at Libby's heart.

She checked her calendar quick and replied, "I am. I have the 23rd to 26th off."

"Perfect. Viv will be in touch. You willing to change your life?" Lake spoke the words like he was asking if she wanted a sandwich for lunch.

Libby paused, thinking for a moment. After a breath, she spoke from her heart. "Change used to terrify me, but now, staying stagnant feels a whole lot more terrifying. I guess I'm a bit lost. I just worked so hard for the career and life that I'm living. It's strange to come to the realization that I might have gotten on the wrong path. More detail than you needed?"

"I knew I liked you. Talk soon," Lake said, chuckling.

Before she knew it, the phone had disconnected, and Libby was staring at her device like an alien planet had just made contact.

Libby found herself drifting into a daydream about this future where she was a full-time writer because Lake Sterling's mom had fallen in love with her first novel. Libby's daydreams were vivid, quite like her dreams at night. In a matter of minutes, she had pictured the nook in the waterfront home where she wrote her novels, the numerous book signings where fans told her the impact of her books on their lives, and the pride in her parents' faces knowing their daughter was a success. Libby felt herself smiling, her whole body warming to the enchanted glow of the daydream. Then, as always happened, one seemingly innocent thought transformed her dream into a nightmare. This thought was how Lake's mom would react to her second novel, the sequel to the cozy mystery.

What if the second book is awful? Feels forced and lacking the magic that came from the first?

What if Lake's mom realizes those negative reviews are right? I lack imagination and my writing is a complete waste?

And right on cue, the absolute biggest fear Libby had in life.

What if I sacrifice my future security and independence chasing this dream of being a writer?

It wasn't a novel thought. In fact, from the moment her dad heard she was interested in writing, he had made this point. Independence, stability, hard work, and financial security were paramount to her dad, the opposite of those being the worst fate imaginable for his daughter. Libby remembered the countless lectures growing up, reinforcing this fear-based thought-pattern until at some point it became imprinted on her brain. When she chose her major in college, stability was on the forefront of her mind. Nurses were in demand, and hospitals across the country were looking to hire. Wistfully, Libby wondered what her career may have looked like if fear, aptitude in science, and articles on nursing shortages from her dad weren't the only factors influencing her choice.

Libby glanced up from her seat on her counter and spotted her succulents. Their calming presence stilled her mind and allowed her to slow her breathing.

Thank you. I needed that.

She smiled at the plants as she refocused on her list for the day. There was no use in daydreaming or day-nightmaring. Libby had a glorious day off from work and was determined to embrace every second.

A few hours later, Libby had accomplished a few items on her list and was packing her car with bouquets for her mom and a couple of other places she figured would appreciate them. Of course, she had kept the one bouquet whose design was based on her novel. Fresh flowers had not made many appearances in her home since Drew, but this bouquet looked perfect sitting between her succulents. At the very least, she felt comfort knowing the succulents would keep the flowers in check.

Her list had distracted her enough to stop her mind racing about Lake's upcoming proposal. Unsure of what to say to anyone about the phone call, Libby decided it was best to share the news in person with her mom. She would give a call to Jane later in the evening. They had planned their weekly TV dinner for that night, a tradition that started a decade ago when they no longer lived in the same place. Reality television, combined with a cheeseburger, fries, and a milkshake, plus a strong Wi-Fi signal, allowed the women to trick themselves into feeling like they were right next to each other and many years younger.

Libby's first stop was the local coffee shop, the Bean Scene. The coffee shop had only been open for a year, but it was already a hub of the community. The world felt simpler in the coffee shop. People were kind, laughing and engaged with one another. Libby often wondered if owner Edwin, a retired laboratory scientist with endless energy and enthusiasm for life, was pumping some magical chemical into the air, transforming the mood of every customer.

"Well, what do we have here? Aren't those the most beautiful flowers I've ever seen!" Edwin said, simultaneously pouring an exquisite design into the latte he was working on while engaging with Libby.

The right barista could make each customer feel seen and special while making the caffeinated beverages with precision. Edwin had that ability and then some.

"A friend sent me a bunch of flowers, and I figured these maroon and orange ones would look stunning in this place," Libby said, glancing around at the interior. The coffee shop had an industrial feel with high exposed ceilings and metal countertops. The wooden tables and maroon velvet chairs complemented the design, providing a warm, comforting environment. Libby's favorite part of the coffee shop was the countless plants Edwin had used to fill the space. Succulents and cactuses on each table, a line of plants placed in front of the windows. It was as magical as Libby could imagine a coffee shop to be, and she made it a point to come whenever she could, sometimes reading a book or just taking in the space and watching the endless stream of people. The coffee shop frequently made Libby's list of things to be grateful for when doing her gratitude meditations.

"A friend, huh? I just hope this friend finally takes Thomas out of the running," Edwin said, with an unmistakable twinkle in his eyes.

Libby internally cringed. When your barista knows your on-again, off-again boyfriend is no good, the universe might be sending a clear signal.

Ignoring the comment on Thomas, Libby responded, "Yes, just a friend. Now where would you like them?" Libby had no intention of explaining the true source of the flowers. While Edwin was a world-class barista, he was not the person you should confide in. News from the Bean Scene traveled faster than the internet, and Libby had no intention of releasing this information. While Lake had not explicitly asked her to keep the upcoming meeting or potential proposal a secret, she knew better than to share it with anyone she couldn't trust with a secret. That list of those she could trust was, of course, composed of two people: her mom and Jane. Even her dad had been known to overshare during a pickleball match. Her mom said it was a distraction tactic for the opponent, his tricks necessary to make up for his lack of athletic ability. Luckily, she knew how much her dad avoided talking about the fact that she wrote a book, preferring instead to brag more about her stable nursing career.

After placing the flowers at the checkout counter and getting her complimentary signature soy cappuccino from Edwin, Libby made her way back to the car. If it wasn't for the physical evidence of the remaining bouquets sitting in her backseat, Libby would have started to doubt the conversation with Lake had ever occurred. As she made her way back in the car, she noticed her phone ringing from her bag.

An unknown number appeared, but considering the day she'd had, she felt inclined to answer.

"Hi, this is Libby."

"Ah, the murderous, mysterious lady herself that everyone is telling me about. This is Viv, Lake's magical wizard, or how he insists on referring to me, his assistant."

Libby smiled at the warmness in Viv's voice, while wondering who, other than Lake, was the "everyone" talking about her.

"Hi, Viv. It's a pleasure to hear from you. I would like to emphasize that I do not personally commit any murders," Libby said, smiling.

A loud, boisterous laugh resonated from the phone. "Pleasure is *all* mine. You have no idea how excited Florence was that you gave Lake a call after his fancy letter scheme. She was half sure you'd throw it out, thinking it was a scam."

"Florence?" Libby said, trying to keep up with everything Viv was saying.

"Oh, yes. Lake's mama. You'll love her, or at least you better, because she's in love with your book. Now we've got some work to do. I need to get your travel arrangements organized and I have no idea what you like. Modern or historic? Luxury or cozy? What are we thinking in terms of accommodations?"

Libby had never thought past price and location when it came to booking a hotel. Before she could answer, Viv was on to the next thought.

"And I need to get some restaurant reservations on the books, so what are your dietary restrictions? And ambiance preferences? I know the taste of food is critical, but I must tell you, the setting is just crucial to the experience. Don't you agree?"

Libby sat in her car, unsure of how to respond.

Was this actually happening?

"Libby, have I lost you?" Viv said, with an impressive level of concern in her voice, considering this was their first conversation.

"I'm here. To be honest, Viv, I have no idea how to answer any of your questions except I'm allergic to shellfish."

Another vibrant laugh echoed in her ear.

Great, now she's laughing at me. Maybe I should have said luxury, historic, with a quiet, dimly lit restaurant with oddly friendly and approachable staff.

Libby had always felt uncomfortable traveling in big cities. The pace and crowds felt out of sync with her body, and she always marveled at how others could look so calm in those environments.

"I knew you'd be a hoot. Let me put something together that I think will suit you. I read your book, you know. I gobbled it down in one afternoon, so I have a feel for you now. You trust me?"

"If you read my book, you are one of very few people, and for that I will trust you with anything."

Viv chuckled, and then her tone became serious.

"Don't you worry about that. Once Florence enters your life, magic begins to unfold. I'm where I am today because of that woman and her goofball son. Oh, and I must say, I'm with Lake on the mailman. You really had me convinced he'd done it. Anyways, I must run. I'll get everything sent over to you. Text me your email address and let me handle the rest."

The first thought after getting off the call with Viv was utter shock that Viv was Lake's assistant. Maybe unfairly, Libby had assumed his assistant would be a retired model, of course under thirty years old, with the perfect wardrobe, standoffish tone, and succinct, efficient communication skills. A minute into the call, Libby had painted a picture in her mind of Viv, a habit she'd picked up as a writer, and that picture was the opposite of what she'd assumed.

Look at you, Lake Sterling. Maybe not so predictable after all.

*　*　*

Fifteen minutes later, Libby arrived at her parents' house. Every time Libby pulled into her childhood driveway, various emotions emerged: nostalgia and longing for simpler childhood times, combined with a strong feeling of failure and inadequacy. Libby chuckled to herself, wondering if anyone had ever created a scented candle that evoked such range of emotion. Thankfully, her mom had settled for plain vanilla as the signature candle scent in her home.

Libby spotted her mom gardening out front and gave a wave. Betty made her way over, eyes widening as she took in the beautiful flowers.

"Oh, these arrangements are stunning! Clearly, these did not come from Vera's," Betty said.

Libby's mom and the local flower shop owner, Vera, had a decade-long feud related to the town's winter decorations on the main street. Libby knew she was biased, but Vera's obsession with beach-themed Christmas décor was an odd choice, considering they lived nowhere near a beach.

Ignoring the comment, Libby soaked in the love from her mom's hug and attempted to casually update her on the phone call.

"So, I finally gave the number a call. It was really him, Lake. He wants me to come to Philadelphia on the 24th to meet with him and his mom, Florence, to discuss a proposal. He didn't give me any details, but his lovely assistant, or magical wizard, as she likes to call herself, has booked all my travel arrangements."

Rarely at a loss for words, Libby smiled at the shocked expression on her mom's face.

"You okay there, Mom?" Libby watched as tears started to form in her mom's eyes.

"I'm just so proud of you. My beautiful, talented, writing daughter has captured the attention of a rapper and his mother. I couldn't be prouder."

The bizarre sentence and the quantity of tears coming down her mom's face caused the two to burst into laughter.

"What in the world?" John said, limping as he walked down the stairs of the front porch. No doubt the latest in his endless list of pickleball injuries.

"Oh John, our daughter will be meeting with the rapper and his mother. Her future is so bright!"

The women burst into another fit of giggles as John rolled his eyes and began to unload the bouquets from the car.

"Please leave the pink and orange roses for the library," Libby said, attempting to compose herself.

* * *

After visiting with her parents, Libby made her last stop for the final bouquet. The local library had been a haven for Libby since childhood. The interior was typical for a local library—beige walls, metal racks, and worn carpets—but the people that worked there were exceptional. The current director was Libby's former high school teacher, Miss Willa.

"Well, aren't you a bright spot on this already beautiful day?" Miss Willa said, coming in for a hug.

"Hi, Miss Willa," Libby said, as she attempted a natural hug while holding a large vase of flowers. Miss Willa had a way of making Libby feel loved for simply existing.

"Thought you might enjoy having these flowers in the library."

"Oh my Lord, they are stunning! Not beach-themed, so I assume not from Vera's?" Miss Willa said with a wink. Miss Willa was always Team Betty when it came to the holiday decorations debate.

"The approaching end of the summer always inspires more of these comments from you and Mom," Libby said, smiling widely.

"Never early enough to put a pin in that. I mean truly, when will she give up trying to decorate our Main Street like a tacky beach rental?"

The conversation was interrupted by the not-so-subtle finger tapping of an impatient patron at the front counter.

"I should probably head back before they get their nails stuck in my counter," Miss Willa said, glancing at the patron. "I love these and so appreciate you thinking of us. Your seat is always available if you want to get writing again."

With another hug, Miss Willa took the flowers and walked like a human sloth to the counter.

I love this place, thought Libby. She had written the majority of her first book from the worn chair in the corner by the window. After she'd finished the book, Miss Willa had been one of her biggest fans. Libby couldn't help thinking she let Miss Willa and her loved ones down with the pathetic sales since its release. What started as a joyful activity to distract herself had turned into a chronic feeling of failure and panic about doing it all again. With a final glance at her favorite chair, Libby made her way back home.

*   *   *

That evening, Libby sat anxiously on her couch, surrounded by the cheeseburger, fries, and milkshake, waiting for Jane to pick up the video call. She wasn't nervous to tell Jane about the call with Lake but was starting to fear the unrelenting excitement that was building up inside of her.

Could this proposal lead her to a career in writing?

Could she exist in a world that didn't revolve around rotating day and night nursing shifts?

Could Lake, Florence, and Viv the magical wizard make all her dreams come true?

"Earth to Libby! Come back to me. You have that lost-in-thought face going on again."

"Sorry, sorry. I have some news and it's got my mind racing."

"I can't believe you told your mom first. She told me everything," Jane said, with a fake-disappointed look on her face.

Libby should have known her mom would talk to Jane. Hidden under the excitement and pride she showed Libby at the news was a hesitation about her traveling to Philadelphia to meet with strangers.

"Truly, there are no secrets anymore. Is she worried?"

"It's alright, I talked her down. My favorite part was when she told me she was scared they would take your passport away so you couldn't come home. Of course, I reminded her Philadelphia is still part of the United States, so you'll be okay."

"And I wonder where my anxiety comes from, being raised by those two. Besides months of stalking by Drewy..." The women had added the "y" to make him less scary.

"I assume your mind is nonstop spinning about where this might go?" Jane asked.

"Something like that. Maybe all my dreams will come true, or I'll be the laughingstock of writers everywhere when the prank comes out. I can see the summary of the episode now: 'Cozy-mystery writer thinks rapper will propel her career, only to find he's messing with her because he's rich and bored.'" Libby ended with a sigh.

"Uh, I think we can assume it will end up somewhere between those two scenarios. I've said this a million times and I'm going to tell you again. You are a talented writer, and you could absolutely do this as a career. Just take this one step at a time."

"Thanks, Jane. Now, my next step is eating this elegant dinner and dissecting our brilliant taste in television. I mean seriously, did he think he wouldn't get a drink poured on him when he said he enjoyed cheating on her?!"

CHAPTER THREE

Two nights, Libby. It's packing for two nights in Philadelphia. You can do this.

The pep talk she was giving herself hours before her plane left felt grossly insufficient. Libby was officially in her head. After three night-shifts in a row, Libby was exhausted, frustrated, and incapable of putting an outfit together. Thankfully, Jane answered on the second ring of her video call.

"I have no idea what to wear. What do serious cozy-mystery writers look like?" Libby said, jumping right in.

"Honestly, I would imagine they look like they are always planning a murder in their head. So maybe lots of black, thick-rimmed glasses, and a knife?" Jane was able to get the entire statement out without even a hint of a smile.

"Very funny. You've got to help me. At this point, I might just wear my scrubs," Libby said, panicked.

"Deep breaths. We'll get you in something better than that." Jane's voice was full of confidence and calm, a trait she'd perfected in her stressful line of work.

With Jane's unmatched ability to recall most pieces in Libby's wardrobe, it took twenty minutes to put together stylish outfits that made Libby feel confident and comfortable.

"How do you do that so effortlessly?" Libby sat on her bed, stunned, as she surveyed the perfect outfits.

"I just remember the outfits you smile the most in and then trend toward blues and greens when I can. Brings out those stunning eyes of yours. You got this, my friend. Whatever proposal Lake and Florence have for you, you'll know what to do."

"Seriously, what would I do without you? Thank you," Libby said, feeling better than she had all morning.

*   *   *

The travel to Philadelphia was unlike anything Libby had experienced in her life. A private town car had arrived promptly at Libby's treehouse with a friendly and capable driver. It felt monumental, since she and Jane had always joked how Libby managed to get the world's worst rideshare drivers. At the airport, Libby was shocked to see how different the experience was as a business-class passenger. Shorter check-in lines, access to the business lounge, and the most com-fortable plane ride. It was remarkable what a glass of champagne and legroom could do for the flying experience.

Libby walked off the plane and went immediately to the restroom. She had packed an outfit to change into once she arrived in Philadelphia. The descent was unfortunately equally nerve-racking in business class as anywhere else in the plane, and Libby had sweated through her blouse. After negotiating her body into her new outfit in the confined bathroom stall, she took a few breaths.

I can do this. It's an adventure. Just like in one of my books. Minus the murder. I think. I hope…

Libby made her way out of the terminal and looked around for her driver holding a sign with her name on it, as Viv had promised. To her surprise, Libby spot-ted a short older woman with bright-red hair holding a sign with the name of her main character from her first book. Next to her was an elegant-looking tall woman dressed in a black dress and vibrant scarf, most likely designer.

"Hi, I'm Libby," she said, as she approached nervously.

"What an absolute honor to meet one of my new favorite authors," the elegant woman said, extending her hand.

"It's my pleasure, honestly. You might be my first fan I've met in person that wasn't a family member or friend," Libby responded, with genuine gratitude, shaking her extended hand while simultaneously scolding herself for failing to show an air of confidence.

"So formal, you two. Come on in," the redhead said, pulling Libby in for an aggressive hug.

The elegant woman shook her head. "You're going to scare her, Viv. I'm Florence and this enthusiastic redhead is Lake's assistant, I mean magician, Viv. Now let's get you to the hotel." Florence began walking at a brisk pace to the exit.

"It's 'magical wizard.' Why is it so hard for you and Lake to get that title correct? Weren't the business cards I printed helpful?" Viv asked, keeping pace with Florence.

Libby enjoyed watching the two women talk back and forth. They were clearly close and had developed an ability to banter that was show-worthy.

As the three women made their way to the airport exit, Libby struggled to keep up. She was not used to the pace of city walking.

"Should we find our driver?" Libby said, feeling the need to fill the silence as she jogged to keep up.

Viv glanced back at Libby. "Don't you worry about a thing. I'm multi-talented and will be serving as your transportation. Before being Lake's assistant, I was his driver."

This woman is full of surprises.

When they settled into the large black SUV with Viv at the helm, they fell into a comfortable conversation.

Libby learned that Viv had been working for Lake for five years. His first splurge in lifestyle was to hire a personal driver so he could work on lyrics in the car, apparently a place he could find a flow, free of distractions. Viv had been a random assignment from the car service, but they'd fallen into an immediate friendship. Viv had proven capable well beyond safe transportation, and when Lake needed an assistant, Florence suggested Lake choose her.

"We've been incredibly blessed to have Viv in our lives. She's a part of the family now," Florence said, smiling lovingly at Viv.

"Quit it with the mushy stuff while I'm driving, Florence. I need to focus on embarrassing the crap out of these inadequate young drivers," Viv said, as they weaved smoothly through the traffic.

Libby couldn't believe how the nerves had settled as she sat there with Viv and Florence. Their enthusiasm about her book was obvious, and she felt a sense of pride as they discussed her writing process and character development.

"Now, do you see me more as a murderer or a detective?" Viv said, cutting off yet another driver as she maneuvered the SUV through traffic.

"Definitely a murderer," Libby said, confidently adding, "You've clearly got a wide range of skills and I've already determined that I'd never want to be on your bad side."

"Ah, you're right about that. Luckily, I've decided I already adore you, so there's no need to worry about that. Unless you decide to stop writing, in which case Florence has given me strict instructions to torture you until you change your mind," Viv said, in a serious tone.

Florence chimed in, "No more book discussion until we're with Lake and the others. I want to make sure everyone is together when we get into the details of this proposal."

Libby wondered who the "others" were, but her thoughts were quickly interrupted as Florence continued talking.

"Now tell me about your family, Libby. They must be so proud of you."

"One out of two," Libby responded, providing a brief background on her parents and their conflicting opinions on her writing pursuits.

Florence listened intently as Libby explained. Libby noticed a flash of emotions crossing Florence's face when she talked about her dad's input on her career.

I wonder what that's about.

Florence responded with empathy after Libby finished explaining. "That must be hard. Not getting his support for something you love and clearly have such talent for."

"It is." Libby found herself feeling more emotional than she expected. This had been the dynamic for years, but seeing the compassion in Florence's expression made her feel seen. Validation was a powerful gift humans could give one another.

"Lake has experienced something similar from family members. That was, until the money came pouring in and their attitude shifted," Florence said, with a hint of irritation.

"Losers," Viv added, getting a laugh from Florence.

"She has a beautiful way with words, doesn't she?" Florence joked.

Libby smiled and then asked, "Did you always believe he would succeed in the industry?"

Florence thought for a moment, then responded, "I'm more of an action-oriented person than a believer. Lake expressed his interest and showed talent from a young age, so I did what I could to support him. There are so many talented people in this world, but they don't all get their chance. I put my energy into helping Lake get a chance and let him prove the rest."

Viv chimed in once again, "Our Florence is a fierce, no-nonsense dream-maker, Libby. Don't be fooled by her classy exterior and poor choice in coffee. Once she gets on your side, you'll see the world shifting in your favor."

Florence shook her head, smiling. "Alright, Viv. Let's not overdo it. I do my best for those I care about, but let's not set expectations too high."

Libby found herself tensing. Was that a subtle clue that Florence wasn't going to do much for her writing career? As much as she tried to be casual about this trip and mysterious proposal, her heart felt like it'd fully committed to this being a life-changing experience.

Viv shouted, "Made it!" cutting off Libby's anxious thoughts.

Viv skillfully maneuvered the large SUV into the front of a stunning tan stone building, positioned on the corner of two streets.

"This is beautiful," Libby said, reminding herself to close her gaping jaw. She'd never stayed at such a luxurious hotel before and felt the newfound ease she'd been experiencing during the car ride suddenly fall away as she wondered how badly she would stick out.

I don't belong here.

Interrupting her negative self-talk, Viv added, "Just wait until you see the inside of it. There's a quiet nook in the library that has your name on it. I could picture you writing the sequel while sipping tea and being fanned by a glorious half-naked body builder."

Florence laughed and said, "Please excuse Viv, she's been binging body-building competitions and reading up on ancient Egyptian history."

"Hey, nothing wrong with studying some material to come up with a few naughty daydreams," Viv said.

Libby joined in on the laughter, feeling slightly better. No matter what came of this proposal, she was determined to remember every moment of this experience. At least she'd have some material she could use for a new book. Viv and Florence were character gold, as far as she was concerned.

* * *

The hotel looked like the setting of a high-budget romance film. There was a massive water fountain out front that seemed to cascade the water in an elegant way other fountains could not dream of. Surrounding the water feature was a meticulously maintained garden bed that housed numerous colorful plants.

Despite sitting directly in downtown Philadelphia, the hotel had a charming European flair. Once inside, Libby looked around the glamorous lobby, filled with natural light from massive windows. Her eyes were drawn to tropical-looking flowers in large vases on seemingly every flat surface in the lobby.

Those vases are probably worth more than my treehouse.

The next thing she noticed were the intricate light fixtures hanging from the ceiling and the luxurious furniture that filled the space below. Viv led Libby to the library she had mentioned while Florence remained in the lobby, checking Libby in. Libby had to actively stop herself from shrieking when she saw the library and spotted the nook that inspired the selection of the hotel.

"Based on the look on your face, I'm going to say you're happy with my choice." Viv stood proudly while patting herself on the back.

"Happy doesn't quite describe the level of joy I'm experiencing right now. Thank you so much, Viv." Libby felt tears coming to her eyes.

"It's a pleasure. It was nice to book a place for a woman that wasn't inspired by 'the most Insta-gram-able picture locations,' like most of the women Lake has me booking hotels for. Quite frankly, I still don't know what that even means." Viv rolled her eyes.

"Thank you. Just, thank you so much," Libby said excitedly.

"Don't mention it. Now, we should get back to the lobby. The hotel manager has had eyes for Florence ever since she started coming here for afternoon drinks, and she's terrible at shutting down a flirt," Viv said.

As they approached the lobby, Libby stifled a laugh as she watched the hotel manager attempting to charm Florence.

"Is Mr. Sterling still in the picture?" Libby asked Viv quietly.

A sadness flashed across Viv's face for a moment. Recovering, she replied, "No. He passed away a few years ago. It was sudden and very hard on Florence and the kids. It happened around the same time Lake's career really started taking off. If you ask me, he's never been able to devote the time and energy to grieving that loss. Of course, I couldn't be prouder of the strength and character that boy has. Sometimes that level of depth in a person can only come from tragedy. Crazy how things work, huh?"

"Yeah," Libby responded, simply at a loss for words. Her lack of research on Lake and his background was beginning to feel ignorant rather than respectful.

Viv gave Libby a puzzled look.

"You really don't know much about Lake or the family, do you?"

"I'm sorry. I should have known that," Libby said.

"Two things, Libs. One, never apologize for things that don't need an apology. And two, you're a breath of fresh air. Most people feel like they know everything about Lake because they can read some posts on social media and gossip columns. Your job isn't to research Lake. It's to write another incredible book so our Florence can experience that joy of reading your writing again," Viv said, with a serious expression.

Libby appreciated Viv's kindness, but the ever-present anxiety about whether her next book would be good enough crept in. "Stalking Lake on social media seems a lot easier than writing, in this moment. I don't want to let Florence or any of my loved ones down."

"It'll come. I'm no writer myself, but I imagine it can't flow all the time. You just get your butt in that nook and watch the words appear. Along with a yummy drink—these waiters are attentive here. Now come on, let's get Florence before that hotel manager starts flexing his biceps."

"That cannot be a thing," Libby said, as she jogged to keep up with Viv's quick pace.

"Don't doubt the draw of that woman. Happened last week at the Ritz. Don't tell any of these guys, but she's more into legs than arms, and that guy has the legs of a chicken."

Libby shook her head as she watched Viv guide Florence away from the manager. She'd never thought about it before, but was she more of an arms or legs girl? Something to discuss with Jane the next time they talked.

"Legs or arms, Libby?" Florence said, as they walked away from the check-in counter.

Can this woman read my thoughts?

"Uh, I honestly have no idea. I like all the limbs, I guess." Libby couldn't believe the words leaving her mouth.

Viv laughed, clearly enjoying observing the awkward exchange.

"Do you have a boyfriend with notable legs or arms?" Florence said, keeping a neutral expression on her face.

"Smooth transition, Flor," Viv said, as she scanned her phone.

"I don't. I used to, but we're off right now," Libby said, unsure of how much to explain about her history with Thomas.

"Ah, on-again, off-again relationships. Not that you're asking for my opinion, but relationships shouldn't be like light switches," Florence said.

"Preach," Viv chimed in again.

"It doesn't feel right, but the comfort of someone who knows you is hard to close the door on," Libby admitted, wondering how these women managed to get her to reveal so much about herself.

"I understand that. You'll find your way. Something to ponder, I guess. Legs, arms, and light switches," Florence said, with a perfectly executed wink.

Libby smiled politely while wondering if she'd find her way out of the relationship cycle she'd gotten into with Thomas.

Florence continued on, "Now, why don't you get settled into your room and I'll swing by to pick you up for dinner at seven, yes?"

"Oh sure. That'd be great. Thank you. I hope you don't feel the need to take me to dinner. I can just grab something in the room." Libby felt like she went from talking to a lifelong friend to an intimidating stranger in a matter of milliseconds.

"There is no sense of need. You know you're a delight to be around, yes? And ever since I read your book, I've felt like we could be friends. At least give me a chance to win you over," Florence responded.

Libby wondered what alternate universe she had landed in where Florence was hoping to win Libby over. The hope of the proposal came roaring back to life.

"I'd love that. It's about time I had another friend. Adding you would double my number," Libby replied.

"Quality over quantity. I too am a member of that club. See you in a couple hours." Florence leaned in for a hug.

"Absolutely." Libby felt giddy with excitement as she made her way up to her room. Nothing quite compared to feeling a genuine connection with another human being and the promise of a better future.

*   *   *

Once her hotel door closed, Libby immediately dialed Jane. It took half a ring before her friend picked up.

"Tell me everything," Jane said right away.

Libby felt a wave of gratitude, hearing her friend's voice. She told her all about the travel and conversation with Florence and Viv.

"So, you still don't know a thing about the proposal?" Jane asked.

"Nothing. When Viv hinted at talking about my book, Florence shut it down, saying Lake and the others wanted to be there. I have no idea who the others are or if that's a good or bad sign. What do you think?" Libby always appreciated her friend's insight.

"I think my best friend sounds happy and, in this moment, that's what she should focus on. I truly think everything else will sort itself out. And when it does, you call me immediately," Jane said, emphasizing "immediately."

"I will, I will. The meeting is tomorrow at 10 a.m., so I promise I'll call you. You think maybe you could show up as my representation, so I have your support?" Libby said half-jokingly, half-seriously.

"This isn't an interrogation, it's a business proposal about something you love to do. You got this," Jane replied with confidence.

"I'm terrified, Jane. What if I can't do it?" Libby asked.

"We're talking about you writing the next book now, right?"

"You really are quality over quantity," Libby said, grateful her friend was so in-tune with her fears and dreams.

"Uh, thanks?" Jane said, confused.

Libby smiled and went on, "Yes, that's my fear. I mean, I'd be disappointed if this whole proposal turns out to be nothing, but more than anything, I'm terrified I need to write my next book and it's going to suck."

"Girl, do you remember what I said when you first told me you were going to write a mystery novel?" Jane said, in her signature business tone.

"You said you'd always be honest with me." Libby could remember exactly where the two of them were when they talked about it. Jane had flown to visit Libby at home and they were taking a walk in her neighborhood.

Jane went on, "Before you sent me the first few chapters of that book, I had thought through how I was going to tell you kindly that this might not be the path for you at this moment. I literally had points written down on how I could communicate it in a kind but factual manner. Then I had a list of resources where you could take beginner-level writing courses for adults."

"That sounds like you," Libby said.

"Always prepare, yes of course. But I didn't need even one of those points, because from the moment I read it, I knew it would work. The story flowed, the characters were relatable, and most importantly, I felt something. Your writing makes me smile, and when I finished the first draft of your whole book, I felt comforted and better about the world. You can do this, and I will be here to remind you as many times as you need it," Jane said.

Libby felt tears coming to her eyes as her friend's kind words soaked in.

"Thank you," was all Libby could say.

Jane went on, "Always. Remember, your mom bought my friendship when she got me that bracelet ten years ago, so I'm in it for the long haul."

The girls had gone to the mall with Betty and joked about Jane needing to be compensated for being such a good friend to Libby. Two minutes later, Betty bought Jane a bracelet she'd seen her eyeing and said it was payment for the past and future of their friendship.

"Do you even still have that bracelet?" Libby hadn't thought of that bracelet in years.

"Not sure, my closet is an absolute mess, but the deal is still on. Now go get yourself cleaned up and ready for this fantastic dinner. You think Lake will be there?" Jane said.

"No idea, but I promise I will let you know. Thanks for the pep talk. I'll have to tell Mom you deserve a new bracelet," Libby joked.

"Not necessary. Love you, my talented and capable-of-writing-an-incredible-sequel best friend," Jane said, before hanging up.

The next morning, Libby walked into the hotel breakfast area with a spring in her step. She was still giddy from dinner the night before. It had just been her and Florence that evening, and the conversation was delightful. They had discussed their life's passions and laughed their way through the meal. It was the perfect combination of fun and meaningful conversation that Libby so rarely could achieve with someone new.

I'm on my way to friendship with a famous rapper's mother, and it's only Wednesday.

Interrupting her thoughts, a waiter appeared from nowhere. "Good morning, Miss Libby. We have your table right over here. I'll get started on your soy cappuccino right away."

"Oh. Yeah, that'd be lovely," she said out loud, while simultaneously thinking, *dear sir, how did you know my name and favorite coffee order, and did you walk through that wall?*

One of her three questions was answered as she watched another server emerge through a hidden doorway on the side wall. Taking in the space around her, she felt like she had fallen into a secret garden. Wrapping vines were visible from every window, and each table was strategically placed to provide privacy and outdoor views. The tables had simple rose flower arrangements in bursting shades of pink and red.

The waiter returned with her cappuccino and Libby found herself saying, "I don't know if I could be any happier."

The waiter smiled politely as he walked her through the menu options.

After indulging in the world's best mushroom and cheese omelet, so many mouthwatering miniature croissants that she lost count, and another soy cappuccino, Libby felt full and content. The waiter and she had bonded over their love of plants, and he had shared his favorite plant store in the city. Libby hoped to stop by in the afternoon. Viv had kindly booked her another night at the hotel, even though the meeting would be over by 11 a.m.

As she made her way up to her room to freshen up, the nerves started creeping back in. The hotel was exquisite and had a way of soothing your senses, but as the meeting drew closer, Libby felt her whole body tensing. After finishing her final touches on her makeup and packing her bag, Libby focused on calming her mind, practicing the breathing techniques she'd learned in her yoga class. She did multiple rounds of box breath. Breathe in for four counts, pause for four counts, breathe out for four counts, and pause for four counts. She stretched her body and stood in her power pose, hands on hips, spine drawing tall, feet rooted.

I can do this.

With as much confidence and ease as she could muster, Libby grabbed her bag and made her way downstairs to meet Viv. Viv had insisted on driving her to the meeting. Libby sensed that Viv understood the gravity of this meeting for her, and appreciated how much she was looking out for her, despite the fact they had just met.

The first words out of Viv's mouth, however, did not help.

"Well, don't you look like the perfect combination of professional and comfortable."

"Oh God. You make me sound like an office chair. Should I not have worn these flats? My feet and heels don't get along but—" Libby said, looking down at her feet.

Cutting her off, Viv laughed and guided Libby outside. "Not at all. The shoes are perfect. My compliments don't always hit right, but you look good. You're going to be okay, you know. Florence adores you and I might just have a sense that this 'proposal' is going to make you happy."

"You know what it is, don't you?" Libby said, getting impatient.

"I do. And no, I won't tell you what it is, but you'll be happy. I'm pretty sure... Won't know till we get you there!" Florence said, opening the passenger door for Libby.

"Okaaaay," Libby said, settling into the car, buckling up, and preparing for Viv's aggressive driving style.

Viv got into the car and smiled as she observed Libby gripping the door with one hand and center console with the other.

"Don't worry, sweet thing, I'm going to drive calmer today. I did my morning lovingkindness meditation. For now, I see my fellow humans as good and worthy of love."

Libby stifled a laugh as Viv started yelling at the slow pace of the car in front of them.

"You sure you're doing that lovingkindness meditation right?" Libby said, as seriously as she could muster.

"Alright, alright. You caught me. Maybe I fell asleep during the morning meditation, but I was really hoping it would still soak in," Viv said, watching Libby smiling out the corner of her eye.

"I like you, kid."

"I like you too, Viv, the magical wizard," Libby said, feeling gratitude for life bringing them together, even if just briefly.

* * *

Viv helped keep Libby's nerves at bay as she had her laughing all the way up the elevator to the conference room.

"So you're telling me that Florence chose her three children's names because a New Orleans psychic said only water-related names would bring her grandchildren one day?" Libby asked, as the elevator doors opened.

"Yep. It was that and deliver them via water births, which she drew the line at. She also likes to be called Aquababe when she's feeling down," Viv added, as they left the elevator.

"You did not." The sound of Florence's voice surprised both Libby and Viv.

"Oops. Caught again. That's my cue. Good luck, Authorbabe! Aquababe will take good care of you." Viv winked and practically skipped back to the elevator.

Libby laughed and turned to speak with Florence. "I must say, I'm surprised we never got to your other children's names during our dinner last night."

"Ah, yes. That felt like second-dinner conversation. I'm one of those modern moms. Trying to show off my non-mom side before launching into fifty stories about my children," Florence said, with another flawless wink.

I wonder if she took a winking course. The execution of those eyelids is next level.

Libby's wink analysis was interrupted by Florence. "Now, Lake said he's running a bit behind with traffic, which translates to he's in a zone with lyrics and wants to finish up. But my other two children, Ocean and River, should be up in a moment."

Libby stopped walking as her mind attempted to reboot from the shock of those names. Naming one child Lake was bold, but she didn't think she could keep her composure when being introduced to Ocean and River.

Florence stopped walking and looked back at Libby's face, grinning widely.

"Kidding, dear. I see you don't know the actual names of my other two yet. Truly, you and your lack of researching my family is refreshing. Right in here." Florence led Libby into the last conference room in the hallway.

Libby walked into the light-filled room and found her eyes widening. The view of Philadelphia was astonishing from the forty-sixth floor. Despite not being a city-loving woman, she appreciated the view from high up, skyscrapers blending with the sky, cars that looked like toys busily driving through city streets, and countless people confidently navigating to their destinations.

"Beautiful, isn't it?" Florence, too, stared out at the view.

"It is. Almost makes me feel calm," Libby said, as she stared at the large conference table, trying to decipher the best seat to sit in.

Florence turned back to Libby. "Come, sit right here. If I didn't feel like I was starting to know you, I would have guessed you had some nerves meeting my famous son. But I'm guessing it has more to do with the proposal building up a bit in your mind?"

"A bit. I might have written a mystery, but I don't embrace mystery in my own life quite as enthusiastically," Libby responded, trying to calm herself by tapping her finger and thumb together.

Florence chuckled. "Makes sense."

A soft knock echoed at the door, and Libby's eyes locked with the tall, handsome man standing in the doorway.

Is it just me or is light radiating off that man?

She had seen enough photos of Lake to know this wasn't him. This man looked slightly older and had similar features, but in contrast to Lake's light hair and eyes, he had dark hair and brown eyes that reminded Libby of freshly brewed coffee.

After a few moments of locked eyes, Florence spoke. "You'll need to introduce yourself, darling. It appears Libby here is the only remaining woman in her generation to not have social media or know every written detail on our family."

He walked into the room with a quiet presence, leaving Libby breathless.

Outstretching his hand and waking Libby out of her stupor, he said, "I'm Wade. It's a pleasure to meet one of my mom's favorite authors."

"As in, you wade through water?" Libby said, immediately regretting the comment as soon as it left her lips.

Florence laughed loudly, bringing her hand to her mouth to soften the sound.

"Viv may have shared the family secret on our water-themed children's names," Florence finally said, once the laugh had settled.

Wade smiled widely, causing a new, wonderfully intense sensation to erupt throughout Libby's body.

"Ah, yes. I often think about the psychic who sealed the fate of me and my siblings. Thankfully, Mom saved the most creative of the names for our talented artist."

"I love the name Wade. It suits you," Libby said, falling into the wonder of his brown eyes once again.

Interrupting their moment, a squeal came from the conference room door.

"It's her! Really her! Oh, Libby, I'm so excited to meet you!" The new woman at the door shook from excitement as she leapt into the room. Her clothes complemented her bright demeanor in vivid shades of orange, blue, and green. Her hair was cut to shoulder length and had orange highlights that were bold and stylish.

"I'm Brooke, and after Mom, I'm your second biggest fan."

Brooke immediately launched into questions about the book. Brooke's energy was so endearing that Libby forgot about the intensity of the draw she had to Wade's eyes and the nerves about the meeting.

After Libby had answered a few of Brooke's questions, Florence chimed in.

"Alright, Brooke. Let's let Libby take a breath before we get started. Lake said he's on his way up."

Libby immediately felt the gaze of Wade's eyes and attempted to casually glance in his direction. The brief moment she allowed herself to watch him, it appeared as if he was deep in thought, like someone trying to decipher where the next piece of a puzzle went.

Was it possible he felt us vibing?

Since when do I use the word vibing?

Concentrate, this is your future writing career.

Libby silently scolded herself for losing focus. She smiled, took a breath, and looked over at Florence.

Florence smiled at Libby with a knowing expression.

Oh God. What is that woman thinking?

Breaking her train of thought, Libby watched as Lake appeared in the doorway.

"And here I am. Apologies for the tardiness, but I can't control when my creative brilliance strikes." Lake entered the room with an energy and confidence reserved for those few humans used to thousands of fans screaming their names.

Like synchronized swimmers, Brooke and Wade rolled their eyes and waved casually at their sibling.

"Libby, I'm so glad we can finally meet in person. I really enjoyed talking with you the other day. You match exactly the picture I had in my head." Lake shook Libby's hand and took a seat between his siblings. Libby noticed how Wade's expression had changed slightly when Lake spoke.

Libby smiled and found herself once again speaking and immediately regretting the comment.

"I appreciate it. I think. Although, Viv told me I looked like an office chair earlier, so I'm hoping that's not coming through."

Lake and Brooke laughed, very similar to their mother's laugh, as Libby's eyes drifted toward Wade. His expression remained focused, watching Libby with a continued sense of curiosity.

"Nah, more like contemporary dining chair than office chair," Lake said with a wink.

Another perfect wink. The whole family must have taken the class.

Watching Lake and Wade seated next to each other, it was obvious the brothers brought the opposite energy, with Lake filling the space, while Wade was a strong, calming presence. Libby had to focus on anyone in the room but Wade, to keep herself breathing normally.

Just wait until I tell Jane about this.

The meeting hadn't officially started and Libby had a million things she wanted to tell her friend.

"Well, let's get started," Florence said, once again bringing Libby's attention back to the matter at hand rather than sneaking looks at the freshly-brewed-coffee eyes of Wade.

"Now Libby, as you know, I loved your first book and would love to read a million more of them. So, we have a way we may be able to encourage that while also furthering a mission dear to our hearts."

Here we go.

Lake took over and confidently explained the proposal. "We are starting a Badass Lake-ified Library and want you to be a pivotal part of its vision."

"We aren't calling it that," Wade with the beautiful coffee eyes interrupted.

"Yeah, yeah, Wadester. We're still having some creative differences on what to call it."

Libby smiled at the playful back-and-forth between the brothers. She'd always wondered what it would be like to have a sibling, and watching their dynamic brought that longing to the surface.

"Let me take it from here before this ends in a wrestling match between you two," Florence said, playfully glaring at her sons.

"Now Libby, we are in the process of upgrading a library and expanding its offerings. We're hoping it will play a central role in the community."

Brooke stood up out of her chair, enthusiastically adding, "It's going to be amazing, Libby. It's going to be a stunning building with books, computers, huge rooms for community activities, and a café like no other, thanks to my brother here," she said, and squeezed Wade's arm.

Libby tabled the mystery of Wade and focused on where she fit into this vision. "Oh wow. That sounds like a great thing for the community, but I don't understand where I come in—and my writing, of course," Libby said shyly, still trying to get used to thinking of herself as a serious author.

Of all the potential proposal ideas Libby had come up with in her mind, this was not one of them. She had a strong desire for community and was a strong proponent of libraries, but she had no idea where the dots were going to connect back to her next book.

"You are going to be one of our literary inspiration models," Lake said, like he was talking about something as basic as the grass being green.

Libby couldn't help the self-deprecating scoff that came out of her.

"I have never associated myself with any of those words," Libby replied.

Lake laughed and continued on. "Don't worry, young bird, Lake's got you. I'll get you fully into yourself before you know it."

Matching eyerolls came from the siblings once again.

Libby waited for the cameras to burst into the room, telling her she'd been punked. But outside of the eye rolling, the rest of the family's expression remained serious.

"Uh, thank you. I agree confidence is not in my top one hundred traits, but what exactly does a literary inspiration model do?" Libby felt even more lost than before the meeting.

"My turn," Wade said, drawing all of Libby's attention to the man. The rest of the room fell away as she watched him. Lake may be the celebrity, but Wade commanded her attention in a way Libby never thought possible in the real world.

"Ignore the terminology my brother is using. Quite frankly, none of us knows what that means. Our mission is simple: create a place for the community to turn to that builds pride, strength, and genuine connection for the town while providing the setting for you to write your next book. Once that's complete, the best new literary agent will take it from there." Wade pointed to Florence.

Despite her shock, Libby was able to ask, "You're a literary agent?"

"I'm on the path. After my husband Noah passed, I started taking classes in journalism, business, and of course, literature. I interviewed a hundred different authors to try to understand if there are any themes on what creates success. I'd always thought about a career as a literary agent, but my grief propelled me to fight for it. I've educated myself, built a strong network, and now, thanks to you and a couple of others, found some clients I'm excited about. You wrote an incredible mystery book as a side gig on top of a demanding career as a nurse. I see such promise and passion in your writing. I want to propel your writing career, if you'll have me." Florence continued watching Libby's expression closely.

"We would ask that you devote a portion of your time to the library," Florence continued, "and the rest to writing your next novel."

"What exactly would my responsibilities be? As a literary inspiration model for the library?" Libby cringed as she said the last sentence.

"Dress in fashionable attire and walk around reciting your superior capabilities as a human," Lake said, managing to keep a neutral expression.

"Lake, seriously?" Brooke said, playfully hitting her brother.

"What he means to say is outlined in our proposal." Florence pulled a folder out of her bag and walked it over to Libby. She turned to the second page and pointed out the core responsibilities.

With her type A personality, Libby felt relieved seeing the well-written list of responsibilities outlined on the paper. Her eyes focused on one of the core responsibilities for her role within the library.

Develop a workshop specific to the mystery genre

"Oh thank goodness. I don't need to know the Dewey decimal system," Libby said out loud, as her shoulders visibly relaxed.

"No, no knowledge of Dewey decimal system required," Florence confirmed with a chuckle.

"I still don't completely understand why you want me to work in the library. I imagine there are a thousand librarians that are better suited to execute the vision you have," Libby said.

Florence smiled. "You'll be working with a group of highly experienced librarians, so don't worry about that. When I was studying in my courses and talking with countless authors, I learned the power of creative space and setting. I wanted to not only provide dedicated time for you to work on your book but also a setting that's inspiring and new. Working on the creation of this new library is very important to our family and we think it could play a pivotal role in bringing the community together, something that is really needed right now. I thought, why not combine these two passion projects? Plus, I think you and the other authors will be a huge inspiration for the community, thus the 'literary inspiration models' terminology my creative son termed."

"Other authors?" Libby asked nervously, wondering if this was a reality TV-show competition.

Like she could read Libby's mind, Florence responded, "Don't worry. This isn't a competition. They are in completely different genres."

"Okay. I'm sorry if I missed it, but where exactly is this library?" Libby asked, silently hoping it wasn't in the middle of a major city.

"The charming town of Willowston!" Brooke said enthusiastically.

"Is this where you all grew up?" Libby asked.

"You don't know my hometown?! Track 2, in my second album? Track 4 and 6 from my third? The references are everywhere." The shock emanating from Lake was palpable.

Libby cringed. "I'm not the most informed on your music. But I have a friend that likes your stuff."

A charming chuckle came from Wade, who was clearly enjoying the moment, while Brooke was laughing so hard, she almost fell out of her chair.

"Rap isn't my typical genre," Libby added.

"Unbelievable. My music is more than a genre. It's a movement," Lake said as he stood, passionately reciting the words.

Brooke spoke up through a giggle.

"I think your enormous ego is starting to show. Libby, you are perfect just the way you are," Brooke said, still attempting to regain her composure.

"Appreciate that. You are incredibly validating, Brooke. So, what exactly is the connection to Willowston and where would that be on a map?" Libby's knowledge of geography was dismal.

Florence spoke as a mix of heavy emotions built in her eyes. "It's where my late husband Noah grew up before he relocated to Pennsylvania. When the kids themselves were growing up, we used to take them there a lot. It's a small town in North Carolina near the mountains. I think you're going to love it," Florence said.

"Eh, might be selling that a bit hard, Mom. I don't want you to get your hopes up too high, Libs. It's not brimming with energy like Philadelphia or New York," Lake said, drawing his arms high above his head like he was in the middle of one of his shows.

Libby watched as Wade's features seemed to tense and Brooke lightly patted his arm.

Pulling herself back to the conversation, Libby replied, "Oh, that's okay. Big cities haven't really been my happy place."

A small smile slipped through Wade's serious expression, throwing Libby off focus once again. Taking a breath, she started again.

"I've heard a lot about western North Carolina. It's supposed to be beautiful. Is it like Asheville?"

"Oh absolutely. If you take away all the restaurants, personality, and activities, it's practically the same," Lake said, inviting a stern stare from his mother.

"Well, are there lots of trees?" Libby asked.

The moment she asked the question, Lake got quiet and seemed like his mind went elsewhere.

Maybe he just thought of some new lyrics?

Brooke was the first to respond. "Oh, so many! The new library practically sits in a forest."

Libby noticed Florence and Wade wearing a similar confused expression, while Lake still seemed lost in thought.

"I enjoy them. My friends joke that I live in a treehouse right now. I just vibe with trees," Libby added, trying to explain herself.

Again with the vibe?

Florence spoke up, putting Libby out of her misery. "I truly think you'll find happiness in the town for the months you're there."

"How long is that?" Libby asked, trying to check off all the questions popping into her mind.

"It's all outlined on our proposal, but we were hoping for an eight-month commitment from you. The library is still under construction but should be open in a matter of months. How about you take some time to review the proposal and we'll connect this evening?" Florence said.

"That sounds great, Florence. Thank you. All of you," Libby said.

Especially you, you coffee-eyed god, Libby thought as she glanced back in Wade's direction.

Lake had finally come out of his silence and added, "Libs, you've got talent. And from what we discussed, it sounds like nursing isn't inspiring your flow state. So I really hope you accept our offer. If the numbers aren't right, we can be flexible," Lake said, leaning back in his chair like he owned the place.

Libby smiled, thinking how no one other than Lake could get away with saying "flow state" in normal conversation.

"Well, let's give Libby some time to think this over. Viv will be downstairs waiting to drive you back to the hotel." Turning to stare at Lake, Florence added, "Our next author is in thirty minutes, so make sure you all get back here on time."

Libby gathered her things and made her way out of the room. She felt shell shocked as the full weight of the proposal began to register.

Brooke pulled her from her thoughts as she came in for a tight hug right outside the conference room.

"I'm seriously so glad we got to meet. Please, please, please accept the offer," Brooke said, reminding Libby more of a sweet toddler than a woman that appeared to be in her twenties.

"Let her breathe, Brooke!" Lake playfully pushed Brooke aside and gave Libby another handshake.

"Give me a call if you want to talk any of it through." With that, Lake took his energetic self down the hallway.

Libby looked over and saw Wade and Florence deep in discussion back in the room. For a moment, Wade looked at Libby and gave her a subtle but powerful nod.

He was the most unexpected part of that meeting, and that's saying something.

CHAPTER FIVE

"How'd you like that proposal, Libs?" Viv leaned casually against the wall in the lobby, grinning widely.

"It was a lot." Libby was squeezing the proposal folder to her chest.

Viv studied Libby for a moment and pressed on.

"What'd you think of the water-named family members? Anything unusual?"

Libby gathered it was entertaining for Viv to hear about how people reacted to meeting celebrities for the first time.

"Well, Lake radiates energy and knows how to fill space in a room, Brooke may be sunshine personified, and Wade..." Libby found her mind drifting to the look he gave her as she'd left the room.

Viv chuckled and guided Libby back to the front entrance of the building.

"Wade, huh? Guess I should have seen that coming," Viv said, as they walked out the tall glass door.

"Seen what coming? I was just simply trying to find the right word for him."

"Maybe tall, dark, and delicious?" Viv ventured, watching Libby's face turn beet red.

"Don't you want to ask me more about the proposal?" Libby attempted to change the subject, praying her face would return to its normal shade of not-red.

"Yes, yes. Of course. Whatever will you do?" Viv exclaimed, dramatically throwing her arms in the air.

Without giving Libby an opportunity to respond, she continued, "Come on, let's get you back to the hotel so you can pretend to make a decision."

Humph. Little does she know I'll be writing a detailed pro–con list when I get back to the hotel.

* * *

A few hours later, Libby's pro–con list had a dozen positives and only three cons.

Tell Dad.

Have to leave my treehouse and plants.

Figure out how to not damage my nursing career by taking the time off.

Libby was jolted out of her staring contest with the list when her phone rang.

"I waited patiently, but 3 p.m. was my limit." Jane's tone was almost serious.

"It's 3 p.m.? I've officially lost track of time." As if on cue, Libby's stomach rumbled nosily.

"Pro–con list?" Jane knew Libby so well.

"If you can call it that. This may be the clearest decision I've ever made. Other than choosing a college outside of my hometown," Libby said, reaching for the room service menu. "I'm starved. Mind if I order lunch and call you back?" Libby scanned the menu.

"Um, who are you and what have you done with my best friend? You're acting casual about this whole thing and choosing your lunch instead of freaking out and telling me every detail?" Jane sounded concerned.

"I don't know what to tell you. I feel good about this. Call you in a minute." Libby laughed, imagining the shocked expression on her best friend's face.

It wasn't that she was taking the decision lightly. But after looking through the proposal and staring at her pathetic excuse for a pro–con list, she knew what to do. Libby would be working at a library, writing the next book in her mystery series, and moving to a town called Willowston.

Let the adventure begin.

*   *   *

By the evening, Libby had updated Jane and her parents and was getting ready to meet Florence downstairs to officially accept the proposal. Only with Jane did Libby share the details of her surprise connection with Wade. To her credit, Jane remained focused on hearing about the proposal and didn't harp on the details of Wade for too long. She did, however, google Wade while they were talking and confirmed he was gorgeous and a chef. Libby told Jane she didn't want to know anything else about Wade or any other family member that an online search could find.

Although her mom and Jane had been enthusiastic and encouraging of her decision to agree to the proposal, her dad was not. He'd already sent a dozen emails with articles, blogs, and podcasts warning her about how difficult it was to make it as a writer and how imperative nurses are in the country. If she weren't so annoyed with him, she would have given him credit for his persistence and ability to find so much evidence that she was about to make a "massive life error."

Her phone pinged with a message from Jane.

DO NOT SECOND GUESS YOURSELF. Check your email.

Jane had sent Libby an equal number of articles and blogs making the opposite argument of her father's. Libby found herself laughing loudly as she read through the titles, particularly the last one.

How to Successfully Pivot Your Career.

The Positive Impact of Fictional Writers.

Following Your Intuition More Than Your Parents' Voices.

Her best friend was a treasure, always knowing what Libby needed to hear. Libby picked up her things and headed downstairs to the lobby to find Florence, with a renewed sense of confidence in her decision.

* * *

Florence and Libby settled into two comfortable chairs in the special library room of the hotel. The stacks of books, charming bold patterns, and plush furniture gave the room a magical feeling. Libby wondered if Willowston would have any space like this that she could write in.

"So tell me. What will it be?" Florence asked, her full attention on Libby.

"Well, I would—" Libby had only gotten a few words out before Florence interrupted.

"This is so wonderful! I am thrilled you're accepting!" She was beaming as she threw her arms enthusiastically in the air.

Libby replayed the last few seconds in her head. After Florence finished her celebrating, Libby said, "Uh, did I tell you my decision without knowing it?"

Libby watched as Florence processed what had just happened. "Oh my. I didn't let you tell me your decision, did I? I'm sorry, I just got so excited. I saw your face when you walked into the lobby, and combined with Viv's confidence, I basically assumed what your answer was."

She signaled to the approaching waiter, who was holding a bottle of champagne and some dessert with candles, to hold off a moment, and focused her attention back on Libby.

"Let me try this again. What are you thinking about our proposal?" Florence said, with as serious an expression as she could muster.

Libby cleared her throat. Despite Florence already knowing what she would say, the moment felt important.

"I would be honored to accept your proposal, move to Willowston, and write the next book in my series. After reviewing the documents, I have a list of questions that I'd like to discuss." The sentences came out sounding more formal than she anticipated, but a deep sense of pride radiated through her. Despite her fears and insecurities, she had a real opportunity to make it as a writer.

Florence stood up from her seat and playfully jumped in the air. The image brought such joy to Libby, and it gave her a better understanding of where Brooke's bright personality had emerged from.

Florence sat back down, smoothed her skirt, and readjusted her blouse.

"Let's get to work," she said, waving the waiter back over.

*   *   *

The two had spent the next couple of hours enjoying decadent desserts and sparkling drinks, reviewing the details of the contract, discussing more about the library project, and mapping out next steps. By the time Libby got back to her room, she was exhausted but wired. She knew it was important that she get some sleep, but it felt impossible in that moment. Her life was changing dramatically in the next month in ways that felt unreal.

Florence and Libby had drawn out a preliminary timeline that had Libby moving to Willowston in six weeks. Florence said Viv would be handling the housing for all three writers. Libby learned that the other two writers had accepted on the spot. Nathanial Norris was a fantasy writer from North Dakota and Paige Raine, a romance writer from New York. Like Libby, Nathanial and Paige had written only one book so far. Libby was dying to know more about Nathanial and Paige, but Florence assured her she would have ample opportunity, once she got to Willowston. Florence did say that she sent copies of their books to Libby's house so she could get a better sense of their writing style.

All the details Libby had to sort out before she left were enough to keep her up at night, but the looming deadline for her book is what really shook her. Florence asked that all three authors have a first draft completed in a matter of months. Then they would each work with editors, designers, and marketing to prepare for the release of their book at the end of their contracts. It had taken Libby over a year to write her first book. The rational side of her brain told her that was due to her full-time job and other commitments, but the emotional side of her brain said it was because she was inexperienced and lacked true talent.

Florence had said all the right things when Libby expressed her concerns on the timeline. Florence clearly had a knack for building one's confidence, but it felt like all that positivity went away the moment they separated. Libby knew her confidence as a writer was going to be one of her biggest challenges. It was clear that sleep was going to escape her for the next couple of hours, so she changed out of her pajamas and made her way down to the hotel library.

The room was quiet, illuminated by a soft light coming from the decorative lamps. A surprisingly chipper hotel staff member appeared and asked Libby if she'd like a drink. After ordering an herbal tea and some more of their miniature croissants, Libby settled into the comfortable armchair and took out her journal. She had written her last book on a computer but found her journal to be a useful way to brainstorm or clear her mind through the writing process. Libby loved drawing and found herself sketching various outdoor scenes into her journal to reset. After sketching a picture of a crescent moon over a charming hotel similar to the one she currently sat in, she felt calm enough to begin thinking about her next book.

She started by writing down all the elements from her first book that she loved and wanted to include in the sequel: humor, relatable characters, and of course, a shocking twist to her mystery. Next, she wrote down what she wanted to do differently in the sequel. She wanted the book to stand on its own and not feel like an attempt to recreate the same mystery with new elements. Thanks to her interaction with Wade, Libby also found herself thinking about weaving in some romance to her next book. Libby jotted Paige's name down, thinking she might be able to offer some suggestions.

Hours passed before Libby looked back at the clock. The familiar feeling of time falling away while she wrote, even though she was just making notes and jotting down potential characters, was nostalgic. Exhausted, she packed up her things and made her way back to her room. Sleep no longer escaped her as she melted into the buttery soft sheets and drifted into a deep sleep.

*   *   *

The weeks following the trip to Philadelphia passed quickly. Libby's rotating nursing schedule was more aggressive than usual, giving her little time to think. When she told the scheduling nurse that she was taking the time off to pursue her writing career, she knew she'd be punished. The response from the supervisor was seared in Libby's mind. "How lovely for you to take months off to play writer while we sacrifice our lives to saving others." Libby had just walked away, unsure of how to respond. The next day, her schedule had been updated with the most ridiculous night and day shifts she'd ever had. Jane had wanted Libby to sue and quit immediately, but Libby felt a responsibility to the hospital. Despite the misalignment with her dreams, nursing had provided a stable career, and she wanted to give them as much time as possible to find her replacement.

The evenings Libby could swing it, she spent with her parents. To say Betty was thrilled for Libby's opportunity was an understatement, but Libby could sense her mother's sadness at their being in separate towns for such a long time.

Even her dad had started to come around to the idea. Libby had Jane to thank for the way she skillfully framed the opportunity to her father via strategic resume writing, somehow convincing him she would be an even better nurse after the months spent in Willowston.

*   *   *

Libby's final weekend before moving to Willowston was planned to the hour. Her last shift at the hospital was Thursday night to Friday morning, and Jane was flying in Friday afternoon after Libby had some time to sleep.

At exactly 3:30 p.m., Libby heard her friend knocking on the door. Libby smiled, thinking of all the times her best friend had come to visit, once she bought her beloved treehouse. Libby was going to miss this house but was grateful to the young dentist that had agreed to rent it for the full eight months. She was elated when the woman told her she was as passionate about plants as she was about teeth.

Libby opened the door and burst out laughing.

"What are you wearing?!" she finally managed to say.

Jane stood with a serious expression. "I have no idea what you are referring to."

Between giggles, Libby was able to get out, "I am referring to the murderous outfit you are wearing. Seriously? All black, thick glasses, and where did you even get a knife between here and the airport?"

"What can I say? My best friend is my ultimate inspiration. Fashion, life, and all. It was either this outfit or dress up as an office chair, so I went with this. I will not reveal my knife sources, even if it is Betty who drove me here from the airport." Jane made her way inside, carefully holding the knife that looked ridiculous sticking out of her belt.

"I thought I was going to help you finish your packing this weekend." Jane looked around in disbelief at all the perfectly organized boxes and the meticulously cleaned house.

"Sleep's been a little rough lately. Between my crazy shifts and my mind spinning about this life change, I've had plenty of time to pack up. So maybe instead, we can go get some coffee?"

"Never said no to caffeine in my life," Jane replied, heading back out of the house to Libby's car.

* * *

As they walked into the Bean Scene, Jane leaned to Libby, whispering, "Ever figure out which chemical concoction he's pumping into this air? It's literally impossible to find someone not smiling in this place."

The women laughed as they watched the joyful patrons throughout the coffee shop.

"Ah, our famous author, gracing the doors of my quaint coffee shop. It must be my lucky day," Edwin said, as he poured an intricate flower in the latte he was working on.

"I'm literally here every day, Edwin," Libby said, as a smile spread across her face. She was going to miss his coffee and personality more than she wanted to admit. Luckily, she found Willowston had a coffee shop that she could turn to for the duration. She prayed the coffee was remotely close to the perfection in a mug she got from Edwin.

After enjoying their coffees and attempting to frown for thirty minutes, the women made their way to Libby's parents' house. John insisted on cooking for his "favorite daughter, Jane." It was also his favorite joke.

The dinner conversation remained light, avoiding the topic of Libby's upcoming move. That was, until John brought up his latest source of anxiety.

"Now Libby, are you sure about this writing? I was reviewing your contract, and I just don't see you being able to write the book in the timeframe they're asking. You've always written the way you played soccer, slow and lacking enthusiasm."

Jane choked on her water. Betty playfully threw a dinner roll at John and Libby just stared.

Sensing Libby needing a moment, Betty spoke up. "Oh John. How many times have you read that contract? It's like every time you read it, you have another thing to worry about. I do wish you'd spend as much time practicing your pickleball as nagging our daughter."

Despite decades of marriage and completely different personalities, John and Betty had a loving and playful connection. Libby was always surprised at the comments the two would say to each other that only resulted in the two looking lovingly at one another.

Jane regained her ability to breathe and chimed in, "I agree the timeline looks aggressive, but this is also Florence's first time working with these authors.

I imagine, like what happens with timelines in many fields, these timelines can be massaged to accommodate different paces. And as for soccer, I believe Libby spent most of the time on the bench, so it's hard to say what kind of player she would have been."

"Very helpful, Jane and Mom," Libby said, finding her voice and remembering what techniques her therapist had taught her when triggered by her dad. Thankfully, her dad provided ample opportunity to work on these skills.

"Dad, I know you're nervous. This is a huge change, and it takes time for us to get more comfortable with it. But I believe in myself and trust that Florence knows what she's doing. And no matter what, I'll always have my nursing career to go back to." Libby's heart always sank when she talked about going back to nursing, but she knew validating her dad's feelings and mentioning her nursing career was the magic formula to appeasing his anxieties.

"Humph," John said, returning to his dinner.

Betty tossed another dinner roll at him, and he added, "And we can't wait to read your next book."

Betty nodded proudly. She had clearly coached him through that line a million times, since these conversations always ended the same way.

*　*　*

That evening as Libby was getting ready for bed, Jane knocked on her bedroom door. She was holding a beautifully decorated present with intricate gold and silver ribbons. Jane had the same level of wrapping expertise as an elf.

"What is this?" Libby said, taking the present from her friend.

"Just a little something to keep your spirits up," Jane replied, taking a seat on Libby's bed.

Libby unwrapped the gift and saw a vibrant pink air plant with a business card underneath.

"What is this?" Libby said, seeing her name written on the exquisite business card.

"This, my friend, is your business card—Libby Autumn: *Author of the Award-Winning Series* Surprise Mystery Solvers," Jane said proudly.

"I don't have any awards," Libby responded, confused.

"Well, it's manifesting. You, my friend, have a remarkable future ahead of you as a novelist," Jane replied.

"You seriously believe in me more than I do, and it means the world. I'm nervous about moving, but Florence has made me feel so supported through all this that I know she'll find a way to make it feel like home. Plus, I'm hoping Paige and Nathanial will want to be my friends. They are so talented, it's absurd."

"Slow your roll there. Friends are acceptable, but you better not find anyone that wants to compete for bestie with me," Jane said.

"I promise to not replace you," Libby said, smiling.

"That's what I like to hear. Goodnight, my talented friend. Get some sleep." And with that, Jane headed to her room across the hall.

• CHAPTER SIX •

Saturday came and went in what felt like a single breath. Jane and Libby enjoyed the beautiful end-of-summer day outside, walking to their favorite park, drinking coffee, visiting with Libby's parents on their back porch, and parading Libby around town like it was her final bow of a performance.

Libby had shed more tears than she expected when she said bye to Miss Willa down at the library. Miss Willa was so proud of Libby getting an opportunity to work on her next book, but she was equally excited about her working in the newly renovated library in Willowston. Miss Willa had instilled a love of libraries in Libby and Libby felt a responsibility to contribute to the success of this new library.

* * *

When Libby opened her eyes on Sunday, she felt an excitement that was usually only reserved for Christmas morning. The anticipation of what lay ahead made every cell of her body feel energized, practically pushing her out of bed.

This must be what Lake feels like every moment of every day.

Libby took extra time picking out an outfit she loved, a comfortable, long, flowy maroon dress with delicate white flowers, wanting to feel confident and beautiful as she moved forward with her big adventure. After she finished her makeup and packed up her final items, Libby walked into the kitchen and froze when she saw what awaited her there.

"Look who came to take a road trip with you," Jane said casually, although the higher pitch of her voice cued Libby that she too was freaking out.

As if the whole thing was planned, Lake spoke up equally casually. "So, this is the famous treehouse."

Did I somehow manage to summon him here when I thought of him this morning?

Lake strolled around the house with his usual confidence and energy.

Finally, regaining her senses and concluding that she did not in fact have the ability to transport people via her thoughts, Libby replied, "This is not what I was expecting this morning. A cappuccino, dramatic goodbyes to my loved ones, and a music-filled car ride were on the agenda. The famous Lake Sterling in my treehouse, not so much."

"Oh, I intend on keeping up with that agenda. Of course, I'll oversee the music. It will be heavy on the rap, which I know isn't your 'typical genre,'" Lake emphasizing "typical genre" with air quotes.

Jane laughed from the other side of the kitchen, enjoying the banter.

Libby glanced at the clock, grabbed a few final items from the kitchen, and said, "Well, we better get going, then. Our coffee shop run may take an extra moment with all this," she said, gesturing to Lake's presence.

Libby felt embarrassed as she showed Lake to her car. Her ten-year-old Subaru was a far cry from the black SUVs and stylish coupes Lake was accustomed to.

He took a moment assessing the car and smiled at Libby. "Yep, this is exactly what I would have thought you'd drive. Living in a treehouse filled with plants, driving an old Subaru that's cleaner than 99 percent of other people's vehicles, yep, that fits."

Jane, feeling protective of Libby, chimed in. "Libby is not as predictable as you think. I'd be careful putting her into a box."

Jane and Lake held each other's gaze for a moment, with Lake finally breaking the silence.

"Your friend is a bit feistier than I expected," Lake said, and chuckled as Jane playfully threw a shoe at his head from the basket she was holding.

"Alright, alright. Please don't leave any of my shoes in the driveway," Libby said, waving them into the car.

Thankfully, the car ride was less dramatic. Jane and Lake appeared to have the same ability to transition from mild conflict to friendliness in a matter of seconds. Libby knew her friend had honed this skill between her high-pressure job and acting as the peacekeeper in her parents' relationship all her childhood. Libby had no idea how long Lake would be in her life, but she found herself hoping he and Jane could genuinely enjoy and appreciate one another.

Libby pulled into a parking spot in front of the Bean Scene and the three got out of the car. Jane said she had a few work calls to make, so she waited by the car as Libby and Lake made their way inside.

It was exactly how Libby pictured it, walking into a coffee shop with a famous person. The typical buzz and energy of the place dimmed as Lake strolled in, everyone taking note of his presence in their small-town shop.

A loud laugh echoed from behind the bar as Edwin waved them over.

"Today's the big day, huh Libs?" Edwin handed Libby her cappuccino with an elaborate design of a book poured on top.

"Edwin, this is gorgeous. Thank you. I'm going to miss you and this drink more than you realize." Libby's eyes were getting misty.

"You know where to find me when you get back," Edwin said, then turned his attention to Lake.

"What can I get you, sir? You seem to have hit the mute button on my coffee shop," Edwin added, chuckling once again.

"Triple-shot latte, whole milk. Great place you've got here," Lake said, as he took in the details of the coffee shop, immune to the stares and whispers directed at him.

"Keeps me out of trouble. So I assume it was you who gave Libby all those flowers weeks ago and not Thomas?" Edwin added under his breath, "Guy never deserved our Libby."

Lake laughed as he witnessed Libby's face transforming into a bright, red apple.

"Story for another time," Libby said quickly.

"Ah, good thing we've got hours upon hours on the road ahead of us," Lake replied, his curiosity piqued.

Turning back to Edwin, Lake fell into a comfortable conversation, getting details about Edwin's history that even Libby didn't know. Libby was impressed how easy it was for Lake to get people to open up to him. After grabbing a latte for Jane and saying their goodbyes, they left the coffee shop.

Once they were within earshot of Jane, Lake said, "So, Thomas. I would love to hear more about this obviously revered man from your life."

The annoyance of hearing his name flashed across Jane's face.

Perfect. Lake's on a roll with Jane…

"Please tell me he didn't text you," Jane said to Libby, eyes pleading.

"He did not. Edwin decided to bring his name up. I'm not talking to him. I would tell you," Libby said, focusing on her friend.

Libby's on-again, off-again relationship with Thomas was one of the few things that had caused a rift in her friendship with Jane. Jane had always felt Libby deserved better than him and despised the way he treated her. The last time Libby had gotten back together with him, she'd kept it secret from her best friend, not wanting to hear her disapproval. That secret lasted two days, thanks to Betty.

"Man. He sounds like a great guy. Wish I could leave that kind of impression," Lake said, drawing their attention back to him.

"I'm sure you leave plenty of an impression," Jane said curtly, as she got into the car.

"Sorry," Libby mouthed to him.

"I have a sister. Trust me, I get the protective instincts, and I love the energy she brings." Lake winked and climbed into the back seat of the car, seemingly unfazed by the interaction.

Libby took a few sips of her drink before getting into the car. If she thought the coffee shop with Lake was interesting, her parents' house was sure to entertaining.

Thankfully, the car ride had dimmed the tension between Jane and Libby. Lake had talked nonstop about everything he was seeing out the window. They had laughed at his enthusiasm regarding the smallest of things.

"Do they even let you out, or do you have to spend all your days in a recording booth?" Jane had joked.

When they got out of the car, Libby asked Jane for a moment to talk, wanting to address the ever-annoying topic of Thomas before going inside.

"I'm sorry I didn't tell you the last time Thomas and I got together. It was a mistake. I won't hide that from you again, okay?" Libby said.

"Oh God, that makes it sound like there'll be an again." Jane shook her head.

Obviously eavesdropping, Lake chimed in from where he was leaning next to the car. "Oh, I wouldn't worry about that, Jane. Libby here made quite the impression on my brother. Thomas isn't going to be making a reappearance."

Libby's jaw dropped as she looked to Lake. "Do you just say everything that's on your mind?"

"Pretty much. Now that that's settled, let's go meet the parents." Lake headed to the front door like he'd lived there.

"Interesting," Jane simply said, following after Lake.

Libby stood there in shock. She'd thought about Wade countless times since leaving Philadelphia but had chalked the whole thing up as a fantasy she had imagined. Libby knew she was beautiful and had a lot to offer, but she also had this deep-seated belief that she wasn't worthy of exceptional love, and Wade was nothing if not exceptional. As she stood there daydreaming about his coffee-brown eyes and strong, quiet presence, she heard the shriek of her mother.

Better get over there before my mother blows his famous eardrums.

*   *   *

By the time Libby made it to the front door, Lake and Jane were inside, standing by the kitchen bar, looking at Libby's childhood photo albums.

"Jeez, Mom, do you keep these in the kitchen drawer if by chance anyone wants to see them?" Libby asked, grabbing a glass of water.

"Of course not, dear. I have it right by the front door in case a celebrity comes in asking more about your past." Betty leaned in closer, attempting a whisper which she never quite mastered. "He seems quite interested in you, dear."

Of course, hearing that, Lake chuckled and said, "Libby is quite fantastic. You both clearly did an exceptional job raising her. I look forward to learning all about her, especially if she's going to be in the family."

"Oh God." Libby dropped her head in her hands.

Betty walked over to Lake. "Tell me everything."

"Let's just say, my brother has never been so interested in reading," Lake said, as he began to share more details about his brother.

John made his way over to the coffee pot, saying to no one in particular, "Why are we always talking about Libby's love life?"

* * *

Over the next hour, Lake showed pictures of all his family members (lingering on photos of Wade), talked in detail about Libby's contract (nothing Libby hadn't read a hundred times), and looked through endless pictures of Libby's childhood. Even John seemed won over by Lake by the time they said their goodbyes.

Libby gave each of her parents a long, loving hug. She would miss the weekly dinners, spontaneous pickleball matches with her dad, and shopping trips with her mom. It was a matter of months away, but it felt momentous walking away from them, the town, and treehouse she called home.

Surprisingly, it was her dad that shouted from the front porch as the car pulled away. "We're proud of you, Libby."

"Damn," Jane said simply, from the passenger seat.

"What am I missing?" Lake said, sprawled out in the backseat.

"He's never said that about anything that has to do with my writing," Libby replied, waving at her parents as she drove on.

"Must have been my charm," Lake said, fully believing every word.

*   *   *

Libby and Lake dropped Jane off in town before hitting the road. She had some work to do before heading to the airport that afternoon and loved to spend as much time as she could in Libby's hometown.

"You are going to do great, got it?" Jane said, as they hugged.

"I hope so," Libby replied, and then added, seeing the reprimanding look in Jane's face, "Yes, I got this. I am a talented writer with a promising future in this industry." She stood up taller.

"That's my girl." Jane gave Libby one last hug, said her goodbyes to Lake, and walked back to the coffee shop.

"Well, shall we get going? I've got the most incredible music lined up, all recorded by yours truly, and I know you are dying to hear. In a matter of hours, I will have you transformed into my biggest fan."

"Maybe we should adjust our expectations, yeah?" Libby said, somehow pulling off a charming wink.

"Looks like my confidence is already rubbing off on you." Lake winked right back as he eased his way into the car with that signature confidence.

See? I don't even need the winking class now.

* * *

Seven hours later, Libby desperately needed two things: a faster car and ear plugs. Lake, with all his radiating energy, had managed to exhaust both Libby and himself. Now he was leaning up against the center console, snoring so loudly Libby could barely think.

As good a time as any to take a break.

She took the next exit promising greasy fast food, and she tapped the brakes a bit harder than normal when they reached the restaurant.

Lake woke from his slumber. "Whoa there, Libs. Precious cargo right here."

Feeling short on patience and in need of food and space, Libby responded, "How does anyone sleep in the same building as you?"

Stretching his limbs, Lake replied with amusement, "I take it Thomas's only redeeming quality was his ability to sleep quietly."

"What is your fascination with my ex?" Libby said, making her way out of the car.

Lake took as much time stretching as a cat after a long sun-kissed nap. "I happen to believe your exes say a lot about you. Just trying to figure you out more via Thomas."

"And what do yours say about you? Viv seems to recall 'Instagram-able picture spots' to be a top requirement of your many suitors," Libby said.

"I have to admit, this hungry, frustrated side of you is incredibly endearing. Not sure how it would mix with Wade's dark temperament when he gets cranky, but I'm sure you two will figure it out. As for my past, exes and brief encounters are very different things. I have one ex and she's magnificent, further adding to my appeal."

Libby rolled her eyes and made her way into the restaurant, not looking back at Lake. Maybe he was slightly onto something with her hunger, but his "I'm so awesome" attitude was exhausting.

The two sat in silence, eating their burgers and fries. Lake occasionally glanced over at Libby as if he was waiting for a signal that she was ready to play nice.

"I get this from my mom," Libby said simply.

"Your big blue-green eyes? Yeah, I noticed," Lake replied, taking another bite from his burger.

"Well, yes, that and the slight moodiness that happens when I don't eat for a while," Libby said, feeling more like herself as she took another bite.

"Brooke's got the same condition. It can be debilitating, and I have first-hand seen the destruction. My thoughts are with you and your loved ones."

Libby threw a fry at Lake, grateful for the returned playfulness in their interaction.

"I've never had so many things thrown at me in one day. I have to admit, I kind of like it," he said, eating the fry Libby threw.

"Come on, a few more hours to go. Think you can keep those eyes open?" Libby said, standing from the booth.

"For you, I will do anything," Lake said, bowing dramatically.

*　　*　　*

Lake did in fact remain awake for the final three hours. The canopy of trees and distant mountains had given Libby comfort as they had driven into North Carolina. They arrived at their destination, the home Florence was renting out for the near future, right after the sunset. The home was on the outskirts of the town, so Libby hadn't seen anything beyond the beautiful scenery of Willowston.

Hearing the car arrive outside, Florence and Viv made their way outside to greet them.

Viv was the first to speak. "I've got to admit, I didn't think you two would have a chance of making it here on time, let alone with smiles on your faces."

The food, combined with conversation over the last few hours, had restored the relationship between Libby and Lake. They discussed more serious topics like the death of Lake's father and Libby's fears related to her dream of being a writer. It felt like they had crossed into genuine friendship by discussing what truths lived deep in their hearts.

Libby was surprised to learn how much the two of them had in common, despite the radically different lifestyles they led. Both expressed a loneliness in their lives that weighed heavily on them. Lake admitted most of his social media was done by other people and that he, too, had a hard time authentically connecting to this virtual world. Lake thoughtfully articulated why he understood her fears around timelines and creating something "good" the second time around. He felt that way every time he released new music, this pit in his stomach as he awaited feedback from the public. The smiles they both wore stepping out of the car were genuine.

"A warning on Lake's award-winning snoring would have been appreciated," Libby said, stretching her sore legs.

"I think what Libby is trying to say is how much she loved my award-winning rap music. This is for the fry," Lake said, tossing a piece of candy at Libby.

"Alright you two," Florence chimed in. "We've got dinner shortly and I want you to have time to freshen up. Libby, if it's okay with you, we thought you could stay here for the night, and we'd show you your accommodations tomorrow."

For a moment, Libby found herself looking to the house, hoping someone else was there. Detecting the hesitation and giving Libby an out in case anyone else had noticed, Viv added, "Nathanial and Paige will be arriving in a couple of days, so tonight it'll just be us."

Libby tried to hide the disappointment she felt. Thoughts on Wade came suddenly. She'd be completely occupied by a task and then in a flash, his coffee eyes would appear. It was incredibly annoying and, as Jane had said, completely transparent.

Lake chuckled as he grabbed the bags from the car. Libby figured he knew the person she was looking for was not Nathanial or Paige, despite Viv's quick thinking. Even though Lake had mentioned Wade's name often, Libby hadn't worked up the courage to ask how he fit into the library project, if at all. Thankfully, the company combined with the setting was enough to bring Libby back to the present moment. After freshening up in her room, Libby made her way back downstairs. She had debated changing into another more formal dress, considering how fancy the house was, but had decided to stay in her maroon one. Even after ten hours in the car, she felt beautiful in that dress.

Based on the size of the home Florence was renting, Libby expected an elaborate dinner cooked by a well-trained chef. She was pleasantly surprised to find out they were making their own pizzas, the crust of course having been premade by the chef.

Libby always found it so profound how comfortable it was to spend time around Lake, Florence, and Viv. The four fell into an easy conversation as they began to make their pizzas. The pizza-making started in a civilized manner until Viv and Lake got into a disagreement over the appropriateness of pizza toppings.

"I know these are fighting words, but anyone who endorses fruit on pizza is a monster," Viv said emphatically.

"Hate to be the bearer of bad news, but those tomatoes you're laying down are technically fruit, due to the seeds inside the chamber," Lake said, smirking, knowing full well that he was provoking Viv.

"Did you just mansplain the definition of fruit to me? That's it!" and without a moment to defend himself, Viv grabbed a handful of mozzarella and tossed it at Lake's face.

Libby stood frozen, watching the scene play out in front of her. Her mom had been the one to cook the most in her family and took a very clean approach to cooking. As she finished using a pan or utensil, it was washed immediately, so by the time dinner was ready, the kitchen was radically clean. This interaction before her felt more like performance art than reality.

Florence spoke up in a stern voice, a voice Libby hadn't heard until that moment.

"I will not allow this type of behavior in this house," she said.

Libby was shocked seeing this side of Florence, and for a moment, she was terrified that she would one day be on the receiving end of it because of her inadequate second book.

Before Libby's mind could go too far, she watched as Florence picked up a handful of mushrooms in one hand and spinach in another, throwing them at Viv and Lake.

The laughter and joyous energy in the room was palpable. After recovering from the shock, Libby too started tossing ingredients. After tossing the cheese and bowl of onions near her, Libby spotted a can of tomato sauce that was half-used. She picked it up and splashed it onto Lake's face and hair.

Everyone stopped and turned to Libby.

"Damn, Libs. The tomato sauce? That's cold," Viv said, as she burst into laughter.

"You certainly know how to play dirty. Remind me to pick your side the next time we get into a food fight," Lake said lightly, as he licked the tomato sauce dripping toward his mouth.

"You know, maybe you should ask Yousuf to add some red highlights into your hair at your next appointment. It looks good on you," Florence said, as seriously as she could muster.

The rest of the evening was filled with an equal amount of fun. They grilled the pizzas together outside and ate under a canopy of twinkling lights. The whole evening felt surreal, and Libby hoped it was a positive omen for the months to come.

That night as Libby settled into her luxurious bed, she read through the endless notes she had made in her journal. She hadn't yet started writing the next book, despite the weeks that had passed by. Her head told her she should get something done, but her heart told her to wait, take in her surroundings in Willowston, and then begin. Tomorrow she would see the place Viv selected for her to live and hopefully find a spark of inspiration to begin.

CHAPTER SEVEN

"Rise and shine," Viv shouted, outside Libby's door.

Thankfully, Libby was ready to go, propelled out of bed early in the morning, excited to see Willowston and Florence's house in the morning light. The view out of her window was a familiar one, being surrounded by trees like her treehouse. However, the view from this window felt elevated, the details more radiant than she remembered at her house. Tall, impressive trees sparkled with the morning dew reflecting off their delicate leaves. A blue sky, which somehow appeared more vibrant and expansive than Libby was used to, filled the rest of the window, with the faintest view of mountains towering in the background. For a moment, Libby wished she could stay and write her book from this very room, but after the gorgeous hotel Viv had selected in Philadelphia, Libby felt confident in Viv's ability to find the right place in Willowston.

Libby opened the door seconds after Viv's shout startled her.

"Well, well, well. I thought you were still snuggled in the sheets, but it looks like you've been up for a while. Thinking about someone?" Viv said, with a grin.

"If you are referring to the characters in my latest book, then yes. They are constantly in my mind. I have been thinking about adding a character that nags the main character about her love life, someone short with bright-red hair and a booming voice mismatched to her small frame. Remind you of anyone?" Libby responded, not waiting for an answer as she looped her arm through Viv's and started walking downstairs.

"Touché. And just so you know, I'd be honored to be in your book. The biggest honor being the murderer, of course," Viv said seriously.

"Of course. But if this nagging, booming-voiced redhead was the murderer, no one would be surprised, and I've read that's an important element of mystery books," Libby said, matching Viv's serious tone.

Viv laughed loudly as they reached the bottom of the stairs.

"Ah, the soothing sound of Viv cackling in the morning. What a beautiful way to transition from my dreams to reality." Lake appeared at the top of the stairs, drawing both Viv's and Libby's gazes to him, with his hair disheveled, still wearing his pajamas. Libby tried to keep her face neutral as she took in the bold print on his silk pajamas, a button-up short-sleeve top with matching shorts. It was most likely as expensive as her car, and it fit his big persona, but it truly looked ridiculous.

"I'd be careful, Lake. I think we have an extra to-mato sauce left over from yesterday that'd go great with that outfit," Viv responded, pulling Libby from her shock and into the kitchen.

Florence sat at a barstool, looking refreshed and elegant as the morning light poured into the kitchen. Seeing Libby's face, she started chuckling. "You saw my son in his pajamas, yes? You have that stunned look that we all had the first time he started buying those."

"It complements his energetic personality," Libby said, taking the seat next to Florence.

"Yes, but why shorts? Silk pajamas are one thing, but shorts? Fashion truly has taken turns down roads I wish we could block," Florence said, shaking her head.

"You know, Libby, Wade wears normal-people pajamas, if that's something you're worried about." Viv poured herself a coffee, ignoring the piercing stare Libby was returning to her. This was the first time someone mentioned the potential of her and Wade in front of Florence, at least as far as Libby knew. She paused for a moment as she waited to see how Flor-ence would respond.

Florence took a sip of her drink and then replied, "Last I checked, matchmaker was not in your job description, Viv. Now, let's eat breakfast so we can show you your home for the next few months." Florence's facial expression remained unfazed, which either suggested she'd heard this before or she had an incredible poker face.

Libby repeated the mantra she'd be working on to refocus. Between the mention of Wade and the pressure of seeing her new place, she was getting antsy.

I am a professional writer who creates magnificent mystery novels.

Libby smiled to herself, remembering what Jane had said when she told her about her endless mantras: "After these months in Willowston, you'll be able to fill a book with the mantras alone."

*　*　*

By the time they were finished with breakfast, Lake had made his way downstairs. Thankfully, he had changed out of his pajamas and was wearing linen shorts and shirt in a neutral shade of tan that allowed Libby to look at him without laughing. Lake casually mentioned wanting to tag along when Libby saw her new place. Libby might have imagined it, but from the corner of her eye she thought she saw Lake and Viv exchange some sort of look.

The view from the car ride was beautiful. Viv suggested she drive Libby's car so Libby could enjoy the scenery while Lake and Florence followed in their own car. Libby hadn't spent time in western North Carolina before, but she found herself falling in love with it. The setting was stunning, with endless trees, impressive mountains, plentiful wildflowers, and winding streams. Viv remained oddly quiet for the car ride.

Maybe she doesn't know what to do without endless cars to weave through and honk at.

"Ah, here we are!" Viv pulled Libby out of her trance as she drove down a hidden dirt road. Turning a corner, Libby saw it and almost choked on the water she was sipping.

"What do you think?" Viv said cheerfully.

For a moment, Libby thought she was seeing something different from Viv. The house was atrocious. It looked old, and not in a charming way but in a "is the roof going to hold up" kind of way. The siding was worn, and even the property surrounding it seemed rough. Overall, it looked terrifying.

Viv didn't miss a beat. She parked the car and made her way out, occasionally glancing over to Libby.

Maybe the inside is better?

Libby tried to give herself a pep talk, but as she stepped out of the car, she felt as steady as the failing foundation on the house in front of her.

Lake came up and wrapped his arm around Libby's shoulder.

"I think it's perfect for our mystery writer. Great find, Viv," Lake said, grinning.

Clearly Lake had the same vision Viv had. Libby looked back to find Florence, but she was still in the car on her phone.

Hopefully she is calling a local real estate agent because she doesn't want her mystery writer to die under that collapsing roof.

After a few moments of listening to Viv and Lake talk about the home like it was a completely normal place to stay, Libby made her way to the front door. About to turn the doorknob, which shockingly looked intact, Libby heard Florence shout.

"Good Lord, don't go in there! I'm not sure the house can take the impact of the door opening." Florence walked up to Viv and Lake, smacking them lightly.

"You two have had your fun. Can we please make our way to her actual place?"

Oh, thank goodness.

Libby almost collapsed in relief, hearing Florence's words. Catching herself, she felt it appropriate to return the favor.

"This is a perfect setting for some of my writing. Viv, Lake, would you two mind joining me here tonight so I can write? Just like Lake gets inspired writing in the car, I find myself propelled to greatness when I write in the middle of the night near a terrifying house," Libby said, keeping her face neutral.

Florence smiled, adding, "I can see it now. You all can camp right here by this side, make a small fire but nothing that attracts too many large animals. I know there are bears around here. Lake, if I remember correctly, you feared bears, growing up."

Viv chuckled. "No worries on that. With those pajamas he's wearing, the bears will be naturally repelled."

Viv glanced at Libby, knowing full well she was kidding. The topic of camping had come up during one of their car rides in Philadelphia, and they had bonded over the fact they both hated it. But Lake's facial expression was hesitant, like he wasn't sure Libby was joking.

Libby walked up to Lake and wrapped her arm around him like he had done a moment ago.

"Oh, come on, you can't fear bears anymore. And you know how important creative inspiration is for us artists. Between this spooky setting and your jammies, I'll have more inspiration than I could have dreamed of," Libby said, looking at him innocently.

"You're kidding, right? We don't even have rights to this property, right Viv?" Lake spoke in a concerned tone Libby hadn't heard before.

The three women burst out laughing, the sign of relief showing on Lake's face.

"Very funny. I will let you know that fear of bears is very reasonable, and many women have said my pajamas are sexy," Lake said, standing taller.

Libby, Viv, and Florence laughed louder as they all made their way back to the cars.

Lake drove the one car while Florence joined Viv and Libby in Libby's car.

"I want to see what you think of the place we actually picked," she said, giving a stern look over to Viv.

"Oh, come on, don't I deserve to have some fun occasionally? It's been a long time since you all let me do this, and I knew Libby would be a good sport," Viv said defensively.

"What Viv is skirting around is that she once did this 'you're going to stay in this horrific place' with one of Lake's lady friends, and she ended up screaming at Lake for the remainder of the evening. Sometimes I really question my children's taste in partners," Florence said, sighing.

"Hey, better he find out now that she was no good." Viv leaned over to Libby as she drove, adding, "It was worth every moment of the silent treatment Lake gave me. It was nice to have a break from all the blah, blah, blah."

Hearing that, Florence laughed loudly.

"Yeah, my son hasn't quite grasped the power of silence, has he? Not like my Wade, who could get anyone to listen to him from his stare alone," Florence said, glancing at Libby.

Oh, not you too.

At the mention of Wade's name, Libby had blushed, which Viv had clocked immediately, smirking from her seat.

The three sat in silence as they took in the canopy of trees they drove under.

A few minutes later, Florence excitedly pointed out her window up ahead. "We're almost at Main Street. Now, I know it's small, but it really has a lot of charm. And as you'll see, the people here are just incredible. There are pharmaceutical and medical device manufacturers in this region that have increased the population of this little town. Then, of course, you have people who work remotely that wanted to relocate near the mountains, and those that commute to the larger cities like Asheville. All to say, the demand for public services like the library have increased substantially, and we're hoping our project will meet that demand and exceed expectations."

Libby listened intently as she watched Main Street emerge. Like Florence said, it was small, but there was a lot of activity for such a small town. The buildings were mostly red brick, but some were recently updated with brightly colored awnings, meticulously curated planters, and delightful store signs done in cursive font. Libby spotted the coffee shop, eager to see if the inside was done as well as the outdoor area.

"Anyone up for a run to the coffee shop later?" Libby asked, unsure what the rest of the day held.

"Absolutely!" Florence said.

"Good luck ordering your usual here," Viv added, to Florence.

"There is nothing wrong with whipped cream on drip coffee. It's a completely reasonable coffee order," Florence replied.

*   *   *

It didn't take long to drive through the small downtown area. A couple of miles later, they turned off the road onto a long cobblestone driveway marked with the sign "Mountain Stream Inn."

Libby simply said, "Please tell me this is really where I get to stay," as she took in the enchanting inn in the distance.

Viv and Florence smiled at each other, appreciating the validation of their choice in accommodations.

The first thing Libby noticed as they drove up to the inn was the massive wraparound porch filled with planters, porch swings, and rocking chairs. It was as inviting as a space could possibly be, and she found herself fantasizing about writing from one of the porch swings in the corner. She couldn't wait to get out of the car and see more.

As they parked and made their way out of the car, Viv said, "The owners are obsessed with plants. They have gardens throughout the grounds. Figured that detail may make you feel at home. Go wander, we'll get you checked in."

Libby smiled widely and took Viv up on her offer without a second thought. Noticing a rock pathway to the left of the inn, Libby wandered that way. As she turned the corner by the house, she almost collapsed from pure joy. Calling what she saw "gardens" was an insult to the exquisite scenery in front of her. Scanning, she could see dozens of varieties of plants, countless bird baths and houses, and best of all, a stunning water feature. It was like someone carved a small creek into the sloping grounds, with multiple miniature waterfalls that ended in a small pond. Libby could see fish swimming around the pond, water lilies floating majestically, and three large bowls seemingly suspended in the water, with tall flames coming out of them. Libby had seen these once in an outdoor landscaping magazine, and they were even more stunning in person.

Finally drawing her eyes away from the water feature, she took in the cozy spots peppered throughout the property, with plush outdoor furniture and pillows in earth tones, perfect for an afternoon of writing.

"You do know, you need to sleep inside the inn, yes?"

Libby had been so focused on taking in the property, she didn't notice someone swalk up behind her. His voice was exactly how she remembered it from that day in Philadelphia. Turning, she had to concentrate to keep a neutral expression on her face.

"After the first place they showed me, I'd be thrilled to sleep in one of those fire and water bowls over that terrifying dilapidated property." Libby hoped Wade didn't pick up on the nervousness in her voice.

It's a human being you're talking to, for goodness sakes. Not one of those magical man-gods Nathanial writes about.

Libby had read Nathanial's book, which was over six hundred pages, in a weekend. His description of the man-gods was enough to excite anyone.

Ah, but the man-gods didn't have Wade's eyes. They're so brown and beautiful and look like swirly coffee.

"What are you thinking?" Wade asked, eyes fixated on Libby as she tried to return to the present moment.

"Need coffee." Not a complete lie, but Wade's eyes were the sole focus in her mind, not the charming coffee shop on Main.

Great, I sound like a cave woman. You write books, you can speak a full sentence.

Lake came up from behind them. "This garden looks enchanted, like one of those fairytales Mom used to read us. Can't tell if it's the gardens or the magical romance spinning circles around the two of you ... Oh man, that's good. I like that. I got to get that down on paper." Lake was gone as fast as he had come.

Even with Lake's awkward interruption, Wade's expression remained curious and calm. Libby, however, felt immediately embarrassed at Lake's comment, as her face got redder and redder.

Before they could say anything, Viv and Florence came out to see how Libby was liking it so far. Hard to tell if they were referring to the inn's gardens or Wade, but either way, Libby appreciated the interruption. She had no idea what the next words out of her mouth were going to be, but considering her face was now the color of the red poisonous apple from Snow White, she knew it wasn't going to be pretty.

* * *

Everyone made their way inside the inn, Libby anxious to see her room and other indoor spaces that would be useful for her writing. As they walked through the front door, they were greeted by two men who would have given Brooke a run for her money as the giddiest.

"Here's our star!" the man with the perfectly coifed white-and-gray hair said.

The other man, taller, with black wavy hair, joined in with equal interest but spoke in a calmer tone. "Your book is one of our favorites. I mean, the way you created those characters was inspired, and the murder, it's exactly how I wanted it."

From the corner of her eye, Libby saw Lake, Viv, Florence, and even Wade smiling.

"Gani, you can't say you wanted a murder. Please don't send that up into the universe. It's always listening," the shorter man said, waving his hands dramatically upward.

The men started bickering, seemingly forgetting the people in front of them. Libby stood watching the playful interaction. Without an introduction, she had to assume they were the ones running the inn and had probably been together a good amount of time. Even though she just met them, she looked forward to seeing the two of them every day.

"Oh, we've completely forgotten our manners. We started out so well and then someone dragged me back down the foxhole," the man named Harrison said, turning his attention back to Libby. He reached his hand out to shake Libby's hand while the other man said, "It's rabbit hole, my love. I'm Gani, and we are your innkeepers extraordinaire."

Libby smiled broadly and shook their hands. "I'm never going to want to leave this place. The gardens out back are a dream. Did you do that?"

"Execution is all me, but the idea was all him. You can surmise who had to work harder," Gani said, teasingly.

"Oh, Gani, Libby is a literary artist, she understands the difficulty involved in creatively shaping an idea into reality," Harrison said.

"I can attest to that. Creative brilliance challenges you in many ways," Lake said, from behind.

"Is it the lyrics bragging about your rap skills, sleeping with multiple women, or the burden of all your excess cash you're referring to?" Viv said with a smirk.

Florence smiled and shook her head, then said to Gani and Harrison, "Thank you both for everything. Our writers are so lucky to be staying here with you. My sons and I are going to head out to meet with the librarians."

Turning to Libby, she added, "If you need anything, just give me a call. Paige and Nathanial will arrive tomorrow. Take your time, get settled, and work on that creative brilliance."

After saying their goodbyes, Florence, Lake, and Wade made their way out.

"Whoever ends up with them will be some lucky ladies." Turning back to Libby, who was trying hard to suppress the blush once again emerging on her face, Harrison added, "So, how about the grand tour?"

The interior of the inn was equally as appealing as the outdoor space. The inn was a wonderful balance of open concept and cozy spaces. The kitchen, dining room, and patio mixed modern touches with classic design. Every counter, corner, and table held various plants. The greenery combined with the endless windows made the indoor space feel part of the outside. Next, they walked to the downstairs rooms. Gani explained that typically they would use these as additional guest rooms, but thanks to Florence and her generous compensation, she asked they be reserved as workspaces for her authors.

Finally, they went upstairs; a cozy shared living room space greeted them at the top of the stairs. Rooms were laid out on both sides, as Libby wondered what her room would look like.

"Now, based on what we've gleaned from you, Miss Libby, I think this room will be perfect for you." Gani walked toward the right, to the room at the end of the hallway.

Libby gasped when Gani opened the door. The room was spacious, with an immaculate canopy bed at the center. A large bay window in the corner with a small wooden desk placed in front of it offered a view of the backyard garden. Small vases filled with dried lavender, fresh flowers, and delicate greenery were placed throughout the room.

"Just wait until you see the glorious bathroom, designed by yours truly," Harrison said, dancing to the bathroom door and opening it with a "Ta-da!"

"You cannot be serious," was all Libby could say.

The bathroom was huge, with an arched cathedral ceiling of wooden planks stained in the most beautiful shade of dark brown. There was a tub centered on a large window, and a shower with tiles in various earth tones.

"This can't be my room. This must be your room or the room of the prince of a small country," Libby said, turning to Gani and Harrison.

Viv, who was working on her phone, smiled as she watched Libby walk in disbelief around the space.

"Give her a moment. She doesn't get out much," Viv quipped, smiling.

"Oh shoot. Gani, she's right. We accidently showed her our room. Must be our age showing again," Harrison jokingly said.

"It's absolutely yours, and it's also the best one, so try not to brag to Paige or Nathanial," Gani said, with a kind smile.

*   *   *

After Libby's breathing returned to normal and she managed to pull her jaw off the ground, Viv, Gani, and Harrison left her to get settled. Viv and Libby planned to meet up in an hour and head downtown to the coffee shop.

Libby lay down on the bed and focused on her breath. She couldn't believe it: the inn, the connections she was building, and the promise of dedicated time to work on her dream of being a writer. After confirming that she was not, in fact, in a dream, thanks to giving herself a strong pinch on her arm, Libby texted her parents and Jane. She sent pictures of her room and the backyard, and a selfie from the night before when they had dinner outside. Responses of varying enthusiasm came from Jane, her mom, and her dad, but it was clear, all of them were equally shocked how nice everything was.

After putting her phone away, Libby started to un-pack, giddy at the small details she discovered. There were scented pillows in the drawers, lavender pillow spray in the side table, and bath products with floral scents, beach scents, and earthy scents, each to use depending on her mood. The bath had glass jars with different salts and small bottles of essential oils. Libby even found "recipes" of how to mix the salts and es-sential oils for different scent combinations.

Now this is the kind of recipe I can really get behind.

Glancing at the clock, Libby saw she had another fifteen minutes before she had to meet Viv. She set her laptop on the small desk and stared out the window at the perfect scene below. After pulling her gaze from the outdoor paradise, Libby opened the single drawer in the desk. She burst out laughing, seeing the single knife lying in the drawer with a note, "For inspira-tion, love, G&H." Gani and Harrison were quickly becoming two of her favorite people.

CHAPTER EIGHT

Sitting across from Viv at the coffee shop, Libby found herself with a permanent smile and a sense of serenity she hadn't expected this quickly in the new town. The coffee shop was small on the inside, with only a few tables and a little bar with some chairs. However, that seemed sufficient, because it appeared most people just grabbed their coffee and left. It was a stark contrast to the Bean Scene, where people would linger for hours on their computers, talking to one another, or reading books. This coffee shop looked recently updated and had a modern farmhouse feel. To the side, Libby noticed an impressive picture wall showing various mountain scenes framed with gorgeous metallic frames, and next to that, a beautiful hanging wooden bar with various dried flowers. The counter was made of a rich dark-stained wood, and the wall behind it was a jade-green tiled stone. The space was immaculate.

"You look pleased with yourself," Viv said, sipping her triple-shot cappuccino.

"How could I not be? The cappuccino is delicious and this place is beautiful. Although I'm surprised more people aren't sitting here and enjoying their coffee." Libby nodded at the latest group of customers who ordered their coffees to go.

"A lot has changed around here lately, the worst being people not caring about anyone but themselves." An older woman with long gray hair stood up and walked over to Viv and Libby. She had been sitting at a table in the corner, the only other customer sitting inside.

"Oh hi. I'm Libby," Libby said cheerfully.

"Hi," was all the woman replied, as she looked Viv and Libby over.

"Care to expand on your comment?" Viv said, returning her stare. Libby had to hold back her laughter at the stare-off the two older women were engaging in.

"Just trying to sort out where the two of you fit around here. Name's Carrigan."

"Pleasure, Carrigan. Well, my friend Libby here is going to be helping with the new library while writing her next novel. I'm Viv." Viv maintained the stare.

"Humph. Still don't know how that's going to work out. Some fancy new building funded by a rapper that's supposed to be the 'center of the community,' as our mayor can't shut up about. Doesn't matter. I bet it'll be a complete waste. People around here now don't linger, don't talk, just live in their own little worlds on that screen." Carrigan signaled to the latest patron who walked in, almost tripping as they stared at their screen.

"It wasn't always like this?" Libby asked, bringing Carrigan's attention back.

A scoff came out of Carrigan. "Not at all. This coffee shop has been here for decades. It was so local that you couldn't find it listed on any map or anywhere on the internet. Every day, it was filled with people. I liked to think it was the heart of this community. But the owners got old, had to sell, and that perky little thing in the back now owns it. Thought our old place wasn't 'cute' enough, so she bedazzled the crap out of it, and now I feel like I'm sitting in a day spa. Ridiculous. Course, you probably like it being all sunshiny and all that." She stared at Libby for a moment longer and walked away, mumbling something as she went.

"Looks like not everyone is appreciating the change around here," Viv said.

"What do you think she meant by 'all that'?" Libby said, looking down at her outfit.

Viv laughed as she watched Libby try to decipher which element in her look had contributed to Carrigan's comment.

"What?" Libby said, feeling suddenly insecure.

"Oh, now don't start overthinking your entire sense of self. Carrigan was just in a mood. Promise I'll tell you if you start looking like the mascot for sunshine and need to dampen down your look," Viv said.

"I appreciate that. I can always bring back more of the office-chair look if needed. Anyways, it looks like we're going to have our hands full with this new library. I'm guessing Carrigan isn't the only one questioning its value. We really need to focus on how our offerings can inspire connection in this town," Libby said, settling back into her chair.

"Oh no, no, no. I know that look. You're commanding the army in your brain to start strategizing. Your primary focus is the book. The mere presence of this library will be more than enough to help the community," Viv said, sipping her coffee.

"I'm not so sure. It's one thing to offer a space and create programs, but it's another to encourage people to come, especially those that are hesitant. If people like Carrigan feel like they already don't belong, they may never even step foot in the library."

"Here we go . . ." Viv said.

"I really want to help. I get what Carrigan is saying about the loss of community; you can almost feel it when you look around. There are enough people, but you don't see them engaging with one another. Having a sense of connection and responsibility in your community is so important, and I hate hearing that this place used to have it but somehow lost it." Libby felt a fire light up inside of her.

"Love your passion. Let's just save a sliver for your next book, yeah?" Viv said.

Viv abruptly changed the subject. "So, I know you're dying to know. Go ahead and ask me."

"Ask what?" Libby said, knowing full well Viv was not-so-subtly bringing up Wade.

"Uh huh. I saw the way you were looking at him. Seems to me he was looking back at you just as intensely." Viv chuckled as Libby's face began its predictable blush.

"Fine. I'll play along. What is Wade doing here in town?" Libby said, with her best attempt at casual.

"Well, he lives here, for one. And two, he's a chef, which even you, the world's worst stalker, must know by now. He's in the process of opening a restaurant here, which he balances with his consulting business that takes him all over the country. And to add to his wonderfulness, he's volunteering his time to help get the library café up and running." Viv smiled at the look of shock on Libby's face.

"Oh, come on, you didn't know any of that?" Viv said.

"I knew he was a chef. My friend Jane looked him up and told me that. But no, I had no idea about the rest," Libby responded.

Those coffee-inspired eyes live here? And I now live here?

"Yep, our Wade is an impressive man. He has more to offer than those gorgeous brown eyes," Viv said, as she watched Libby blush yet again.

"I have no idea what you're talking about," Libby said, knowing her face had so rudely given away her true feelings.

"Uh huh. I'm not even going to acknowledge that blatant lie. According to Florence, Wade had a knack for cooking from a young age. She said by six, she and Noah used to joke he cooked a better meal than the two of them combined. He worked in restaurants every chance he got, but Noah was the one that noticed his aptitude for business. So, with Noah's encouragement, Wade did both culinary school and business school. An MBA chef sounds pretty good for a long-term partner, no?" Viv said, winking.

"Yes, yes. I'm just wondering if you can talk to me about Wade without winking just one time," Libby quipped.

"Impossible. He's wink-worthy, what can I say?" Viv said.

"I can't believe I didn't know he lived here," Libby said, recalling her previous conversations with Florence.

"Yeah, he's been all over the place between school and his restaurant gigs, but after Noah passed, he said he felt drawn here. All the kids had close relationships with Noah, but Wade is so much like him," Viv said.

"So, he was already living here when the idea to revamp the library came about?" Libby asked.

"That he was. As you know, Florence is so passionate about this library, it's her way of honoring Noah by helping the community. But if you ask me, I think she also wanted a chance to spend more time in this town and get Lake and Brooke here so the whole family could be together, at least temporarily," Viv said.

"Where does Brooke live?" Libby asked, making sure she covered the basics to avoid further surprises.

"She's in Philadelphia. Works for a nonprofit research organization focused on healthcare contracts related to chronic conditions. But she'll be coming down frequently to help with the library," Viv said.

"And speaking of the library…" Libby paused, trying to sort out how to ask her question.

"Go ahead, you can ask whatever is on your mind, but I already told you Wade wears normal-people pajamas, nothing like Lake's," Viv said, shuddering dramatically as she recalled Lake's assortment of bold-print pajamas.

"How would that relate to the library? Never mind," Libby said, not letting Viv distract her with thoughts of what Wade wore at night.

"Florence has told me all about the library project, but one thing we haven't gotten into is how Lake is affording to fund the whole thing. I mean, even Carrigan said he's the one funding it, and I know he must be wealthy, but I imagine the cost to do a completely new build, equip all those facilities, and staffing, it's got to be astronomical." Libby looked down nervously at her almost-empty cup. Asking about finances felt uncomfortable, but it was also something she'd been wondering for a while.

"That's a perfectly reasonable question. No need to go crawl into your empty mug. The town was already in the process of planning a major renovation to the library. Wade was the one that first brought the idea to Florence after he had heard about the library needing work done. Apparently, the old building was in rough shape and had this terrible smell." Viv made a face and continued on. "Everything blossomed from there. The town is covering the base expenses, everything they would have paid toward prior renovations, staffing, and maintenance. The 'extras,' as I like to call them, 'unnecessaries,' as the town council likes to call them, are being covered by the family. Lake is funding a significant portion of that, but he's not alone. Florence is contributing a lot too, thanks to decades of successful investing. As you can imagine, the family attended what seems like thousands of meetings with the town. Florence and the children aren't being compensated for any of their efforts, but it's become a way to honor Noah."

"Such a beautiful way to celebrate your late husband and dad. I appreciate you always being so candid with me," Libby said, squeezing Viv's hand.

"It must be the sunshine reflecting off you that forces me to be so honest," Viv replied, with a slight smile.

"Unbelievable. This is the last time I wear yellow," Libby replied as she stood up, straightening her light-yellow cardigan.

*   *   *

Libby and Viv spent the next hour wandering the town. Libby counted a handful of businesses on Main Street that were open and looked recently renovated. However, there seemed to be just as many buildings that were abandoned. It was easy to see the potential for the town, especially with the charming storefronts and active community, but it was clear the town was in the process of redefining itself.

"We've seen most of Main Street and you still haven't pointed out where Wade's restaurant will be," Libby said.

"Oh, I am not showing you that. Take that precious moment away from you and Wade? I think not," Viv said, walking faster and leaving Libby standing there.

"Unbelievable. Might I remind you, I'm not starring in a romance film; I'm a professional writer who creates magnificent mystery novels," Libby shouted after her, causing some patrons around them to give her a confused look, and a boisterous laugh to erupt from Viv up ahead.

* * *

That evening, after spending some time relaxing in her room and looking over her notes for her novel, Libby got ready for dinner with Gani and Harrison. Other than meeting them earlier that day, Libby hadn't gotten a chance to really talk with them. She was happy to hear that she would get their full attention for the evening, as Florence and the others had made other plans.

When Libby stepped into the kitchen, she was greeted by an enthusiastic Harrison.

"Ta-da!" Harrison said, fanning his arms around the over-the-top Mediterranean dinner sprawled on the countertop.

"I hope you like Mediterranean. We weren't sure what you liked, so we made, well, a bit of everything," Gani said, nodding to the food.

"This looks incredible. I love Mediterranean," Libby said, as she started to fill her plate.

After everyone had gotten their food, they sat down at the table by the window. The reclaimed wooden table was decorated with fresh flowers and a subtle vanilla-scented candle that made Libby feel immediately at home.

Gani was the first to speak, since Libby and Harrison immediately filled their mouths with food.

"We're looking forward to getting to know you. Harrison had surmised your entire life story, but it'd be helpful to hear it from you, with actual facts," Gani said, smiling at Harrison playfully.

"Don't listen to him. He loves my imaginative mind," Harrison said, as he chewed his hummus-dipped flatbread.

"Harrison, please remember what the doctor said about being mindful of eating." Harrison rolled his eyes as Gani went on. "He had a terrible choking incident a few months ago, and I'd rather not repeat that." Gani's demeanor remained calm, but it was clear the episode had scared him.

After Harrison finished his bite, having dramatically chewed the rest of the food, he turned to his partner and said, "Some moments require an immediate verbal response, choking be damned."

Gani shook his head. "Yes, I remember you saying that to the doctor as well, but can we please save the drama for non-choking-related things?"

"Fine, but for the record, my choking performance was masterfully executed," Harrison responded proudly.

"Not a performance, dear. Now back to Libby and her true life's story." Gani signaled for Libby to go on.

"Yes, please share, but I'm sure my version is better," Harrison replied shamelessly.

Gani simply shook his head and gave his full attention to Libby.

"Harrison, you're probably right. My life has been a bit uninspired lately." Libby surprised herself with the confession but continued.

"I'm trained as a nurse. I've been working in the same hospital in my hometown since I graduated, and it feels like my soul is depleted at the end of every shift. I wrote my first book to escape, and I fell in love with the process. I self-published, sold a pitiful number of books, and cried an unreasonable amount at the negative reviews that appeared online." Libby cringed, thinking about the moments she sat obsessing about those reviews.

"Well, we both read your book and loved it. After dinner, I shall go online and type up one of my famous reviews. My reviews have been featured on multiple high-profile websites," Harrison said, sitting up straighter.

"He means websites for the local plumber and a restaurant in California that liked his passionate review of their guacamole. No one can quite entice you on the wonders of an avocado like Harrison," Gani said playfully.

"I'll take that as a compliment with no underlying humor," Harrison said, continuing, "Now, as someone who's gotten a lot of negative feedback in my life, the key is to believe in yourself. If you believe in yourself, and I mean really believe in yourself, the universe will respond. It's incredible that at your age, you found your love for writing mystery novels, and that it's something you'll want to pour your soul into for the rest of your life."

"Thank you. Yeah, it's amazing," Libby agreed; but internally, something felt off.

Before Libby had a chance to dissect the source of those feelings, Harrison chimed in, "Now, give us the more personal stuff. Tell us about your parents, friends, and lovers. Emphasis on the lovers, please."

"You don't need to tell us anything more if you don't want to. Of course, if you don't tell Harrison about your love life, he will continue to bother you day and night until you do," Gani said calmly.

Libby laughed. She was really enjoying the company of these two.

"I'm very close with my parents. I'm a momma's girl through and through, but I spend a lot of time with my dad too," Libby said.

"Ah, the parent who was less than supportive, I recall," Gani said, surprising Libby with his knowledge of the dynamics.

"How did you? Ah, never mind. I can guess this one. Viv?" Libby said, smiling.

"Yes, Viv. I apologize if that was too sensitive to bring up. But she shared that detail with us when we were preparing for your stay," Gani said, looking a bit guilty.

"Ah, look who is stirring up the drama now. And with a bite of flatbread in his mouth, I believe?" Harrison said, dropping his napkin theatrically.

"That's my tongue, dear," Gani said, with a subtle smile on his lips. No matter what the two were arguing about, the love and fondness for one another was apparent.

Libby chimed in, "It's really alright. It's no secret my dad thinks writing is a distraction and that I should be 100 percent devoted to my nursing career. I wish my heart aligned with his dream for me, but here we are, so..." Libby's thoughts wandered off.

Gani reached for Libby's hand and gave it a soft squeeze. "We're so glad you're here. Now, leave it to us, this inn, and the town of Willowston to provide everything you need to write this next book."

Libby felt her heart melt, and she squeezed Gani's hand right back.

Harrison sat impatiently waiting for more details on her life, until Libby continued. "As far as friends, I have one that has stood the test of time, Jane. I'm hoping she'll come visit so you can meet her. You'll love her. She's strong-willed, gorgeous, and my best cheerleader."

"Love that for you. And for us. Anytime she wants to come, you just let us know and we'll be ready. Now let's see, we talked about family, friends and hmmm... Gani, what was that last category we were asking about?" Harrison glanced over at Gani innocently.

"Thomas," Libby replied. "My love life can be summed up in one name."

"That's sad," Harrison said, his face full of pity.

Gani shook his head at Harrison as Libby shared more. "We knew each other in high school but didn't date. Then after college when I moved back to my hometown, we ran into each other and started the world's most enchanting love affair," Libby said, with a thick layer of sarcasm.

Harrison made a not-so-subtle cringe face.

"So yes, it's been years and we've dated on and off. I can't seem to get out of the cycle. I guess some part of my brain thinks one day we'll click, and it will turn into something amazing." Libby looked out the window wistfully.

"Ah, so what we're hearing is you can't seem to get off Thomas the Tank Engine, even if another train with a much better caboose is right in front of you," Harrison said, smirking like a naughty toddler.

"Something like that." Libby sighed as she sunk into her seat.

"If we know anything, it's about how to choose great love," Harrison said, looking at Gani sweetly.

"It's true. Of all the decisions I made, choosing Harrison was the most important. Who you choose as a partner in this life matters more than people realize," Gani said.

Harrison shrugged his shoulders happily and replied, "Well said, my love. Now Libby, I know we've just met you, but I'd like to impart this piece of wisdom—"

"It will be the first of many," Gani interrupted playfully.

Harrison cleared his throat, stood up from the table, and delivered his monologue like it was a theatre performance. "You can only choose great love when you feel you deserve great love. Your family and friends can tell you all day long that you are incredible, special, and deserving. But you must feel it inside, the love and self-worth." Harrison pointed to his heart.

Libby found herself clapping, and Gani joined in. Harrison proudly took a bow. The specialness of the moment was clear, based on the joy Libby felt sitting at the table with Harrison and Gani. These were two people she was determined to have part of her life forever.

*   *   *

That evening as Libby was getting ready for bed, she thought about Harrison's words on the importance of self-love. All her life she'd been surrounded by people who made her feel deserving of love, but the one person that never seemed convinced was herself. Perhaps it was time for her to start validating herself rather than waiting for those around her to do it. How she would do that was another story, but she felt a sense of pride for figuring out that this was something she needed to do.

She heard her phone beep and she walked to the side table where it rested, then shook her head when she saw the text. It was like the universe was listening and ready to give her a chance to start on the path.

Thomas: I heard the news about your move to NC. I'm missing you and would love to talk. I want you back in my life.

Over the years, she had gotten countless variations of this message from Thomas that eventually led to asking her to get back together. Libby waited for the familiar feelings to bubble up: relief, excitement, curiosity. But this time, the feelings weren't coming. It was like she had seen behind the curtain. She could literally write how things would go if she answered her usual way. The texts would get more flirtatious, they would meet up, and the familiar spark would come back. They'd go on a few dates, pretending like things were different this time and that they were taking it slow. Then a few weeks later, they would fall into the familiar pattern of being girlfriend and boyfriend. A couple of months would go by before the same old issues brought them back to the same place. And like clockwork, Libby would be crying to her succulents because it didn't work out.

Libby took a breath and decided that this time, she wanted a new path. Maybe it was all the conversations she'd had about the on-again, off-again relationship or the new career opportunity she'd bravely taken. But Libby Autumn wanted more, deserved more, and knew the only way to do that was to try something new.

Libby: We can't keep repeating the same pattern. We both deserve more from a relationship. I wish you a happy life, but it won't be with me as your partner.

She pressed Send, then turned off her phone. That night, Libby slept more soundly than she had in a long time.

CHAPTER NINE

The downside of turning her phone off was clear the moment she opened her eyes. She didn't need the clock on her phone to tell her it was much later than she normally woke up and she was going to need to hurry if she was going to get downstairs at a reasonable time. Libby didn't want Florence to think she was going to sleep through this incredible opportunity she had been given to write her next book. It was important that Florence knew Libby was taking this very seriously. Plus, Paige and Nathanial were arriving today, and Libby wanted to make a good impression. She already admired their talent as authors and was looking forward to collaborating with them as they wrote their next books, but secretly Libby hoped they would also become good friends.

One benefit of working rotating day and night shifts was the ability to get ready in a ridiculously short amount of time. For a moment, her mind flashed back to Thomas's "pretty days and ugly days" comment. A deep sense of pride washed through her for the strength and clarity she communicated in the text to him last night. She deserved more than he was able to offer her, which needed to start with how she treated herself. Libby stepped into her favorite soft light-cream jumpsuit and tied her hair back with a dark-brown-and-cream-checked clip. One final glance in the mirror and she whispered, *they are all pretty days*. She hadn't been paying attention as she ran down the stairs, turned the corner, and slammed right into the unexpecting man in front of her.

"Fire I don't know about?" Wade said, gently holding Libby by the shoulders as she stabilized herself.

"Coffee beans," Libby said under her breath.

"You seem to think of coffee a lot when we meet." A hint of a smile appeared on Wade's lips.

Please tell me no one has whispered a word of my inner thoughts regarding his perfect eyes and my favorite beverage.

"Yes, well I do love—I mean *drink* it, regularly." Libby struggled to form her words, like she was experiencing writer's block mid-sentence.

"Well, by all means." Wade motioned to the kitchen. "Looks like you've got a clear path the rest of the way." He watched her for one more moment then breezily stepped around her, heading outside.

Libby stood for a moment, chastising herself for her inability to act like a human being in front of Wade. She was going to need to learn how to be in his presence without turning into a schoolgirl with a crush.

Be kind.

The reminder to treat herself nicer returned front and center to her brain. Libby took a breath, complimented herself on the fact that she didn't melt into his muscular arms when he touched her, and walked into the kitchen.

Thankfully, Viv, Florence, Gani, and Harrison were in a heated debate on how to prepare a proper crepe and hadn't overheard the interaction with Wade.

"Good morning! I meant to get down here sooner, but I turned my phone off last night and, well, here we are." Libby had no intention of starting the morning with a monologue on her decision to officially stop the cycle with Thomas. Enough of her life had been spent on that relationship, and it was time she made space for something new.

"Wade is here too, if that's at all interesting," Harrison said, getting a stern stare from Gani for his subtlety.

"Yes, we, uh, collided," Libby said, as lightly as she could muster.

"Well, that perfect man came with more plants to help us take my latest creative landscape vision to life," Harrison said, signaling to the large leafy plants by the back door.

"How nice. I'm surprised you can find a spot for more," Libby said.

"My thoughts exactly, but nothing will stop this man," Gani replied, looking at Harrison affectionately.

Libby smiled. "So how did everyone sleep?" It was Libby's best attempt at getting the conversation away from Wade.

"Slept wonderfully. Gani and Harrison gave me some of the lavender spray to take back to my rental house, and I swear there is magic in there," Florence said.

"She's not lying. I fell asleep within seconds. Didn't even get to fantasize about the body builders playing chess, which was a shame, but I guess the night of sleep was worthwhile," Viv added, deep in thought.

While Viv continued thinking, Florence whispered, "Her latest thing is watching a series on chess, but she still can't let go of the body-building competition shows, so alas, here we are, Viv's newest fantasy mash."

Libby laughed like she was ten again. The personalities surrounding her were bringing out a lighter side, like she could let her guard down and enjoy the moment more.

"The man of the hour is here," Lake said, as he slid into the kitchen.

"Oh yeah, and we brought him too," Viv said, indicating Lake, finally out of her daydreaming.

It appeared Lake was unable to enter a room without making a statement. Today's outfit made his pajamas from the other day look subtle. It was a neon-colored romper with a graffiti-type design.

"I know we drove you here, but every time you walk into a room wearing this outfit, I find myself questioning life's purpose," Viv said, as she shook her head.

Harrison chimed in immediately. "Oh Viv, it's fashion. I happen to think you look marvelous, Lake. The haters gonna hate. Maybe you can get me one but more pastel colored?"

Gani choked slightly on his tea.

"Thank you, Harrison. I will talk with the designer," Lake said, then looked to Libby. "Don't you think it brings out my eyes?"

"Totally. You know, this is incredibly helpful. I might just have the murderer wear this as they stab the victim," Libby said, sipping her coffee.

"Can't say they didn't see it coming," Viv added, as the room burst out in laughter.

Everyone settled into a comfortable conversation on the plan for the day. Libby was happy to hear they would drive over to the library construction site to get a feel for the building, once Nathanial and Paige arrived. Ever since Viv and Libby talked with Carrigan, Libby couldn't stop thinking about the potential the library held. She continued writing notes in her journal for her next book, but now the pages were getting scattered with ideas for the library, her mystery-genre workshop, and endless sketches of the outdoor land-scape at the inn.

*   *   *

Two hours later, the inn was bustling with energy. Harrison was preparing a light lunch with an upbeat jazz soundtrack in the background, Gani and Wade were planting the new plants out back, and Lake was discussing his travel plans for the coming weeks with Viv and Florence while simultaneously trying out new material.

Libby was seated by the window, journal in hand, watching the scene play out in front of her. There were moments in her life that felt right, like the puzzle of the universe managed to line everything up exactly as it needed to be, and this was one of them.

Libby was so distracted by her thoughts, she didn't see that Lake had come over.

"Well, my young writer, it is time to bid our fare-wells and leave you to learn how to spread your wings into a profitable second book," Lake said, sitting on the armrest of Libby's chair.

"Love when you call me young, considering you're almost a decade younger than me," Libby said, at-tempting not to laugh at his romper again. "But thank you for all this. Seriously, I feel so lucky to be here and have this opportunity. I'm glad you sent that let-ter to me," Libby added.

"You got it. Anything to make Mom happy," Lake said, nodding toward Florence, who was deep in conversation with Viv.

"I'm curious. Did you do the same thing when you reached out to Nathanial and Paige? Sent them a letter on paper worth more than my car?" Libby said.

"Nope. Just you. Mom reached out to Nathanial and Paige the boring way. Formal email exchange, blah, blah, blah. I asked to handle your case," Lake said, as he got distracted with the latest buzz on his phone.

Don't love that he's referring to me as a case.

"So, why did you do that?" Libby said, bringing his attention back to the moment.

"We were out to dinner one night; I'd just been asked for a thousand photos on our way into the restaurant. I got my hair styled slightly different that day, and people were really feeling me." Lake played with his hair.

"Uh huh," Libby said, wondering if he was going to eventually get to the answer to her question.

"Mom was talking about each of the three authors she found and mentioned that you had no social presence. I asked her if you were sixty, but she confirmed you were a real human woman in her thirties. I got curious and did some search with the help of Viv. Boy, that woman can stalk with the best of the alphas. Found out you were a nurse, lived in the town you grew up in, and were attractive. Enough to pique my interest," Lake said casually, as he once again got distracted by his phone.

"Huh," Libby said, trying to make sense of his answer.

A moment later, Lake put his phone down and focused his attention fully on Libby.

"I told you before, I like different. Thought you deserved a different approach. Just my way of saying, 'I see you and how special you are and shall grant you my time and attention.' It's highly desired, as you know," Lake said, as he sat up taller.

"You realize you manage to compliment yourself in more conversations than not," Libby said.

"Yep. It's so easy to do when you're me. Now before I go, I need to impart my next lesson on confidence," Lake said, sounding serious.

Libby attempted not to roll her eyes. "Go on, oh wise one." Libby opened her journal to a fresh page.

Ignoring her sarcasm, Lake did go on. "Lake Sterling thinks you're special and good enough for his brother. Now write that down. Once it soaks in, you'll be all set on confidence." Lake stared at her and then her journal, impatiently waiting for her to write it down.

"You're serious," Libby said, in a half statement, half question.

Lake took a deep breath. "I don't know how good your memory is, so I encourage you to write it down. You can also record my voice as I impart this wisdom, if that works better for you," he said, again getting distracted by his phone.

"Lake, I'm supposed to be focusing on my writing career and not my love life. You should be building my confidence as a writer and not a future sister-in-law," Libby said, recognizing the ridiculousness of the entire conversation playing out.

"Libby, the sister-in-law. I like the sound of that. Let's put some effort into that, yes?" Without pause, Lake went on., "Did you write that mystery book with your name on it?"

"Well, yeah, obviously," Libby said, trying to follow Lake's transition from Wade to her writing career.

"Then you can write. And not just write but do it well and in a way that makes people want more. You don't need confidence as an author, you need it as a human. Believe in yourself as a whole person, not just as a talented writer, and it'll come. Think on that wisdom I'm dropping and actually write it down." Lake stood up, took a bow, and headed to the door.

Libby sat stunned at the conversation that just took place.

What is happening right now? I'm getting lectured on my love life and writing career from a twenty-something rapper?

"He's right, you know." Florence walked over and sat down in the chair next to Libby.

"Which part exactly? Hard to hear what he was saying with that romper in my face," Libby said, using humor to deflect from the mix of emotions Lake's words had inspired.

Florence chuckled. "We should have warned you about Lake's bold voyage into fashion. Now, I'm going to be here to help you get this book done. I don't want you to feel like you're alone in this. But Lake's right, you've got the talent, you just need to recognize how incredible you are. As both an author and a human being. We all see it." Florence waved her hand to everyone in the house.

"Thank you," Libby said, unsure how else to respond.

Florence stood up and gently placed her hand on Libby's shoulder.

"No time like the present to start loving yourself," Florence said with a smile. She removed her hand from Libby's shoulder and walked away.

Libby looked out the window, processing all she'd heard.

The universe is sending a clear message on self-love right now, as well as the importance of neutrals in fashion.

* * *

Lake and Viv headed out together, needing to review his upcoming schedule on the way to the airport. Wade also left, with some vague answer as to where he was headed.

A short time later, the sounds of a car on the gravel driveway signaled the arrival of Paige and Nathanial. Gani and Harrison rushed to the front porch, excited to meet the two new guests. Libby felt nervous as she saw the two authors emerge from the car.

Nathanial was tall and thin, with a curly mop of strawberry-blond hair. He had black-framed glasses and wore jeans with a short-sleeve button-up in a subtle floral print. He looked acutely uncomfortable coming out of the car, his tall frame slouching as he smiled shyly. Libby's first impression was that he was adorable and was going to be even more overwhelmed when Harrison introduced himself with his intense level of excitement. Nathanial wasn't at all what she expected after having read his fantasy book filled with magic, horror, and incredibly vivid scenes of steamy romance. The contrast between his shy exterior and inner world made her even more curious to get to know him.

Paige, on the other hand, seemed like the female version of Lake, exuding confidence and style out of every pore. She was tall, with long black hair that flowed in the wind as though she were in the middle of a photoshoot. Libby laughed internally, imagining how overwhelmed shy Nathanial must have been when the two of them met up at the airport. Paige wore a dark navy-blue blazer-dress, something Libby had never seen worn in person. The dress showed off her perfect legs, which managed to be even more perfect because of the tall navy-blue heels she wore with it.

"Fabulous!" Harrison shouted, as he tore down the porch to greet Paige. "You, my dear, will be going shopping with me. I can't wait to see inside your suitcase." Harrison grabbed Paige's hand and spun her around like it was a choreographed dance scene.

Gani sensed Nathanial's unease and calmly walked over and introduced himself. Florence followed behind and greeted Nathanial. His shoulders began to relax as Gani and Florence talked to him. Libby took a breath and walked down the porch.

Paige and Harrison were deep in conversation, so Libby decided to greet Nathanial first. Florence made way for Libby and handled the introduction.

"Nathanial, this is Libby, our mystery writer. I think the two of you are going to get along wonderfully." She grabbed Gani's arm and walked to greet Paige, giving Nathanial and Libby a moment to talk alone.

"I thought your book was incredible," Libby said, stretching out her hand.

"I appreciate that. I read yours in one sitting. I never really got into mysteries before, but the way you wove the story, developed the characters, and revealed the mystery was super cool."

"Well, I'd love that in writing as a review. I need to hear that more than the negative reviews that haunt me," Libby said, smiling as she realized how comfortable it was to talk to him.

"Right? I can recite word for word the negative reviews I've received. It's part of the reason I've been struggling to write my next book. I'll be typing, and then suddenly the negative reviews pop in my mind and the story just shuts down," Nathanial said.

Libby knew exactly the struggle he was experiencing and was grateful she could talk to someone who understood how impactful the negative reviews could be. Florence was right; they would get along great and probably be better authors for it.

"Libby in the flesh. I have been dying to meet you." Paige walked over to Libby and wrapped her in a hug.

Libby almost fell over in shock. She had expected Paige to be more cold with her, maybe give her a once over and a few fashion notes, but instead she was hugging her with the intensity of a bear.

"Oh hi. Wow, you're strong," Libby said, as she felt her breathing strain from the tight hug.

"Pilates!" Paige said, mid-hug, like it was the obvious answer to all life's mysteries.

Paige finally released Libby and went on. "How did you do it? The way you put the mystery together, laying out small clues while making you absolutely fall in love with the characters. That mom? I mean, I wish she were my mom. Hilarious, sassy, and just perfect. Libby, you are a true talent." Paige waved her hands around as she spoke. Libby had just met the woman, but she already loved her.

"I don't know, and I don't know if I'll be able to do it again," Libby said simply.

"Ridiculous. You were meant to be a mystery writer. Alright, we have got to see the backyard. Harrison told me it's enchanting, and I could use the inspiring scenery for my book." With that, Paige looped one arm around Libby and the other around Nathanial and guided them to the backyard like she owned the place.

"Those three are going to do great things. Now let's give them some time to get acquainted," Florence said, smiling at the backs of her three authors.

* * *

Viv had returned to the inn after dropping Lake at the airport, as she had decided to stay a few more days in Willowston. After a light lunch and tour of the inn for the new arrivals, the time to visit the library site had come.

As the three authors waited outside for Florence and Viv, Libby started sharing her excitement for the library project. Immediately, she felt out of sync with her fellow authors.

"I never realized the power a library held in a community until I spent more time in the one at my hometown. They can offer a safe space for people to work, dream, and connect. For this town especially, you'll see how much it's needed. The town is dealing with a ton of change, and from what I've heard, there haven't been many opportunities for people to connect in a meaningful way. The scope of offerings the library is going to provide will enhance people's minds, health, and spirit. It's so great to get to see it." Libby paused as she noticed Nathanial and Paige looking at Libby like she was from another planet.

"Um, no offense, but I'm seeing this as more of a job requirement. Check the boxes, obviously do it well because that's the only way I do things, and move on to writing," Paige said, glancing to Nathanial for comment.

"Yeah, I mean I think libraries are valuable institutions, but I'm with Paige. Just get it done and focus on my next book." Nathanial's expression was apologetic as he looked at Libby.

"Oh sure. I wrote my first book from the library in my hometown, so I guess I'm just feeling more nostalgic," Libby added, hoping to regain her composure as her mind spun.

"Oh wow, yeah that makes total sense. I love that for you," Paige said sincerely to Libby.

"Yeah," Nathanial added, with a double thumbs up.

The women burst out laughing, and Paige went on to discuss the proper use of a double thumbs up to Nathanial, notably *never,* unless interacting with a small child. As Nathanial defended his use of thumbs up, citing its origin during World War II, half of Libby's mind stayed curious about the library project and wondered if her excitement about it would dissipate as her writing got underway.

· CHAPTER TEN ·

An hour later, the three authors, Viv, and Florence stood in front of the library. The exterior looked near completion. It was a sizable building tucked perfectly into the forest.

"Isn't it wonderful?" Florence said, radiating excitement.

"It certainly is wood-forward," Viv said, getting a glare from Florence.

"It's reclaimed teak siding. We wanted to make it as eco-friendly as possible and have it blend in with the setting," Florence added as she went into the details of the material and color choices.

"It's mesmerizing. Makes me want to spend all day here," Libby said, unable to take her eyes off the building.

"Yeah, you and the beavers," Viv said, and received another glare from Florence.

"Don't mind Viv here. She is still processing the fact that we didn't make the building bright red to match her hair," Florence said.

"They did it in San Antonio, I don't know why we couldn't do it here. Red is a powerful color. How can you not look at my hair and want to use it as inspiration?"

"Yes, well, fire stations have taken you up on inspiration for decades, so we can go visit one of those later," Florence replied with a smirk. Then turning her attention to the authors, she said, "Let's head inside so you all can get a better feel for the space."

The inside was unlike any library Libby had experienced. Even with the ongoing construction and lack of books, computers, or furniture, she could visualize the potential. Wood panels, combined with light-green paint and the use of stone, brought the beautiful outside setting in.

"Using her better judgment, Florence listened to me on the water features," Viv said, noticing Libby's eyes focusing on the far wall, where the water would cascade once the installation was complete.

"It's gorgeous," Libby said, as if in a daze.

After a few moments of wandering, Florence gathered everyone to show them the activity rooms in the back. The first few were smaller, appropriate for study groups or other small meetings. The last room, positioned in the back corner of the building, appeared to be spacious. Before they went in, Florence proudly shared the hopes for the use of the room.

"This is where we'd like to do book readings, storytelling, exercise classes, and inspiring art classes. We are thinking of this room as the heart of the library, where the community can really come together," Florence said proudly.

She motioned for them to step inside. Paige had stopped suddenly, causing Nathanial and Libby to bump into one another.

"Oh, look at that incredible romper," Paige said, standing up even taller.

Libby and Nathanial peered around her and saw Lake, Brooke, and Wade standing by the far wall. Of course, Libby's attention went to the non-romper-wearing brother.

How are his eyes glowing even from this distance? Maybe it's the reflection off Lake's romper...

Nathanial spoke up, interrupting Libby's thoughts.

"What's behind that paper hanging on the wall?" Nathanial said, pointing to the wall where Florence's children stood.

"Seriously? You see the talented, gorgeous, world-known rap artist Lake Sterling, and you want to know what's behind the paper?" Paige looked genuinely shocked.

"What? We met during the interview process." Nathanial waved at Lake like they were old friends.

"Fascinating. You get shy around the squirrels outside, but a world-famous celebrity results in a casual wave. Nathanial, you are truly something," Paige said, shaking her head.

"Alright, everyone." Florence projected her voice in a strong and formal way, causing all to turn with their full attention.

"As you noticed, Nathanial, there is something behind that paper on the wall."

Florence paused, looking to Viv with love and admiration.

"Now, although your fabulous hair did not inspire the exterior, we thought we might draw some inspiration here." Florence signaled to her three children to remove the paper.

What remained were bold red letters with the words "I love my community" surrounded by impeccably drawn flowers in shades of red, purple, and blue.

"No. No, no, no. You didn't. Oh my God, you did." Viv practically sprinted to the wall to touch the flowers and letters.

"Wow," Nathanial said, as they watched Viv rolling her body sideways along the wall.

"So, what are we missing?" Paige said, turning to Florence. "I mean yes, the letters are red, and this room now looks more Viv's style than the rest of the space, but what is causing that woman to rub her body on a wall so passionately?"

Florence laughed as she watched Viv's enthusiasm fill the large space. Her children had descended on Viv, giving her hugs. The display of love in front of Libby made her catch her breath.

Florence turned to explain to the three confused authors. "Years ago, when Viv's mother's health began to decline, the two women decided to get matching tattoos. If you think Viv is a hoot, her mother sounded like she was on a whole other level. I never met her, but every story Viv has shared makes me admire her mother even more. Now, they had no idea what they wanted to get tattooed on their bodies that day, but as they were about to walk into the tattoo parlor, they saw these beautiful flowers in shades of red, blue, and purple. Her mom literally plucked them out of the planter and brought them into the tattoo parlor and said, 'We want these permanently displayed on our luscious bodies.'" Florence laughed.

Viv walked over, adding, "Despite everything, it was one of the happiest days of my life. We got our tattoos and then planted flowers in her garden. Mind you, none of them ever bloomed, because we had no idea what we were doing, but we laughed and enjoyed that day. Things went downhill fast after that with her health, but no one can ever take those memories away from me. Here, take a look." Viv took off her jacket and rolled up her sleeve, revealing the tattoo. It matched the design of the flowers on the wall perfectly, resulting in everyone getting misty eyed.

"Well, damn. Now I want to get a tattoo," Libby said.

"Give us some more time together and that very well may happen," Viv said, winking at Libby.

Lake, Brooke, and Wade then joined the rest of the group. Libby enjoyed watching the way each of them interacted with people. Lake was his typical outgoing, high-energy self, flowing in and out of conversation with those around him. Brooke squeezed the authors with endless enthusiasm and spoke with such sincerity about her excitement for their next books. Of course, Libby's attention kept floating back to Wade, who was talking with everyone but her. When he finally came over to her and said hello, Libby felt her breath catch. The intensity of the stare from his deep brown eyes seemed to reach a part of her that hadn't been touched before.

"Hi," Libby said, simply.

Wade nodded hello and, for a moment, looked nervous as he stood close to Libby.

Is he nervous ... because of me?

An instant later, the nervousness seemed to disappear as he asked casually, "What do you think of the library, Libby?"

I dunno, what do you think of me?

Refocusing, Libby replied, "I love it. Of course it's beautiful, designed with incredible, talented eyes."

Stop talking about eyes around this man.

Libby cleared her throat and went on, "But it also has this warmth that reminds me of the library in my hometown. There is something special about a library, the way it welcomes people into a safe and inviting space. I find it inspiring."

Wade's only response was another small nod of his head and he went to talk with the others.

Great, you bored him away.

Libby turned and saw Lake with a smug smile on his face.

"Oh don't give me that look," Libby said to Lake. "I thought Viv took you to the airport."

Lake chuckled, allowing Libby to change the subject away from his brother. "Yes, that was a bit of a ruse. I had to be here. Nothing quite like making our Viv happy. Especially when it has to do with honoring a parent that passed away."

For a moment, the grief of losing his father was written all over Lake's face as he glanced back at the flowers drawn on the wall.

"I'm glad you were here," Libby simply said.

For a few seconds, Lake continued to stare at the wall, seemingly lost in his pain. Turning back to Libby he added, "Yeah, same. Glad I was here."

His expression changed quickly as he nodded toward his brother. "Might want to dust off your flirting game, sis-in-law." He chuckled at his own comment and strolled off to talk with the others.

Can someone get him on a plane and keep him there?

* * *

After some time, Florence's children said their good-byes. Lake promised to leave for real this time after he gave a loving and funny speech about Viv's greatness. Wade was driving Brooke to Florence's house so she could get unpacked for the next few days she spent in town.

After the three children left, Florence showed the rest of the space, including the impressive café area. Libby could almost picture Wade behind the counter, crafting coffees to match his eyes.

Smooth, creamy, dreamy brown coffee. Ahhh...

"Are you alright?" Nathanial's voice pulled Libby from her daydream. "You look kind of weird," he added.

Libby cleared her throat. "Yes, I'm fine, just feeling a bit low on caffeine," Libby replied, hurrying to catch up with the rest of the group before Nathanial could say anything else.

By the time they were ready to leave, even Nathanial and Paige seemed inspired by the new space and were excited to start working from there. All three authors had picked a special spot to do their writing. Libby chose a quiet area by a window at the back end of the library, far away from the café, to minimize distractions. Nathanial wanted a table at the café itself, citing how his best writing was done in coffee shops. Paige picked the corner near the waterfall wall, where she could position herself to write while simultaneously featuring her best side, apparently the right. Libby had no idea which side of her face was the best, but truthfully, her favorite photos showed the back of her head, which perfectly highlighted the difference between her and Paige.

* * *

Once outside, Florence updated the group on the timing for the completion of the space. "We're hoping the library will be open in a little over a month." As she spoke, her brow wrinkled, revealing some lingering concerns on the timeline.

Viv sensed the worry and added, "No worries on that. Thankfully, the contractor, Bill, has taken to our dear Florence and is hellbent on impressing her. It'll get done. Florence here has a way of inspiring men to achieve the unachievable."

"Oh! Spill!" Paige said, hooking arms with Viv and wandering back in the direction of the car.

"Ignore her. Bill is a professional and I trust he'll get it done," Florence said to Nathanial and Libby.

"He hopes to get a lot more done than the library," Viv shouted from up ahead.

"Ugh, that woman's hearing is annoyingly robust," Florence said, as she waved them to the cars.

* * *

The group stopped at the town coffee shop on the way back to the inn. Carrigan was nowhere to be found, but Libby was happy to see a few more tables occupied. Viv and Florence ordered first and said they wanted to grab a table outside to talk. Viv hadn't had the opportunity to talk with Florence one-on-one since the reveal of the wall. Nathanial, Paige, and Libby said they would order and enjoy their coffees inside.

When it was Nathanial's turn to place his order from the barista, the next happy surprise of the day came.

"Oh hi." Nathanial immediately looked extra shy as he took in the beautiful, cheerful barista in front of him.

"Hey to you. I'm Grace, the owner and barista of this little coffee shop," she said, with a curtsy that somehow felt normal from her. "What can I get you today? You look like the kind of guy that knows his way around a coffee shop," Grace said flirtatiously, causing Nathanial's face to turn the shade of red Viv had hoped for the outside of the library.

"I would like a coffee in a cup, please." Nathanial's brain was fizzing out in front of them. Recognizing the condition, being a recent victim herself, Libby stepped in.

"Nathanial, you were just telling us how much you love an extra-sweet mocha," Libby said, helping him with not just his order but also providing his name for Grace as she watched him with curiosity.

Paige chimed in, "It's true. Libby and I here just recently met Nathanial, but we can tell you with confidence that he really appreciates sweet things."

"Oh God. Mocha, your largest size please," Nathanial said, immediately turning to walk to the farthest corner of the small café.

Paige smiled at Grace. "I'm Paige. Are you single, Grace? Because Nathanial over there is a special man, and he's also an up-and-coming writer with an impressive imagination." Paige's forwardness was shocking to Libby but well-received by Grace.

"Lovely to meet you, Paige, and Libby, I know I've seen you before, so welcome back. I am single. Well, this café is my one true love that I've poured most of myself into, but I'd be lying if I didn't sometimes wish for more. Are you three just here visiting or . . .?" Grace paused.

Paige jumped right in with her response. "We just moved here. The three of us will be staying at the inn up the road. We're going to be working in the new library while writing our next novels. I'm a romance writer, Libby here crafts an incredible mystery story, and Nathanial writes daring fantasy books that keep you up at night, if you catch my drift." Paige winked at her, getting a laugh out of Grace.

I wonder if Paige is a professional wing-woman on the side.

"How amazing. Can you tell me the names of your books? I love to read," Grace said, as her face lit up.

"We'll do you even better. Nathanial will drop off copies for you tomorrow. Now, I would love a twelve-ounce oat milk latte with caramel," Paige said, transitioning the conversation with ease.

"I'll do a twelve-ounce soy-milk cappuccino please," Libby said.

"You got it. I'll be right out with your coffees." Grace danced to the espresso machine as she worked on the order. She seemed to have even more pep in her step after the conversation.

The second Libby and Paige got to the table where Nathanial was pretending to look at his phone, he immediately asked, "What'd she say?"

"That she's single, poured her heart into this café, and is definitely interested in you," Paige said, as she applied a deep-purple shade of gloss to her lips with the precision of a surgeon.

"Really? Libby?" Nathanial's eyes were pleading for more information.

"She's the romance writer, and based on Paige's skills as a wing woman, I think you've got a chance with Grace. And tomorrow when you drop off our books, you'll get another chance," Libby added.

"Drop off books? By myself? What are you talking about?" Nathanial's return to panic was swift.

Interrupting them, Grace called from behind the counter, "Nathanial, soon-to-be-famous fantasy writer, your drink is ready."

Libby and Paige looked at Nathanial as he sat frozen. Thankfully, his back was facing Grace, so she didn't witness how nervous he looked.

"What do I do?" he said, trying to disappear under the table.

Paige, looking directly at Nathanial, spoke in a calm but stern voice. "You take three deep breaths, remember that you are a talented writer, and strut your handsome self over to that bar and get your extra-sweet mocha."

"Huh. Talented and handsome. Wish I saw that written in my reviews," Nathanial said, as he stood up and walked to the counter, looking surprisingly confident.

"I don't understand," Libby said to Paige, as they watched Nathanial retrieve the drink and actually manage to thank Grace without stumbling over his words.

Paige smiled and replied, "He just needed to hear he was handsome. Works wonders to build a man's confidence." Then they saw Nathanial trip over a chair on his way back. Paige quickly added, "The effects are temporary," and looked at a message on her phone.

As Nathanial worked to place the chair he tripped over back at the table, Libby spoke to Paige in a quiet voice.

"Can you teach other people how to be confident when they have a crush, with maybe more lasting effects?"

Paige glanced up at her, eyes sparkling. "I knew it."

Their conversation was interrupted by Nathanial as he sat down at the table with a deep sigh and stared into his mug. Libby and Paige followed his gaze and saw the small heart design Grace had poured on top of his mocha.

"Well, that's adorable," Libby said.

"I'm sure she does this on all her drinks," Nathanial said, attempting to sound casual.

"Libby, Paige, ready for you," Grace called from behind the counter.

"I'll grab them while Libby catches you up on why she needs some romance help from yours truly," Paige said, grinning.

"What's she talking about?" Nathanial asked, grateful for the conversation change away from him.

"I like someone and I'm struggling a bit to interact with him. It's becoming a distraction and I need a boost of confidence so I can get on with my life," Libby said.

"No offense, but I really don't see you and Lake working out," Nathanial said.

"She's not interested in Lake," Paige said, as she returned with the two drinks.

She nodded to the design Grace had done in their mugs: beautiful flowers, but no hearts in sight. Nathanial again tried to look casual, but excitement was written all over his face.

Returning his focus to Libby, he said, "Not Lake?" looking completely confused.

"Wade," both women responded.

"Huh. The serious and mysterious brother. I should have guessed, but to be honest, I was distracted by Lake's romper." He went on, sounding slightly frustrated, "Girls always like the mysterious type. I mean, I wrote my first book dreaming up the male character I wish I was." Nathanial's honesty was endearing.

"Well, we like you just the way you are," Paige said, immediately resulting in a smile from Nathanial.

"Thanks. You two are pretty great yourselves," he replied.

Paige then turned to Libby. "Back to you. I think what Nathanial is referring to with Wade is that he has some walls up. Nothing wrong with that, but it does make it hard to know what he's thinking. For most people. But of course, I'm not most people."

"What exactly are you saying?" Libby said, bracing herself to hear Wade wasn't interested in her.

"It's mutual. The attraction, that is," Paige said, casually sipping from her cup.

Nathanial chimed in before Libby could say anything. "How could you possibly know that? You watched them together for all of ten minutes." He looked at Paige like she was a magical sorcerer.

Paige chuckled and replied, "The obvious things were the eye contact and how he positioned his body when talking to her. The more subtle cues were the crease in his brow and how his gaze drifted to her when they weren't talking. Almost like he was trying to figure her out. Body language is incredibly revealing, if you know what to look for. And I'm happy to teach you both," Paige said.

"When can we start?" Libby and Nathanial said together eagerly. The three laughed before Paige dove into her first lesson.

As the weeks went by, a few things became apparent to Libby. First, her lessons with Paige were paying off, because she was finally conversing in complete, logical sentences with Wade. He, on the other hand, remained consistent with his perfect dreamy eyes, friendly conversation, and promising body language toward Libby, as interpreted by Paige, but made no verbal romantic declarations, as witnessed by Libby.

Second, Libby was becoming even more passionate about creating the mystery-genre workshop for the library. While Nathanial and Paige struggled to put together enough material for their three-part workshop, Libby had decided to expand hers, securing multiple mystery-writer speakers and developing a list of books and talking points for an ongoing mystery book club series she wanted to provide, once the workshop was complete.

Third, Libby was happy to a degree she hadn't thought possible.

"Libby, I appreciate that you need to whisper, since there are gossips infiltrating your current residence, but I cannot hear you one bit," Jane said, exasperated, on the other line.

"Sorry, sorry, I know. Okay, let me move to the bench by the garden." Libby hopped off the front porch and walked into the ever-transforming landscape. The cooler, shorter days of autumn brought about magical shifts in the garden beds and tree line. With a last name of Autumn, Libby's love of the season was pretty much set in stone the day she was born.

"Okay, I'm safe. Unless they have this bench miked, which I wouldn't put past Harrison. That man loves gossip more than anyone I've ever met." Libby looked under the bench, confirming there was no obvious listening device.

"Let's go with Harrison hasn't crossed that line and tell me what you were saying," Jane said, anxiously waiting for her friend to share. Based on the panic text, combined with Libby's nervous voice, Jane knew her friend was struggling with something.

"Oh Jane, it's worse than I thought possible," Libby said dramatically, finally settling into the bench.

"We talk daily, and you've been sounding happy. Did something happen? Who do I need to destroy? I'm ready. Just say the name and consider it done. I will turn their life upside down in ways you wouldn't dream of." Jane had shifted from the loving, kind friend to the murderous maniac in a matter of a few sentences.

"Whoa there, bestie. Stand down. I repeat, stand down. The problem is, I'm deliriously happy, and it's unsustainable. My bar on happiness is rising, and I can't keep this up," Libby said in a panic.

"Oh, dear Lord," Jane said, rolling her eyes.

"This is serious. My days of happy are numbered. I'm living in a fantasy. I literally wake up to a gorgeous sunrise, jot notes on ways to improve my mystery workshop while simultaneously avoiding looking at my computer—which I should be writing my novel on—and get ready in the bathroom of renovation dreams. Then I go downstairs, enjoy a leisurely breakfast talking to Gani and Harrison, who I fall more in love with every day, then I write, sort of, which eventually leads me to wandering the gardens behind the inn. At some point Nathanial, Paige, and I go grab coffees and stroll around town while harassing Nathanial to finally make a move on the barista. We come back to the inn, do some more writing—or in my case, anything but—and then have dinner with everyone like we're one big, happy family."

Libby paused. "Are you still there?" she asked Jane, wondering if the line was dropped.

"I'm digesting what you're saying while simultaneously wondering how you wrote a book with no run-on sentences," Jane replied.

"Very funny. What do I do? How do I stop being so happy, so I don't hate my life when this is over?" Libby said, as her mind spiraled.

"Whoa, whoa, whoa. I have seriously never heard you like this. Did you finally sleep with that gorgeous chef with the perfect cold-brew eyes?" Jane said.

"What? No! We're still at the 'I try to apply the lessons Paige has taught me and not melt or mention coffee around him' and he's all, 'stares deeply into my soul, asks me questions and then does his confused eyebrow crease and wanders away,'" Libby said, after confirming there was still no one within earshot.

"Ah. So basically, you and Nathanial are in the same place in terms of romantic progress," Jane quipped.

"Something like that. Now can we get back to my life crisis please? I need a plan, like, right now," Libby said.

"Yes, yes, one minute. We'll get back to the, 'ah, help me I'm so happy' crisis. You mentioned a few times about not writing much. Aren't you supposed to be close to a quarter of the way done with your next book? This explains why you haven't been sending me any chapters. Your 'happy issue' was my last clue. We both know you tend to hide the actual issue, leave some verbal crumbs, and then set the stage for a dramatic distraction. Which, by the way, is why I believe you're such a good mystery novelist, but I digress," Jane said.

"Yes, well it's not ideal. I'm a bit behind. Paige has a ton of chapters done; Nathanial has completed his insanely detailed outline and doesn't seem nervous about finishing on time; and I'm on page… I can't even say it." Libby slumped down in the bench.

"Please don't say it. You know how seriously I take deadlines, so I don't want to know. So, what's going on?" Jane asked.

"The truth is, I have no desire to write. I'm both deliriously happy with my present life and more lost than I've ever been about my writing. Which makes no sense, because this is the first time in my life I've had dedicated time to focus on it. But to be honest, I just want to spend time at the library developing my workshop and talking with the librarians. But my book? Every time I think about it, I'm just getting that horrible stomachache I get," Libby said, rubbing her belly.

"Breathe, Libby," Jane said, waiting to hear the audible exhale from her friend.

Once she heard it, Jane went on. "I think that's incredible, how passionate you are about the mystery workshop. But you're in Willowston to work on your next book, which sounds like it's not happening, and you're trying to hide that fact. We both know your sensitive stomach struggles whenever you try to hide something," Jane said, remembering the countless secrets Libby had told her over the years to relieve the tension of holding them in on her own.

"I can't. I don't want to let Florence or Lake or everyone else down. They believed in me, and now I'm just a wannabe librarian who doesn't know the Dewey decimal system," Libby said, feeling defeated.

"Why did you write in the first place?" Jane asked.

Libby thought for a moment and responded from her heart. "When I wrote my first book, I felt like I was transported to a kinder, happier world where I could flow freely with the thoughts in my head, rather than the panic and struggle I felt day to day."

"And?"

"And I guess, I'm just worried that I only wanted to write because I hated my job and schedule so much. Now that I have a meaningful role in the library developing the mystery workshop and enjoying my day-to-day life, I'm scared the appeal of writing has just, 'poof,' gone away." Libby motioned the "poof" with her hand like an explosion, though Jane couldn't see her.

"Did you poof with your hands?" Jane said, smiling.

Libby laughed. "Yes, you know I can't help myself. Plus being around Paige all the time has started to really increase my use of hand motions. They're just so effective in getting your point across," Libby said.

"Libby? You're allowed to enjoy your day-to-day life and successfully write a mystery novel. Your life situation doesn't need to be the same to result in another great book. I mean if that was the case, you'd have to forget about dreamy coffee-bean corneas and go back to, ugh, dead-eyes Thomas," Jane said, shuddering at the thought.

"At this rate, there will be no eyes. I just feel like I'm taking too much happiness from the earth joy bank, you know?"

"Oh Libs, that scarcity mindset hasn't done you good one time in your life. There is no 'earth joy bank' that you are overdrawing from. We both know life can change in an instant, so please, for both of our sakes, suck up as much joy as you can," Jane said.

"I know you're right. It's just been hard to watch Paige and Nathanial find their flow with writing their next books so easily. They are enjoying everything around here, but they are always dying to get back to writing. I'm just starting to wonder if it's my path, Jane," Libby said, placing her hand on her chest at hearing the words out loud.

"That's okay," Jane said simply, finally understanding the source of Libby's struggles.

"How is that okay? This is all I thought I ever wanted, and it's been handed to me on a silver platter, or antique floral plate because that's Florence's favorite, but you get my point," Libby said.

"I think you were so focused on this dream not being a possibility that now that it is, you must figure out if it's what you want. But may I also say, that just because you write your next book, it doesn't mean this is what you'll do for the rest of your life. You get to change your mind, you know," Jane said.

"Great. I don't want to be a nurse, and now maybe I don't want to be a writer, and I refuse to learn the Dewey decimal system, so I guess I'll just live with you and tend to your plants," Libby said.

"You know I don't allow real plants in my house. After the one hundredth one you convinced me to get died, I've decided that's my good deed: to never kill another houseplant. And quite frankly, I like it that way," Jane said.

"You killed the air plant I got you for your birthday? How do you even do that? It was only three months ago."

"Let's not lose focus here. Back to your future," Jane said.

"I'd rather not," Libby replied.

"Look, I've seen you force yourself into boxes that don't fit you all your life, because you're trying to please everyone around you. Now you've made a commitment to write this next book. You can do it, and you can do it well, but stop telling yourself that you need to fit into the latest box of being a professional mystery writer, no matter how flashy and appealing you once thought it was," Jane said.

"I just wanted this to be it. So badly, you know? And the thought that maybe this isn't the path for me is terrifying, because it feels like I'm more lost than I've ever been." Libby felt weighed down by the thought.

"I know. But isn't that part of life? Trying different paths, seeing what works and doesn't? Life isn't about finding that one thing and then everything fits. You're going to be okay," Jane said confidently.

"Thanks for saying that. But you're right. No matter what, I need to deliver this next book. Any brilliant ideas on what my next book should uh, I dunno . . . be about?" Libby said, as she checked in on her mind, which remained empty on fresh ideas.

"Actually, I do," Jane said, sitting up in her chair.

"Oh, not this again. I'm not making my ex-boyfriend the victim of a gruesome murder in my next book," Libby said.

"Not that, although I still think the best friend murdering the ex-boyfriend makes logical and appealing sense for our demographic. No, I'm thinking you should make your two worlds collide. Write the next book in the setting of a brand-new library, in a charming town set in the mountains, with a romantic lead that has incredible brown eyes." Jane mentally patted herself on the shoulder for the brilliance.

Libby thought about it for a moment. She had written notes over the past months, but she hadn't finalized a setting.

"That might work," she said finally.

"Of course it does. I'm a walking inspiration everywhere I go," Jane said, glancing down and admiring her manicured nails.

"Jane, the floodgates are opening. The next mother-daughter mystery can be a body found at the site of a library when they're doing a renovation. Okay, I must go. I love you and owe you," Libby said, feeling a faint sense of relief.

"You got this. And Libby? You deserve spectacular overwhelming joy in every aspect of your life. You will find your path, but it's not as a caretaker to my dying house plants," Jane said.

"Well, they wouldn't be dying if I was there, but yes, point taken. Love you, Jane." Libby disconnected the phone and took a breath.

"Floodgates, huh?"

Libby looked up, startled to see Gani pruning a nearby bush.

"How much of that did you hear?" Libby said nervously. She adored Gani and Harrison but didn't want all her inner struggles on display for the house.

"Very little. Gardeners only tend to listen when we hear words related to floods and droughts. Plus, I know you wouldn't know it, being married to Harrison, but I can keep a secret like a CIA agent," Gani said, winking.

"Seriously? How? Secrets melt me from the inside," Libby said, cringing at the thought.

"Guess I think of them as pieces of someone's soul, not meant to be shared unless it's your own," Gani said, with the voice of a wise sage.

"And you manage to stay married to the town gossip, how?" Libby asked, hoping she hadn't offended him.

"To each their own. I'm my own person and Harrison is his. And I love that; it's the mismatch of philosophies that keeps things interesting," Gani said, surprising Libby once again.

"Okay, I think you've just secured your spot in my book, you multilayered innkeeper. Would you like to be murdered?" Libby said, actually getting a look of concern from Gani.

"I'd rather not," he replied, playfully slowly backing away from Libby and taking his gardening shears with him.

* * *

A week later, Libby, Nathanial, and Paige went to Florence's house for dinner. Each time Florence hosted them for dinner, which averaged a couple of times a week, she had someone pick the cuisine for the evening. Tonight was Libby's choice, and she knew it was the right one when she entered the kitchen. Various breakfast foods were displayed on the counter: a quiche, perfectly crisped bacon, hash browns, pancakes, and waffles, alongside some of the very best toppings, like fruits, nuts, chocolate, nut butters, cream, and syrup.

Nathanial, who had turned out to be the biggest eater of the group despite his thin frame, immediately grabbed a plate and started piling food on it.

"Well, it looks like this was a winner," Florence said half to herself, as she chuckled watching Nathanial balance a second plate after discovering one was inadequate.

Once everyone had settled at the table, Florence proposed a toast that quickly transitioned into a longer speech. "To my brilliant authors. It has been my pleasure to get to know each of you more and watch how you've settled into this town. Gani and Harrison are asking if I can extend your stay for the next ten years, so I would say you've left your mark on them. Of course, I could not be prouder of how hard each of you are working. The librarians said your literary workshops are coming along wonderfully, some even expanding dramatically." Florence winked at Libby and continued, "But the time has come that I'd like to meet with each of you and see your progress on your next novels. And yes, I know the word all authors cringe at, but your timelines..." Florence paused as she quickly studied the expressions on each of the authors' faces. She hadn't expected to see Libby looking the most panicked of them all.

"We'll get our meetings set up next week. In fact, we'll have those meetings in the newly opened library," Florence said excitedly.

Everyone cheered, clinking their glasses together as Florence talked more about the plans for the grand opening. Even Libby forgot her panicking, listening attentively to Florence. Libby couldn't wait to see the doors officially opened to the public and hoped the community took interest in the literary workshops she, Nathanial, and Paige had worked so hard at.

Throughout the evening, Libby's mind alternated between her excitement for the library opening and her fears on meeting with Florence to show her progress on her book. Since her conversation with Jane, Libby had officially started her book with the scene set in a small town by the mountains, where a library was being demolished to make way for the new and improved one. Despite her efforts, she only had part of the first chapter and had no idea how to speed up the process. When she wrote her first book, she had crammed it into a busy schedule and that had somehow given her a push. But now, with the flexibility in her schedule and her mind constantly drifting to the library, it was like she didn't know how to embrace it.

* * *

At the end of the evening, Paige, Nathanial, and Libby went to the door to put on their shoes and jackets.

Florence asked Libby if she could pull her aside for a moment, and Libby saw Paige and Nathanial cringe from behind her. The moment felt reminiscent of the one time she'd been called into the principal's office. It was a mistake, of course, because Libby lived her life avoiding getting in trouble.

"Are you doing alright? You looked more overwhelmed than I've seen you in a while," Florence said kindly.

"I am. I am. I am." Libby paused, recognizing the confirmed worry in Florence's eyes with every repeated "I am."

"I just have a lot on my mind with the book. You know us authors, always lost in our fantasy worlds." Libby gave her a goofy grin.

Florence smiled sincerely and said, "I'm here if you need to talk. Next week will be a big week, with the library opening, and of course finally getting a first look into your next book."

"Oh, for sure. I think you'll be pleased. At least more so than the dead woman in my story!" Libby knew the conversation was going downhill but didn't know how to stop.

Florence smiled but with concern written all over her face. "Of course. It will be wonderful. I know it can be difficult to find momentum, so we'll figure it all out. I can see the brightest future for you as a brilliant mystery writer." She gave Libby a gentle hug.

"Same. We are totally on the same page," Libby said, while internally dying.

"You can do this, Libby. We'll talk through it in more detail next week. Just take some time to relax this weekend." With that, Florence focused her attention on Paige and Nathanial to say her goodbyes.

* * *

As Libby lay in bed that night, she felt nauseated, and it wasn't the breakfast food she'd had for dinner. Her mind was spinning in ways she hadn't experienced before. The panic of already being behind, combined with her mind desperately trying to put together the plot for the rest of her book, and the late-night hour, were creating a perfect storm of fear.

Libby pulled herself out of bed and went into the bathroom. Standing below the arched wooden ceiling, she felt like she was in a magical fairy-tale cabin, and as she looked up, her breathing immediately calmed. Ignoring the fact that she felt a bit ridiculous, she grabbed her pillow and blanket from the bed and placed them on the bathroom floor. A few minutes later, she drifted into a peaceful sleep.

Libby woke to sun shining brightly on her face. Rolling over, she bumped into something hard and suddenly remembered where she was. She pushed herself up, careful not to hit her head on the tub, and immediately felt regret. Libby had had occasional problems with her back ever since she turned thirty. There were only a handful of times that she felt the radiating pain, but each one of them was memorable. The pain lasted about forty-eight hours, but it severely limited her movement and dignity. Jane had been a witness to one episode the previous year after the two of them had volunteered to help her mother weed the garden. Jane's initial concern and welcome help in Libby's recovery had transformed into mild harassment once Libby felt better. Every day for the month, Jane sent reminders to talk with the doctor and get a medical massage, along with links to various strength training and stretching exercises to build her lower back muscles. That and endless GIFs of old women and "gracefully aging" humor.

Libby spent the next hour painfully getting herself ready for the day. When she was putting the final touches on her makeup, making her thin, light-brown eyebrows visible to the human eye, her phone buzzed. Seeing the name, Wade Sterling, caused her to drop the eyebrow pencil, where it rolled far under her table.

Libby looked at herself in the mirror. With only one eyebrow complete and the pencil at an unreachable place under her table, she knew the day was going well.

Wade had only texted her one time since she moved to Willowston, with the most benign message known to humanity:

Wade: This is Wade Sterling. Thanks.

Surely, this one would be just as riveting. Taking a breath, she opened the message.

Wade: I'm taking you out today. Wear comfortable clothes for the hike. We'll leave in an hour.

Libby's mind ran rampant.

No. This cannot be right. Wade doesn't take me places. Maybe he texted the wrong person.

As if Wade had sensed her confusion, another text came through.

Wade: Trust me, Libby.

First thought following his message was that she'd follow him and those brown beauties off a cliff, but her next thought was she had one eyebrow and a painful back.

Libby: Can't hike today. Pulled my back in my sleep. Things got wild last night.

"Oh my God. I did not just text that," Libby said out loud, as her face grew hot. She reread the message she sent and sighed loudly. She watched her phone, waiting for Wade's response. After what felt like an hour, but was only five minutes, another message came through.

Wade: No problem. Still be ready in an hour. Bring an extra set of clothes and wear your bathing suit.

Libby reread the message a few times. After realizing the clock continued to move despite how frozen she and her back felt, Libby texted Paige.

Libby: SOS. Please come to my room. I need your long limbs.

A moment later, there was a knock at the door. Libby called for Paige to come in and attempted to sit up a bit straighter.

"I am here with my beautiful long limbs. How can we be of service?" Paige said, as she seductively drew her hand along her legs.

"Oh, sure, rub it in. Not only is your body the easiest to go shopping in because you look good in everything, now you are showing off how well your back functions," Libby said, cringing as she twisted herself to face Paige.

"Uh oh. You look fifty years older. What happened?" Paige said, full of sympathy.

"I can't believe I'm saying this out loud. I had a bit of a freakout last night when I started thinking about the book timeline, and I ended up sleeping on the bathroom floor because it makes me feel like a fairy princess." Libby watched Paige's expression for judgment.

Paige started to walk away from her, causing Libby to panic that her friend was leaving, but instead Paige went to the bathroom. Libby could hear Paige taking a few breaths and looking around the room. A few moments later, she emerged back in front of Libby.

"Same, girl, same. We all need to feel like a fairy princess in our cozy wooden cottage from time to time. I'm going to put aside my jealousy at you getting the best bathroom in the house and help you out. Now, how exactly can I help?" Paige said.

But then she took notice of Libby's mismatched eyebrows. "Ah, say no more. Where did the eyebrow pencil roll?" Paige asked, looking around Libby's seat.

"Down there. Truly evil turn of events," Libby said, and she moved slightly so Paige could reach below the table and grab her pencil.

After Paige handed the pencil back to Libby she said, "So why aren't you resting in bed all day, considering your current predicament?"

Libby simply handed her phone over to Paige so she could read through the messages. Despite the cringy "things got wild" response she sent, she felt like Paige could be trusted, after not judging her decision to sleep in the bathroom. Libby and Jane always joked about their "monumental friendship-building moments," and this interaction with Paige was definitely one of them.

"Oh Libby, this is so exciting! I told you Wade was interested. I'm glad he finally got the guts to ask you out," Paige said, clearly feeling validated.

"I wouldn't go that far. Last night when I talked with Florence, she could tell I was full-on panicking, so she probably just told Wade to let me hug some trees on a nature walk to bring me back to sanity," Libby explained.

"Eh, whatever. There are plenty of trees around here that Gani or Harrison could have let you hug. I think Wade was just waiting for an excuse to spend time with you alone. We see him all the time, but a professional setting with your mom present isn't exactly primed for steamy interactions," Paige said.

"I can't even think about that right now. I need two matching eyebrows, to change into a bathing suit, and to pack a change of clothes for a hopefully back-pain-friendly activity. Oh God, how am I going to get in my bathing suit?" Libby said frantically as she thought of the tight one-piece intended more for swimming laps than hanging out with her crush.

Paige gaped at Libby's extraordinarily terrible gait as she slowly made her way over to her drawers and pulled out the black one-piece.

"Oh my. You can't wear that. It's hideous," Paige said, cringing.

"A bit harsh. It's more for swimming laps. It's practical," Libby said defensively, as more doubt crept in.

"Do you swim laps?" Paige said curiously.

"No, but that's not the point," Libby said, feeling defeated.

"Okay, don't panic. We can do this. You've got me, the long-limbed beauty, in your corner. Just trust me, we'll get you ready in time. Now, where are your other clothes?"

Paige sifted through Libby's clothes with the concentration of a concert pianist. A few minutes later, Paige had put together a few pieces Libby never thought to match.

"This is beautiful. How did you do that?" Libby said, shocked.

"Coordinating various shades of neutral always looks refined. Now before you put this on, I'm going to grab some bathing suit options from my room. I think it's best you put it on under your clothes to limit your movements on your mystery date."

"It's not a date," Libby said half-heartedly, hoping it was, in fact, a date.

"Uh huh, sure," Paige replied, deciding not to push her on it.

"And how will I ever fit in your bathing suit? We don't exactly have the same body type," Libby said, suddenly insecure.

"No worries. I love to mix and match my bathing suits. Before this trip, I went on a shopping spree and got a ton of new ones, so I'm sure we'll find one that fits." And with that, Paige disappeared to perform a miracle.

*   *   *

Forty minutes later, Paige and Libby emerged from the room with Libby feeling twenty years older rather than fifty. Paige had not only picked out a couple of great outfits and a bathing suit but given Libby some of her magical healing balm for her lower back. The pain was very much still present, but she was able to move around without the shooting pain.

When they got downstairs, Harrison, unprompted, said, "Look at you, Libby. You look a bit more like Paige, so put-together and fashionable. Even your body looks tighter. What's the occasion?"

Gani interrupted before Libby could respond, calmly but sternly speaking to his partner. "Harrison, we've talked about making unsolicited comments on people's physical appearances. That statement broke like ten of the rules." Gani mouthed "sorry" to Libby.

Paige spoke next. "Actually, Libby is headed out with our Wade. Maybe someone else in the room with a crush could take some inspiration from the move." Paige stared directly at Nathanial.

"Ah, that explains it. See, I knew something was happening. My effort barometer is never off. I know when something is up, and Libby looks the prettiest we've ever seen," Harrison said shamelessly.

Gani shook his head at his partner and said to Libby, "You look beautiful, Libby, and I'm sure you and Wade will have a great time together."

"I just have one more comment, if you will," Harrison said, and everyone held their breath for his next offensive statement.

Libby motioned for him to continue.

"I think you should stick with your normal walking. I see why you're trying to replicate the way Paige moves with grace and sexiness, but you aren't quite nailing it. It looks a bit painful." Harrison's voice was full of concern.

Paige and Libby laughed, then explained the short version of her back pain, leaving out the "slept on the bathroom floor" bit.

Nathanial, who had been lost in thought, finally joined the conversation. "How exactly did Wade ask you out? Can I see how he worded it?"

Libby tried not to laugh as she passed her phone over to her friend. Nathanial was the most talented writer she had ever met, and yet coming up with the words to ask his crush out was beyond him.

* * *

After eating some breakfast, they heard the steps at the door. Libby's nerves suddenly returned.

"Oh, oh, he's here, he's here!" Harrison said in an attempted whisper that had Libby immediately reddening again.

Wade drifted into the kitchen dressed in a relaxed pair of dark-wash jeans with a caramel-brown sweatshirt that made his eyes appear bigger and brighter.

Harrison nodded to him and said, "Ah, isn't it the handsome face we were just talking about around here. You're looking especially dapper this morning."

Without missing a beat, Wade replied, "I always try a bit harder when I know I'll see you, Harrison."

The way Harrison visibly melted caused the others to laugh.

"So, you ready to head out? I can grab my wheelbarrow if you need transport to the car," Wade said, looking Libby over.

"That won't be necessary. Harrison here was just complimenting me on my gait despite the back pain," Libby said teasingly.

Libby stood up from her chair with as much grace as she could muster and slowly headed to the door. Thankfully, Paige had placed the perfect pair of slide-on shoes at the door, so the embarrassing performance of bending over was prevented. On their way to the car, Wade walked next to Libby, his hand placed tenderly on her back. His touch felt twice as soothing as the balm Paige had provided, and Libby gave herself an internal pep talk.

This is what we've been training for. Paige has taught you how to remain calm despite the hunk of man standing next to you.

Ohh, his hands. They feel so strong yet gentle. I wonder what they'd feel like on other places on my body . . .

"Is this something your body likes to do often?" Wade asked, interrupting her stream of thoughts.

"Not often, no. Most days I'm my typical limber self." Libby shook her head as the words left her mouth.

Clearly, I haven't had enough lessons with Paige.

"I see," Wade responded, with a subtle smile on his lips.

As Libby got into the car with Wade's help, she noticed Harrison, Gani, Paige, and Nathanial peeking out from behind the curtain in the living room window.

"Oh, how embarrassing," Libby said, not intending to say it out loud, as Wade got into the car.

"Pulling your back out is incredibly common," Wade said, missing the circus at the window.

"Not me. Them," Libby said, pointing to the window.

Wade glanced to the window, causing the group to attempt to hide, which meant everyone bumping into each other and Gani eventually pulling the curtain.

Wade chuckled. "What exactly do you think they're looking for?"

"I'm sure they're just concerned about my back," Libby lied.

"I'm sure that's part of it," Wade said.

What the hell; my dignity was lost during last night's beauty sleep. Might as well be honest about this.

Libby went on, "Everyone has their own reasons. Paige is always looking for inspiration for her romance novels and seems to think something could be brewing between us."

First mention of coffee, check...

"Nathanial is looking for tips on how to make a move, since he's been dragging his feet with Grace. Then we have Harrison, who wants drama in every shape and form, and Gani, who pretends to not be interested in it, but secretly enjoys it as much as his partner." Libby stopped and managed to look Wade in the eyes.

A flicker of some sort of emotion flashed on Wade's face. Then he started the car and said, "I suppose you're right. The itinerary for the day had to change due to your back, but I imagine you'll still come back with enough excitement to keep them all happy for a while."

What does that mean?

"Well, on behalf of everyone at the inn, we thank you. So, what exactly are we doing today?" Libby replied.

"You'll see. But I promise to have your back," Wade said with the sweetest smile, making Libby fall even harder for him.

* * *

As they drove on, Wade and Libby settled into comfortable conversation, Libby shelving her confusion on what this day meant and focusing on the moment. The views outside were breathtaking, with leaves in vibrant shades of red, yellow, and orange.

"Do you love living here?" Libby asked.

"I do. The access to a dreamland of outdoor activities, the quiet and the connection you get to nature, and, well, the history with my dad just makes it feel like home in a way no other place has," Wade responded.

"I'm so sorry about your dad. From what I've heard, he was an incredible man," Libby said, not being able to imagine a life without both her parents.

"He was. We were lucky to have him. And I'm sure you can see, he's left a mark on all of us," Wade replied.

A comfortable silence took over between them as the drive continued. Libby enjoyed the scenery both in and outside the car, and Wade played a mix of country and alternative music. Libby felt herself relaxing into the seat. In what felt like a flash, Wade announced they were almost there.

"Hot springs?" Libby said, shocked to see the signs as they approached.

"Ever done this before?" Wade asked, watching Libby's expression.

"I have not, but I've always wanted to. Considering how much I was enjoying these heated seats, I wasn't sure I was going to leave the car, but for a hot spring, I shall," Libby said, getting more and more excited.

Wade chuckled and replied, "Happy to hear it."

* * *

Thankfully, Libby's back was feeling good enough to ease herself into the hot spring without too much pain. It was pure bliss for Libby as she closed her eyes and let the heat melt into her tense body. She was so relaxed that for a moment, she forgot Wade was with her. When she finally opened her eyes, she saw him watching her.

"You always look so puzzled when you're looking at me," Libby said, suddenly emboldened.

Wade chuckled. "You make me curious in a way no one has before. So, are you doing alright? I mean, besides the back."

"Did your mom tell you about my panicked expression yesterday after she brought up the book timeline?" Libby asked.

"She did," Wade said simply.

"And she asked you to take me out to make sure I relaxed rather than furthered my trek down panic lane?"

"Not quite. I was just talking to her about what I was planning for us today and she mentioned it."

Libby internally cheered for a moment on hearing the plan to spend time with her today was previously in motion.

"So are you going to continue to evade my question?" Wade asked, bringing Libby back to the moment.

"I am. Doing alright. I'm a bit behind on my book," Libby blurted.

Wade lifted his eyebrows, waiting for her to expand.

"I've written three-quarters..." Libby paused, adding, "of a chapter."

She held her breath as she waited for Wade's response to her dismal progress.

"Eh, you'll get it done," he said casually, like they were discussing making a sandwich.

"Unless you don't want to?" Wade added, watching Libby closely.

"I know you took me to a hot spring, but I suddenly feel like I'm getting the third degree without a possibility of escape," Libby replied, feeling the heat of Wade's gaze.

"Oh, you absolutely cannot get out of here without my help." Wade chuckled.

"Yes, well . . ." Libby looked away, shocked at the level of connection she felt with him. "I do want to. Finish the book, I mean. I'm just writing a little slower. Think like the turtle, not the tortoise," Libby said.

"You mean hare?" Wade said, smirking.

"Yes. Right. How about you? Did you always know you wanted to be a chef?" Libby asked, shifting the conversation away from her writing.

Wade conceded and answered Libby's question. "I always had an interest in cooking. Took longer to figure out how I wanted to fit it into a lifestyle that worked for me."

"How come you haven't cooked for us any of the nights at Florence's house?" Libby asked. It had been a topic of conversation between her, Nathanial, and Paige. All three of them were confused by his reluctance to cook for them, considering it was his career choice.

"Cooking in Willowston has been challenging lately." Wade looked down and then away.

Libby sensed he wasn't ready to share any more details, so she didn't push.

They relaxed in the soothing heat of the hot spring for a few more minutes before Wade suggested they head out. As they headed to the entrance of the hot spring, Libby got nervous thinking about how her back would manage the exit from the water. Before she could take the first step, she felt Wade pick her up and easily carry her out of the spring like she was a feather.

"Wow," Libby said, staring at his flexing biceps like she was in a trance.

At least I solved one mystery. I am definitively an arm girl.

CHAPTER THIRTEEN

After driving back to Willowston, Wade parked his car in front of a building Libby had noticed during her walks on Main Street. It was up a small hill and had an old-world charm about it. It was a long, narrow building surrounded by overgrown landscaping and low-hanging tree branches. The exterior had intricate stonework and was a faded green color. But despite the charm, it looked worn and like its best days were far behind it.

"Is this your restaurant?" Libby asked, suddenly grateful she hadn't made a joke about the building falling apart.

"Someday," Wade replied.

"Did you know you are terrible at providing answers with sufficient detail?" Libby commented, turning to him.

"It's been said before." Wade pulled his gaze from Libby to the building in front of them.

Libby crossed her arms, waiting for him to say more.

Wade chuckled and motioned for her to go to the entrance of the building. He produced a key from his pocket and unlocked the front door. From the looks of the exterior, Libby was surprised the door didn't fall off when he tried to open it.

When Libby stepped inside, she suddenly understood why Wade had chosen this building for his restaurant. The space desperately needed work, but there was something special about it from the moment you walked in, like a quiet, calm energy that drew you into the space.

A long bar was off to the left with enough space for a few tables. To the right was a most likely unworking but enchanting fireplace with a bench along the wall. A staircase with a worn red carpet was in front of them.

"Where does that lead?" Libby asked.

"To a room we'll use for private parties, small weddings."

Ahh ... maybe we could use it for our wedding.

Libby coughed as she realized the ridiculousness of the thoughts in her head. Wade looked especially puzzled, and Libby thanked the universe that he couldn't read her mind.

He placed his hand on Libby's back and guided her inside to the back.

"This is where most of the restaurant seating will be. The room with the fireplace would be for people who want to just grab drinks and appetizers, and then of course we have the bar room that will hold a few tables as well. What do you think?" Wade watched as Libby took in the space and the windows that displayed the grounds out back.

"I think it could be magical but absolutely would not pass a health department inspection."

Wade laughed. "Clearly."

Even his laugh is sexy.

Libby went on, refocusing on the space around her. "The natural light pouring in from all these windows and a view of what I'm sure will be a breathtaking outdoor space, now that I know you and Gani plant together—just exceptional," Libby said, as she started to walk the space.

Libby could feel Wade watching her as she continued to visualize the potential of the space.

She walked around more, taking in the bar area and fireplace room once again. After a while, Wade asked, "What are you thinking?"

"I can see it. It's like the feeling I get when I'm writing a powerful scene in my book. It's like my brain places the people, objects, and setting right in front of me," Libby said softly, unsure of how Wade would respond.

"Tell me what you see. And please don't make it a murder scene," Wade said.

Libby laughed loudly and admired the expression that Wade wore when he told a joke—a small rise of the outside of his lips and a crease on his forehead that released when she laughed, almost like he was nervous to see how his joke would land.

Libby took a breath, closed her eyes, and shared what she visualized. "I see small, delicate chandeliers on the ceiling that shine over wooden tables decorated with rose-filled vases and soft, simple tablecloths. I see a small fountain outside surrounded by plants, reminiscent of an English garden. I see people at every table, connecting with each other and the food and drinks, laughing, looking light and inspired. And I see this chef, with beautiful brown eyes, standing at the door, feeling pride that he made this all happen."

Libby opened her eyes and looked at Wade. There was no question at the expression he wore, and he stood staring at Libby, full of desire and intensity. Libby's breath caught as the moment stretched between them. Wade finally broke the silence, he himself seemingly also caught off guard.

"That sounds nice." Wade gestured to the front.

After they walked out of the building and he locked the door, Wade said to Libby, "I just wanted to tell you that I understand."

"Understand?" Libby was determined to get him to explain himself before he changed his mind.

"How you can struggle with something you love." Wade paused as Libby's hopes sank that he would finally open up to her, but then he continued, his voice a little lower.

"I bought this building about two years ago, on the first anniversary of my dad's death. I wanted to honor him, create this place to celebrate the dad he was to me and all he did to inspire my dreams."

"That's beautiful," Libby said, desperately wanting to hold him but instead giving him space to share more.

"But then the grief just hit me. The day I signed the purchase of this property, it just paralyzed me. Other than the occasional day I'll spend here picking up or dreaming, I can't take the next step. I just started focusing on the consulting portion of my business, traveling everywhere so I didn't have to deal with this." Wade looked weighed down in a way Libby hadn't seen before.

"And that's why cooking for us here in this town has felt like too much," Libby said softly.

"Cooking for someone is so personal. Growing up, I cooked a million times for my dad. He was my biggest fan and, we used to joke, the worst critic. He loved food, but despite how many times I'd teach him, he would only say it needed salt." Wade's eyes got misty as he turned away from Libby.

Libby could no longer help herself; she walked over to Wade and wrapped her arms around him. After a few moments, Wade's shoulders relaxed, and their breath synced.

"Thank you," Wade said finally.

He gently pulled himself away and looked deeply into her eyes. "You are inspiring me. Seeing you change your life in every way to achieve your dream of being a mystery writer. It's inspiring."

Libby cringed internally.

Great, another family member I'm letting down if I don't become a professional writer.

Thankfully, outwardly Libby retained her wit and replied, "Well, I am an official literary inspiration model, so that makes sense."

Wade smiled. "Are you hungry?"

"I am. Want to grab a bite at the coffee shop? Grace makes some amazing savory scones."

"I have another idea." Wade led the two of them to the car.

* * *

They drove in the opposite direction from the inn, a few miles from town. Wade turned the car down a gravel road, as Libby had flashes of the murder cabin Viv had pretended she was staying in.

What emerged as they drove farther in was a beautiful one-story home set perfectly between a forest of trees.

"This is my version of a treehouse," Wade said, reciting Libby's line from their first meeting.

He remembers.

Inside, the home was bright and soothing, with light creams, greens, and blues. The color choices contrasted with what Libby would have assumed Wade would have chosen.

Wade noticed the surprise on Libby's face.

"Were you expecting a log cabin with animal heads on the walls?"

Libby laughed. "I mean, I wouldn't go that far, but I did expect it to look more masculine."

"Are you saying this looks like a woman's vision?" Wade replied, with a fake offended expression.

"I can't seem to figure you out either," was Libby's only reply.

"Brooke might have helped me out with the décor. Come on, let's get some food," Wade said, leading the way to the back of the home.

Libby found herself relieved to hear it was Brooke who helped with the décor and not another woman.

The impressive kitchen looked out on the backyard, with beautiful gardens and a mesmerizing pool and waterfall.

"You've been holding out on us," Libby said, waving to the pool.

Wade chuckled. "It's not exactly pool season."

As Libby looked around the space, she kept an eye on Wade. He pulled things out of the refrigerator, started preparing ingredients, and looked completely focused and at ease. Libby wondered when the last time was that he cooked for someone in Willowston, considering all he had confessed at the restaurant, but decided it was best to let him focus, and she went outside.

After exploring the outdoor space, she sat down at one of the barstools in the kitchen.

"What's that look for?" Wade said, as he noticed Libby smiling at him.

"Watching you cook, it's ... nice," Libby said, trying not to make things uncomfortable for him.

"Well, don't just sit there and stare, come show me your cooking skills," he said, handing her a spatula.

"Oh no, no, no. I don't think that's something you need to see. It'd be like asking a toddler to write a mystery novel," Libby said nervously.

Wade laughed louder than she had heard from him before. The sound made her stomach do flips, that feeling of alignment returning to her heart.

"Come on, I'll show you," Wade said, waving her over.

* * *

An hour later, Wade and Libby sat at the table overlooking the back patio, enjoying tomato bisque with a pesto topping, gourmet grilled cheese sandwiches, and freshly made mojitos.

"You make quite the sous chef," Wade said finally, as he leaned back in his chair.

"I absolutely do not, but thank you for saying that," Libby said, as she finished up her soup. "Okay, what is that look?" she said, noticing Wade about to say something.

"That's an interesting technique for eating your soup," he said, with a smile.

"What are you talking about? I'm using a spoon," Libby replied, confused.

Wade laughed. "You are scraping your teeth on the spoon every time you take a bite."

Libby rolled her eyes and then took another bite. Sure enough, as she went to remove the spoon she slid it across her teeth.

"What, you don't do that? Everyone does that, I'm sure," Libby said, defensively.

"Absolutely no one else does that. But don't change it. It's adorable," Wade said, his intense stare once again taking her breath away.

"Okay," she said, smiling, once she regained the ability to talk.

* * *

After they finished eating, Wade made a vague statement about needing to get to some appointment, so he had to drop Libby back off. She tried not to overanalyze or focus on the disappointment she felt about the day being over.

Wade parked the car and walked Libby into the inn. Thankfully, everyone had decided to go out to an early dinner that evening. Paige had texted that she could meet them at the pizza parlor, but Libby simply replied she had already eaten and would see them later. She got texts from everyone after she sent that message to Paige—one from Gani, one from Harrison, and one from Nathanial—all with variations of hearts and kissy faces and OMG.

Once inside, Wade and Libby faced one another, seemingly at a loss for what to say next. After a few moments, Wade spoke. "Thanks for your company today."

Libby suddenly felt like a friendly dog and not a romantic potential to Wade.

"Oh yeah, sure. I feel like a completely changed person with my back. Did you see how I took those stairs?" Libby sometimes didn't understand the words that came out of her mouth.

Wade chuckled. "You did great."

He watched her with that intense stare, and then in the next moment, turned and walked away.

"See you later, spoon scraper," he called, as he headed back to his car.

That was his takeaway. Just perfect.

*   *   *

Libby paced around the inn, trying to decipher what the day had meant. After ten minutes of that unhelpful exercise, she dialed her best friend.

When Libby was finished explaining the details of the day, Jane couldn't help laughing.

"Seriously? I tell you this whole thing and you can't stop laughing about the soup eating?" Libby said, exasperated.

"I never said anything because I knew it'd give you a complex and you really do love soup but yes"—her cackling could be heard towns away—"you really do scrape that spoon and it drives me nuts."

"Wade said it was adorable," Libby noted.

"You really *are* adorable. You attack that soup like you're a ferocious dinosaur." Jane's laughing was picking up steam.

Libby shook her head, giving her friend a moment to come back.

"Okay, okay, I'm sorry." Jane calmed her laughter.

"Uh huh. I don't know what to think. Was this just a friendly gesture to help me get out of my head, or is he into me and thought this was a date?" Libby sat down slowly on the closest chair. Her back was better, but she knew it was best not to push it.

"It doesn't matter," Jane responded, her laughing finally ceased.

"What are you talking about? Of course it matters. It matters so very much." Libby was shocked her friend wasn't getting the gravity of the situation.

"As far as I see it, if this guy wants a future with you, he'll have to do more than a half-attempt at a date. Libby, you are incredible in a million ways, and some person out there will see that and do everything in their power to have you in their life. If Wade is that guy, well, like I said, we'll need to see better," Jane said.

Libby always marveled at the way her friend could so practically look at love and relationships. Libby felt all emotion and zero practicality, so having Jane as her confidant was a remarkably good thing to balance her out. Of course, she rarely listened to the advice, but it was still helpful to hear.

"And... may I remind you the importance of not giving away your power. Even if a person has eyes made from the coffee gods, it means nothing unless they are the right one for you. You, my friend, need to be choosy. We don't all end up with the right person." Jane paused.

She didn't need to go on to get Libby to understand where she was coming from. Libby was raised in a happy household with parents that loved each other. Jane had witnessed traumatizing interactions between her parents over the years, and despite her love for both independently, she knew without a doubt they should never have been together.

Libby gently spoke. "I love you, Jane. Neither of us are going to end up in the situation you witnessed your whole childhood. And we have your wisdom to thank for that."

"Ugh, I can't get teary-eyed. I have an important conference call in ten. And yes, before you say it, I am aware that today is a weekend, but my latest clients are as patient as whatever perfect analogy I would fit in here, had I slept more than three hours last night," Jane said, sighing.

"You work too hard," Libby said, concerned about her friend.

"I do. Now, don't you have a book to get back to?" Jane asked.

"Yes. Yes. I'm on it. Thanks for the talk," Libby said, smiling.

"Anytime. Love you. Later, Libs."

Libby truly felt better after talking with her friend. Jane's perspective seemed to widen the lens of a situation, giving Libby a greater sense of calm.

*   *   *

Libby was increasingly grateful for her conversation with Jane regarding the date or non-date with Wade, because for the next few days, she heard absolutely nothing from him. On top of that, he wasn't around when Libby went to the library or had dinner with Florence. If it wasn't for the pestering of her housemates, she would have thought the day had never happened.

Libby had made some more progress on her book, motivated by her upcoming meeting with Florence and the desire to distract herself. Paige met with Florence on Wednesday and Nathanial met with her on Thursday. When they had come home, each spoke highly of their conversations and shared how Florence had further inspired them. Libby's only thought at hearing that was neither Paige nor Nathanial needed any inspiration, considering they were flying through the chapters in their books.

*   *   *

When Friday morning arrived, Libby woke up and immediately grabbed her computer. She opened her laptop and read through her pages, mentally preparing herself for her conversation with Florence. She knew Florence would be kind, but there was no way around the fact that Libby was seriously behind. They had agreed to have the meeting in one of the small conference rooms at the library. Libby got ready, packed her things, and ate breakfast at the counter with Harrison.

"Anything from Wade?" Harrison couldn't help but ask Libby at least three times a day.

"Still nothing. The points are adding up to I don't have a shot," Libby said, with a sigh.

She had shared the details of her day with Wade with Gani, Harrison, Nathanial, and Paige, leaving out the more personal parts, including his taking her to his restaurant and his vulnerability about cooking in Willowston. Nathanial had suggested she assign points to their interactions throughout the day to calculate the chances of him liking her or it just being friendly, which he termed the "Do I Have a Shot" formula.

After about twenty minutes of explaining the points system and getting made fun of for creating this formula in the first place, the group agreed to help Libby assign points based on her memory of the day. Even leaving out the major factors of him sharing his vulnerabilities and showing his restaurant, the points were in favor of him liking her. However, the days between contact were a big part of the formula, which were turning the points into the unfavorable category of being friendly. Paige, who initially made the most fun of Nathanial, had become entranced by the formula and even decided to include it in her book. Libby was grateful at least she had gotten something lasting from that day.

"Well, you know I have a sense about these things, and my fingers get extra tingly when you both are around. Don't lose faith yet," Harrison said, wiggling his fingers dramatically.

"We need to tell Nathanial your tingly fingers need to be accounted for in his formula," Libby said with a smirk.

• CHAPTER FOURTEEN •

An hour later, Libby sat nervously in the library conference room. The moment felt reminiscent of the proposal meeting in Philadelphia. Libby blushed, thinking of her first interaction with Wade.

She was lost in thought when he appeared at the door. For a moment, Libby thought she was hallucinating. Harrison had served her a mushroom omelet and joked about the magic of mushrooms.

"Hey," Wade said, leaning against the door like he was posing for a photoshoot.

"Oh hi, how's it roasting? I mean going?" Libby shook her head at herself.

Seriously? Back with the coffee terms?

Wade chuckled at Libby and walked in, sitting on one of the chairs.

"I officially started the process of getting a contractor to begin the renovations for the restaurant," Wade said proudly.

"That's incredible. I'm so happy for you. Oh, that place is so special, and if your food is anything like that sandwich and soup you made the other day, it will be award winning." Libby felt genuinely proud of Wade for taking that step.

Wade smiled, adding, "I wanted to thank you. Something changed for me after that day." He paused as Libby's heartbeat quickened.

Before he could go on, Florence appeared at the door.

"Oh, hi dear. Here to do last-minute checks on our fabulous café?" Florence said, as Wade stood up, greeting his mom.

"Yeah, we'll be ready," Wade said.

With that, Wade looked at Libby and said, "Thank you again. When this one"—pointing to Florence—"sees it, she'll be eternally grateful for the role you played. For now, let's keep it between us." The way Wade said "us" melted Libby's heart.

"And what exactly are we talking about here?" Florence said, with full attention on Wade.

"All in good time, Mom. Love you." Wade gave an affectionate kiss on Florence's cheek and walked out.

Florence turned back to the sitting Libby, who was trying to get as small as possible in her chair.

"Oh dear, I'm not going to interrogate it out of you. We have your future writing career to talk about. And to be honest, I kind of love the two of you keeping secrets from me." Florence winked flawlessly and settled into the seat across from Libby.

Libby's stomach churned at the words "future writing career," but her excitement for the moment with Wade won out. She couldn't seem to wipe a giddy smile off her face.

Florence began to talk about the agenda for their meeting, with items related to a book launch Libby hadn't ever considered, and including a plan to republish her first novel. As Florence dove into the first item on the agenda, the perfect editor she found for Libby's second book, Libby's eyes kept drifting to item 4, *discuss progress and timeline for completion.* Twenty minutes later, they had arrived on that very item, the giddiness from her moment with Wade officially gone as the reality of her book timeline settled in.

"Well, let's talk about your progress. Now, I know you said it's been slow, so let's figure this out." Florence talked about it so calmly, Libby knew she didn't grasp the severity of the issue.

"Well, I have three chapters and a well-developed character for the victim," Libby said, her voice quiet.

"Okay, and how many chapters are you thinking for this one?" Florence asked.

Libby struggled to get the words out. "Probably thirty."

"Okay, so in four months we need another twenty-seven chapters." Florence paused, deep in thought, as she kept an eye on Libby.

Libby thought for a moment about telling Florence everything. How she was having serious doubts about a career in writing. How this dream she'd had for more years than she can remember had felt unfulfilling when it became her sole focus. She considered confessing how the pressure of writing in a short timeline left her creative mind paralyzed, taking away the magic she once felt.

Florence finally spoke, shaking Libby out of her thoughts.

"I by no means am sharing this with you to provide additional pressure, but I want to let you know what I was planning and why this timeline of completion is so important. We hoped to have the books written by February so that we could have them ready for an April launch. I was going to hold a massive launch party for you, Paige, and Nathanial to create interest in your books and in each of you as new and powerful authors. The angle of having a mystery writer, fantasy writer, and romance writer was paramount to me in terms of market representation." Florence paused.

Tell her. Libby felt her head throbbing.

"What I need to know from you is, can you make this happen?" Florence finally said, studying Libby.

Nope.

Libby instead said, "Absolutely. I understand the importance of this, and I will have the book ready for you. Thank you again for this opportunity."

What?

"Okay, then let's figure this out," Florence said, diving into suggestions for helping Libby get more writing done.

An hour later, they had settled on a plan that gave Libby more time to focus on the book by reducing the scope of her mystery workshop at the library. It was the absolute opposite of what Libby wanted, but it appeared her people-pleasing voice won out during that meeting.

With the grand opening of the library the next day, Libby found herself with little time to obsess over the details of her meeting with Florence. Even though Libby wasn't completely transparent with Florence about her concerns for her future, she was grateful Florence was still confident she could get the book done in time. Libby hoped the details of the book launch and the importance of Libby having a mystery book completed by February would give her an unexpected boost in motivation.

* * *

The next day, Libby, Paige, and Nathanial arrived early at the library to prepare for the grand opening. The energy of the Sterling family and the librarians was contagious, as Libby found herself excited for the day in a way she hadn't felt in years.

An hour after the doors were officially opened to the public, it was a clear success. It felt like the entire community had come out to see the new space. Many patrons had confessed to being more motivated by the chance to meet Lake Sterling, but regardless, it stirred interest.

The librarians worked the large crowd with grace and poise. The literary-focused workshops organized by Libby, Nathanial, and Paige were fully booked by midday. Libby spent as much time talking with the library patrons as the librarians did, while Nathanial hid in a corner avoiding the crowd, and Paige spent the time walking around with Brooke, enjoying the refreshments. Initially, Libby thought she would spend the day convincing people to attend her mystery workshop, but because it was already filled, she ended up talking to them about other programs they'd like to see, gaps in the community, and things they loved to do in Willowston.

Throughout the day, Libby found herself drifting by the café and trying to covertly watch Wade while he worked the counter, made coffees, and guided the staff. It was so easy to see him as a successful chef, restaurant consultant, and soon-to-be restaurant owner. He held a calm confidence that eased the people around him. She heard constant chatter from women talking about how handsome he was and how he was supposedly single. Libby felt more jealous than she anticipated, rolling her eyes and huffing each time she heard the comments.

Lake entertained the crowd like the trained performer he was. Since Florence had anticipated the draw of her famous son, she gave him the job of performing tours of the new space. Libby followed along for one of the tours, and Lake spoke with such enthusiasm that by the end she was even more excited for the future of the library. He did, however, get scolded a few times by the librarians for letting the young children on his tours splash around the water features.

When Libby was free, finally taking a break from talking with people and not-so-subtly checking Wade out, Viv went over to her. Libby expected Florence had shared with Viv about the little progress Libby had made on her next book, so she wasn't really looking forward to this conversation.

"I've never seen someone wear the expressions of joy and heaviness simultaneously the way you are right now. What's on your mind, kid? The constant chatter on Wade's single status getting to you?" Viv said with a knowing smile.

"Wade is single, so there is nothing wrong with that chatter, as you call it. I'm a mere mortal friend of his," Libby replied. Focusing on the Wade conversation felt easier than talking about what really bothered her.

"You've been reading too much of Nathanial's stuff. If it was his fantasy land, both you and Wade would be seducer-witch-warriors, which you know makes a fiery combination," Viv said, with a few winks.

Libby lightly smacked Viv. "Would you stop winking at me? And unfortunately, we're not in Nathanial's fantasy world. He's so talented. No one can develop as enticing a male lover as he can. He's ruined the appeal of a mere mortal man. Well, most of them, anyway," Libby said, as her eyes drifted to the café.

"Spill it, witch warrior. I know it's not just Wade's massive appeal to all women that's weighing you down. What's going on?" Viv pressed.

Libby looked at Viv, knowing she meant business and wouldn't let it go. Nevertheless, Libby attempted to sidestep.

"I'm just taking it in and feeling moved by all this, I guess. The impact the library is going to have on the community is profound. Did you know I saw a few guys in the motorcycle club talking with the librarians about the yoga program? Apparently, all that sitting on their motorcycles messes with their hips. Then, one of the local knitting club members overheard and said she felt the same pains in her body with all her sitting she does while knitting. They all signed up for the yoga class and agreed to meet for drinks at the biker bar after class. I mean, talk about bringing people together," Libby said, with wonder.

Viv laughed loudly, saying, "We've got to put that in the first bulletin they send out for the library. Now go on, I can tell you've got more going on in that constantly churning mind."

Libby decided to reveal some of what she was truly worried about. "It's my book. I'm sure you've heard I'm behind, and I guess the weight of completing it in time is showing on my face. Florence told me about the release party and how important getting all three books done is, so I have no choice but to get it done." Libby held back on her fears about her future writing career.

"Ah, I see. I'm not worried about you finishing your book one bit. You put your mind to something, you'll get it done. You've been working a career as a nurse that drains you for years, and yet you still show up and do it. Now what comes after you finish this book, well, you'll figure that out too." Viv gave Libby a knowing smile and walked away.

Libby stood there frozen after hearing Viv's last comment. Libby thought she had hidden her hesitation about her future well, but apparently Viv's intuitiveness won out. Or had Florence herself figured it out and shared that with Viv? Libby decided there was no point in wasting further energy obsessing about who knew what. She needed to devote her mental space to creating a masterful mystery.

* * *

Later in the day, Libby decided to take a break from the crowd. She grabbed her coat and went outside to sit down by a towering pine tree. The peace of being by the tree released the tension from a day of constant conversation, ruminating about her future, and anxiety on her book timeline.

As Libby sat there, she recognized that guilt was creeping into her mind. She was finally admitting her truth, that she didn't want to write full-time, which left the gap of what she would do, moving forward. Despite all the opportunity and privilege she had gotten in her life, she felt frustrated at herself for not yet knowing what her career path held. Libby so badly desired to wake up every day with a feeling of synchronicity and flow with her calling. Nursing had certainly not been it, but she did miss the way her prior career helped people. The actual reality of that environment did not align with her nature, but that feeling she had at the end of a hard day's work, that she helped someone in a tangible way, felt important. Writing was a solitary activity, and even though she knew people would read and enjoy her effort, it didn't give the same level of immediate feedback that nursing did.

Libby glanced back inside the library. Witnessing the impact the librarians, staff, and Sterling family made today and for the future of Willowston was profound. When talking to people, she had learned how much young parents relied on the library to provide a comfortable space to come to after a sleepless night. She had talked to older adults who shared the chronic feelings of isolation that their participation in the library programs could alleviate. And of course, Libby herself was aware of the impact that books had: unveiling stories that whisk you away, motivate you, or just simply make you smile.

Glancing once again back at the tree, Libby said out loud, determinedly, "I can do hard things. I will both finish this book and find my future calling. Something that allows me to help people while not draining my soul. Sorry Dad, but I'm not going back to nursing."

Libby's profound moment was interrupted by the unmistakable voice of Lake Sterling. "Who are you talking to? Are you talking to that tree?" Libby suddenly felt panicked, unsure how much Lake had heard.

Lake sat down next to Libby, uncharacteristically silent for a few moments, and looked up to the tree. He finally turned his attention back to Libby and said, "Damn. That tree is tall," like it was a shocking new discovery.

Libby laughed, relaxing slightly. "It is. Trees can tend to do that. Grow tall and all."

Lake smirked in reply.

Maybe he didn't hear what I said at all, she thought, relieved.

A few more moments passed before Lake looked at Libby with a serious expression. "Your dad will get over it. You not wanting to be a nurse anymore, I mean."

"You heard that?" Libby tried to respond casually, wondering if he heard the previous part about needing to find her calling.

"I did. You know, me and John are close now. He thought I was brilliant, which naturally, I am. But I know him, and he's going to support you as a writer. I mean, how could he not? You're incredible at it, and thanks to the Sterlings, you're finally going to get noticed by the world. You just focus on pumping those great mysteries out, and we'll take care of the rest," Lake said, with total confidence.

He definitely didn't hear the rest of what I said.

"Thanks for saying that." Libby paused, wondering if she was overstepping, but added, "For what it's worth, your dad would have been so proud of you for how much you helped this community today. You really made a difference, and I'm grateful I was a part of it."

Lake sat uncharacteristically silent for a moment, looking up at the tree, deep in thought. Finally, he stood up, saying, "Thanks for saying that," and he walked away.

CHAPTER FIFTEEN

Two months later, the landscape had transformed from the peak of fall to the beginnings of winter. The trees had fully shed their leaves as the days became shorter and the temperatures dropped. With the month of December finally upon them, the entire town of Willowston embraced the winter holidays. But no one came close to the level of enthusiasm Harrison and Gani had for the merry season.

Harrison had visualized and Gani had executed the beauty of the holidays throughout both the inside and outside of the inn. Twinkling lights greeted all from the porch and were perfectly weaved on trees on both sides of the property. Inside the inn, there were Christmas trees in more rooms than not, decorated with various themes. The one in Libby's room was based on Harrison's favorite Broadway musical, *Kinky Boots*. The top of the tree was the world's most fabulous miniature high-heeled boot in deep red. It had taken Gani ten tries to balance the shoe exactly the way Harrison had wanted, a true testament to Gani's impressive level of patience. The outside gardens were interspersed with lights and various outdoor decorations. Harrison had conceded a small portion of the garden for Gani's love of blowup décor and referred to it as the "less tasteful area." The annoyed huffs that came out of Harrison every time he saw them inflated made it especially entertaining for everyone.

*   *   *

Libby woke up startled every morning when she saw the looming boot out of the corner of her eye. Then she'd laugh, realizing what it was. This was the typical morning routine since the tree was placed in her room the week prior. After getting ready and having her morning coffee with Harrison and Gani, Libby headed to the library. Nathanial and Paige both liked to sleep in and could never understand why Libby insisted on getting to the library so early. But Libby had found this regular routine that got her writing by 7 a.m. was vital in completing pages.

Since the grand opening of the library and the close call with Lake almost finding out the truth, Libby's sole focus had become the completion of her book. Initially the struggle was paralyzing, but over time she began to find her flow, being the most productive in the morning hours before her mind could start obsessing about the fears over her future plans.

Libby found that she thrived when she worked from the library. It also gave her an opportunity to talk with more of the patrons, observe the various programs the library was offering, enjoy the limitless nooks to write from, and, when he was around, observe Wade in all his glory at the café counter. Unfortunately, he was around less and less as he was consumed with his restaurant renovations and consulting gigs.

Libby had become friendly with all the librarians and staff, especially since she got to the library before they were open to the public. At this point, everyone working in the library had become invested in Libby's book and they were constantly asking for updates.

One librarian in particular, Pixie, was Libby's absolute favorite. Pixie was in her late sixties and had worked in libraries all her life. Her haircut was as one would expect with the name Pixie, and her style was "rainbow forward," as Pixie liked to call it. She wore bright colors and bold jewelry, and she frequently donned hair accessories she made herself. Libby often thought only Pixie could pull off the looks she put together. Pixie felt familiar and comforting for Libby, almost like a beloved aunt she never had, since both her parents were single children.

"Tell me my dear, how is the novel coming along? Did the murderer finally get what's coming to him?" Pixie asked, sitting down in the seat across from Libby, having found her in one of her favorite nooks by the romance section.

"Hi Pixie." Libby always lit up when her librarian friend came to check on her. "Considering I'm still debating who the murderer should be in the first place, no, they haven't gotten what's coming to them. But don't worry, I promise Darcy will get justice for her unfortunate ending," Libby replied, with more confidence than she'd had since starting her second book.

"Good. I feel a sort of responsibility to dear Darcy, since she too was a librarian with a vivacious passion for books, like yours truly. As much as being murdered sounds dreadful, I'm glad she was able to rest in the comfort of her beloved library for all those years," Pixie said wistfully.

Libby smiled, placing her hand on Pixie's. "Only you would see the bright side of being murdered and hidden for a decade in a library. Now tell me, how are your knees doing today?"

Over the past weeks, Libby had become familiar with all aspects of Pixie's life, including all the body parts that pained her, her favorite and least favorite family members, and the countless adventures from her travels over the years, including her European lovers. According to Pixie, Irishmen were the best. Libby enjoyed hearing about Pixie's dramatic romances, since her own current romance with Wade was at a standstill and as entertaining as staring at a No. 2 pencil.

Despite many interactions in the library, at the inn, and at Florence's residence, Wade hadn't suggested they spend any more one-on-one time together. And although Libby considered herself a modern woman who could very well initiate plans herself, she was hesitant, questioning if he even liked her. That fear was enough to hold her back from asking him out. On top of that, he was insanely busy, finally signing off on work at the restaurant and still traveling a few times a month for his consulting gigs.

Even still, Libby felt a loss there because of the magnetism she felt every time he was in her presence. As the days went on, she told herself she needed to come to terms with it being only a friendship. And anyway, maybe she should focus on an Irishman, if everything Pixie said was in fact true.

After Pixie gave her health updates, she focused her attention back on Libby's book. "Every time I look, that word count is 'blowing up,' as the young kids like to say," Pixie said, shaking her short hair.

"I'm not sure that's what the kids are saying, but yep, I'm about a third done. It's not bad, either," Libby said, looking proudly at her screen.

"Of course it's not bad. It's perfect. Enticing, charming, and pure joy," Pixie said, smiling.

"Um, you haven't read it, Pixie."

"I don't need to read it. I'm just describing how I feel about you. I'm sure it'll translate onto that screen."

Libby laughed. "I can see the review now: 'Never read it, but based on my opinion of the author, it's phenomenal.'"

"I stand by my review," Pixie said confidently.

"Well, Jane said on her latest read that it was 'captivating,' so I'm feeling hopeful." Libby had talked about Jane so much that Pixie felt she knew her already.

"Well, I know I tell you this every day, but I'd love to read it, so whenever you feel ready." Pixie held hope in her eye that today Libby would concede, but today was not the day.

"Soon. I promise," Libby said, as she always did.

Libby wasn't ready to let anyone else read the pages but Jane, Florence, and her editor. Florence had thankfully been gracious and understanding when Libby asked if she could wait until she was farther along to share it with anyone else. Especially since the other person that was most insistent on reading the latest pages was Florence's only daughter, Brooke. Brooke sent Libby daily texts asking if today was the day she could see what Libby had written. Her texts always included an excessive number of exclamation points and hilariously funny GIFs. Outside of her persistent harassment on reading the pages, Libby had grown fond of the daily texts, which lately had become longer conversations about other aspects of their lives.

Libby couldn't believe that in a matter of months, she had developed more meaningful relationships than she had in her entire life until then. She just hoped that everyone would be understanding when she finally admitted her secret desire to not be a full-time author. Every day she felt more and more confident that being a full-time author wasn't her path in life, despite how much that fact pained her. She was enjoying the writing process again, but the familiar feeling that something was missing remained present, and Libby didn't want to ignore that feeling any longer.

*　*　*

That evening as everyone gathered at Florence's for dinner, Florence was in an especially animated mood. When Libby exchanged puzzled looks with Paige and Nathanial, it was obvious they were sensing the same thing. When they asked Florence what she was so excited about, all she said was, "You'll see, as soon as that magical wizard Viv gets here."

An hour later and two big bowls of guacamole demolished, Viv arrived, looking a bit disheveled. She walked over to Florence and handed her a pile of fancy looking papers. Libby felt suddenly transported back to months ago when she first received the letter from Lake.

"I may have been banned from the UPS store for the near future, so I hope this was worth it." Viv sat down on the barstool and signaled to Nathanial to pour her a margarita from the pitcher next to him.

Florence's positive mood was unfazed. "Of course it was worth it. Now everyone gather around. Viv, drink your margarita and quit ruining the moment."

Viv huffed and took another sip of her drink.

"Well, my author stars, here are the invitations to my holiday soiree. It will be a night to remember, as most of my parties are. However, the three of you will be my guests of honor. I'm inviting a few influential book vloggers and journalists. You can think of this as the first wave of introductions to the world." Florence threw her hands up dramatically, resulting in various reactions from the three authors. Nathanial looked as if every muscle in his body had tensed, while Paige's face lit up excitedly.

Libby, meanwhile, felt her palms start to sweat. "Oh, I thought you were going to wait to introduce us until the spring. After our next books were written. What's the rush, you know?" Libby's attempt at casual failed miserably as everyone in the room turned to look at her, slightly puzzled.

"Oh, you know, just to prepare more. I haven't done much PR. More of an RN." Libby's laugh was forced.

She pressed on, as if it needed explaining, "RN means registered nurse. So that's why that was so funny. Because I'm a nurse."

Thankfully, Florence put her out of her misery and answered her original question.

"Well, waiting was the original plan. But then Lake and I were talking, and as you know, he's an expert in all things marketing, and he suggested we take advantage of the holiday season and throw a memorable holiday party to start the buzz around you three as authors. But there is no need to worry, it's going to be a low-pressure evening with some brief introductions."

Libby was relieved to hear the words "low-pressure." She could sense Nathanial felt the same, as she watched his shoulders visibly drop.

Florence went on, almost as if the next point was a minor afterthought, "Of course, we'd love for you all to do a short reading from your next novels. Really get people talking and see that you're wildly talented. Speaking of buzz, are you feeling better, Viv?" Florence received a nod from Viv and indicated to Nathanial to top Viv off with some more margarita.

"Come now, look at these invitations. Aren't they stunning? Now does anyone have ideas on what section they'd like to read from their book?" Florence asked, scanning the authors.

Viv chimed in before anyone else had a chance to speak. "I vote that steamy scene when the characters unexpectedly meet in the outdoor spa from Paige's, and that part where the sexy lead reveals the extent of his powers with that very detailed description of his male form in Nathanial's. I'd have a suggestion from Libby's if she let me read it . . ." She gave Libby a playfully irritated look.

"Apparently, the margarita has not kicked in completely," Florence said, with a sympathetic glance to Libby.

"I know, soon, I promise." Libby should make a recording of this statement, with the number of times she had to say it in a day.

"Maybe the scene where they find the body? You did such a beautiful job setting the scene and dropping a few clues that draw the reader in," Florence said.

Libby thought for a moment and replied, "Maybe. I could also read the part where the mother and daughter arrive in the town and first learn of the body. I liked the way I wove in humor and think it may pique interest in finding out more as well."

"Brilliant. I think that's perfect. Now, let's get into the main course before we run out of guacamole." Florence waved to the table as she pulled the enchilada dish from the oven.

*   *   *

That night after returning to the inn, they gave Gani and Harrison their invitations. Harrison's squeal reached a new decibel, and after a moment of celebrating, he ran out of the room bubbling something about needing to find the perfect outfit.

Gani with his calm demeanor just smiled at his partner and offered to make tea for Libby, Nathanial, and Paige. The post-dinner tea ritual had become a special part of their life at the inn. Once they were all settled into the living room, the ambiance from the large fireplace easing their bodies, Gani asked for more details about the party. While Harrison was happy to be invited to the grand party, Gani could sense there was more to the evening for the authors.

"It's basically our first introduction to the world. A chance for us to make our mark, let the world know to watch out because we are going to make waves in the industry." Paige spoke without any nervousness.

Gani smiled at Paige. "That sounds like a wonderful opportunity. It also sounds a bit overwhelming. Especially considering it's happening in less than two weeks." Gani looked directly at Nathanial and Libby.

Before either could respond, Harrison's voice boomed from above. "That's what I'm saying. How can I be expected to pull together the perfect look in ten days?"

"Not about you, darling," Gani shouted upstairs before motioning for Nathanial and Libby to go on.

Nathanial spoke first. "It's not my strong suit. I write novels because I like being behind a screen. Being the center of attention and having to read a scene from my book, I don't know if I can handle that. I mean, I can't even ask Grace to go out with me, and I see her *every day* when I get my morning coffee."

Libby's heart went out to Nathanial. His talent as a writer was profound, but she had never thought about how he would react to the marketing piece. Without a word, Libby and Paige went over to Nathanial and gave him a hug.

"Anything we can do to help, we're here," Libby said.

"Agreed. We can rehearse over and over again until you feel like you know the words without even looking," Paige added.

Harrison shouted from upstairs, "And if things go horribly bad, I'll just burst into one of my famous Christmas songs. My baritone is like nothing you've ever heard."

"How is he even hearing us?" Nathanial said.

Everyone laughed and Libby and Paige settled back into their chairs. Gani spoke to Nathanial with a gentleness. "I'm with you; public speaking and asking out someone can be terrifying experiences. Perhaps rather than focusing on the fear of those activities, think more about the possible outcome. You deliver a clear, magnetic read-through of your novel and entice influential vloggers, who have the potential to explode the interest in your book. Then someone, somewhere, who's suffering in their life and needs that fantasy world to reinspire them, learns of your book. You transport them, easing their pain, even just temporarily, and open a window of possibilities for them. And, well, Grace could be the love of your life, and it'd be a pity to miss out on that." Gani sipped his tea with grace as the group stared at him, stunned.

"Well when you put it like that, I have some work to do, rehearsing in my nonjudgmental mirror." And with that, Nathanial left the room.

"And you?" Gani said, turning his attention to Libby.

Libby couldn't tell him about what really gave her pause, being introduced as an up-and-coming mystery writer when she was realizing this wasn't want she wanted to do long-term. So instead, she responded with the next immediate fear. "What if my reading has the opposite effect Florence is hoping for? I mean, instead of stirring interest, the influencers think it's no good and have no interest in helping me?"

Fear flashed on Paige's face. "Oh, I didn't think of that. I mean, Florence wouldn't let us fail. She must know what she's doing, right?"

"I see we've hit a note. I'm glad Nathanial isn't here for you to inspire any more fear in the poor boy. Now, you two listen to me. While you can't guarantee anything in this life, I'm quite sure you can confidently count on Florence Sterling to deliver. She is a force and has that red-headed bulldog by her side, lest anyone fall out of line," Gani said, getting laughs out of Paige and Libby.

Gani pressed on. "You both possess incredible talent as writers. We believe in you, and no matter what, you can count on Harrison and me to cheer you on. So even if you are drunk and only make it through one terrible run-on sentence, we will be cheering like it's the best thing we've ever heard."

"Hear, hear!" Harrison shouted from above.

"Thank you," Libby said, misty eyed.

▪ CHAPTER SIXTEEN ▪

The morning of the holiday party, the excitement could be felt throughout the inn. Harrison had the holiday music blasting by 7 a.m., which corresponded with a text from Gani asking each of the authors to excuse any unfavorable behavior from Harrison due to his uncontrollable excitement. Gani also tailored a kind, heartfelt message to each author, citing specific things he loved about their writing style and why today would be a momentous day in their future as successful writers.

After Libby wiped the tears from her eyes at Gani's sincere message, the familiar unease churned in her stomach. The secret of her uncertainty in her future as a writer was very much not out. She decided she was going to wait until the right moment to tell everyone, but at this point, all she wanted to do was ignore it. Her ever-present stomach, of course, did not sign off on the "ignore" approach, reminding her constantly.

The plan was to have a low-key breakfast at the inn, go to an undisclosed location to relax for a few hours, and then head over to Florence's to get ready for the evening. Thanks to the countless bedrooms her rental residence had, Libby, Paige, and Nathanial had their own rooms for the evening. Florence insisted on making things as comfortable and enjoyable as possible, but it was clear she also wanted to reduce the chances of Nathanial fleeing before the event.

In the days leading up to the party, Nathanial had practiced reading his excerpt multiple times a day. Harrison had taken on the task of helping to prep him by engaging in a variety of seemingly unrelated activities, including caroling at a few of the neighbors' houses, introducing himself to strangers on Main Street, and going to daily coffee runs with Harrison, armed with talking points for engaging in more conversation with Grace.

The result, however, was not what Harrison had intended. Despite having the pages in front of him, during practice Nathanial was mixing up the words of his reading with lyrics from random holiday songs and the talking points from his conversations with Grace. It was like all the stressful events were now jumbled in his mind, creating an oddly entertaining but ineffective book-reading performance.

The night before the party, Florence and Viv had come over for final practice sessions with everyone, and thankfully Nathanial had gotten through his pages without any issues. However, he still mentioned considering fleeing the state before the party began. Just in case, Viv had found a lookalike that could pass as Nathanial, though Florence vehemently refused to go with that option.

Libby finished getting ready in the requested "cute lounge clothes" that Brooke had told them to wear for the day. When she got downstairs, Brooke, Paige, and Nathanial were already there eating their breakfasts.

"Look who's the slow one today," Paige said, nodding to Libby.

"Mom said I should give you and Nathanial a fake time thirty minutes earlier, so technically, she's right on time," Brooke said to Paige, smiling sheepishly.

"Fair," Paige and Nathanial said together.

"Well, get some food in you, we have our appointments in an hour," Brooke said, pulling out the chair for Libby.

"Appointments for what, exactly? Can we please just know what's happening? I can't take any more surprises from your family for the rest of my life," Nathanial said, in the most dramatic tone they'd heard from him to date.

"Fabulous! Keep that level of emotion for your reading later today," Harrison said, as he clapped loudly.

After the laughing settled down, Brooke agreed to share the itinerary with everyone.

"Well, Mom and I thought what better way to get you all in the right headspace than a day at the spa. So, there's this amazing place in the next town over that has a boutique spa that you will love." Brooke looked beside herself with excitement.

"Great, now I have to lie naked with a stranger rubbing my shoulders, on top of all the other horrors of this day," Nathanial said under his breath, but loud enough for Libby and Paige to hear him.

"It sounds great, thank you for this," Libby said, feeling a little excited herself. Her nursing salary hadn't supported frequent spa trips, but she'd attended a few with Jane or her mom for special occasions.

Brooke looked at her phone, lost in thought for a few moments. She turned back to everyone like no time had passed and said, "Alright, heading out in ten. Yay!"

When Brooke walked out of the room, Libby nudged Paige and asked, "What do you think that was about?"

"No idea, but there's something going on. She seems distracted. I saw her glance at her phone, like, twenty times since she got here, which is strange, especially for her," Paige said.

"Agreed. Something is up. She looks at her phone less often than anyone I know of, and that includes me with zero social media presence," Libby responded.

* * *

An hour later, the group pulled up in front of the spa. Nathanial looked relieved to see how outdoorsy and relaxing the environment appeared to be. It looked like a converted log cabin, and didn't look like a stereotypical, overly feminine spa at all.

Brooke was acting stranger with each passing moment. She seemed like a rubber band stretching farther and farther, her energy getting hyper to a level that was unsustainable.

"Uh, are you okay?" Nathanial asked, as Brooke practically tripped, running so fast toward the front entrance.

"Oh, I just love moments like this," was Brooke's only response.

"Like what?" Nathanial said.

But the question needed no response as the doors opened, revealing three very happy faces, the close friend of each author.

"Jane?!" Libby squealed, running up to her friend and hugging her tightly.

"Oh, I did it, it's so wonderful," they could hear Brooke saying to herself as she watched the joyful scene played out in front of her.

Once the shock of seeing their best friends in Willowston had dissipated, they introduced everyone. With how much time Paige, Nathanial, and Libby had spent together, they knew plenty about each of their friends. It was a special moment to finally meet each other in person.

"I can't believe you're all here," Libby said, clearly capturing the sentiment her fellow authors were feeling.

"Well, with all the work this guy has been putting in to prep for his big introduction to the world, I couldn't possibly miss it," Chris said, gripping his friend's shoulder.

"At least I can save the phone call where I tell you how poorly I did now," Nathanial said.

"You will do no such thing," Diti responded immediately.

"I know I'm here to support my favorite person in the world, but we both know Paige doesn't need much support, because you got this, girl." Diti nodded at Paige as she stood there looking perfectly confident, as usual.

"Well, yes, obviously I've got this," Paige said, waving at the crowd like she was the queen.

"She truly is the female version of Lake," Jane said under her breath, so only Libby could hear.

Diti focused her attention back on Nathanial as her voice morphed into a calmer, more professional tone. "Consider me your additional support person. Now, please recite three positive affirmations about tonight," Diti said, taking Nathanial to another part of the spa.

Paige laughed and explained that on top of Diti's successful career as a fashion designer, she also worked as a life coach.

"Thank God for that. My man needs all the help he can get. And I say that in the most supportive way," Chris said, watching his friend with concern.

*   *   *

The next three hours were the perfect combination of relaxation and entertainment. Besides receiving some of the best treatments Libby had ever experienced in a spa, she felt like she bonded with Diti and Chris. It was as though the group had known each other all their lives. Even Nathanial looked relaxed after the spa, which they attributed to the presence of his best friend Chris, the highly trained massage therapists, and his new life coach, Diti.

"Well, are we ready to go to Mom's and dress ourselves up for the evening?" Brooke said, once everyone had gathered at the front entrance of the spa.

"I'd love to stay here a few more hours, maybe until the party is over," Nathanial said, but then after the look he received from Diti, he added, "But I am proud of my work and am capable of giving a dynamic reading to an audience of fellow book lovers."

"Excellent," Diti said, while the rest of the group raised their eyebrows.

"She's intense, yes?" Jane said to Paige.

"Oh, insanely intense. But also, incredibly effective. I have no doubt Nathanial will nail his reading after

Diti works with him for another hour," Paige said, looking over at her friend proudly.

Jane leaned to Libby and whispered, "And you thought I was a lot."

Libby tried to muffle her laugh as they made their way out of the spa.

*   *   *

Libby, Jane, and Brooke rode together in one car, which gave Diti more time to work with Nathanial in the other. Brooke joked that by the time they arrived at Florence's, Nathanial may be a new man completely.

Once they did arrive at Florence's, they hurried inside, pushed by the cold chill in the air. The month of December had officially embraced the winter season with a few light snowfalls and much cooler temperatures. The powdering of snow left on the ground from last night's snowfall created the perfect setting for the holiday party. That, combined with the elaborate holiday lights and tasteful decorations, made Florence's house look more like a movie set than someone's residence.

Florence greeted everyone the moment they walked in the door. As usual, she looked perfectly elegant and at ease meeting her latest guests.

"Well, was this a good surprise or what?" Florence said, finally turning her attention to the three authors.

Libby immediately wrapped her arms around Florence, and Paige and Nathanial followed behind.

"Do not group hug without me!" Viv slid into the room seemingly out of nowhere.

Libby heard Chris ask, "Is that the magical wizard-slash-bulldog that Nathanial is always telling me about?"

"Oh, for sure. There can't be two of her in this place," Jane said, as they all chuckled.

They heard the front door open, and without looking, Libby knew Lake had arrived, thanks to the gasps from Diti and Chris. Per usual, Lake had chosen a unique outfit for the evening. The print on his formal suit was plaid, shiny, and completely over the top. But Libby's focus quickly shifted to the tall man behind him. Wade wore a dark-blue suit that was simple but fitted and managed to make his brown eyes glow even more than usual.

Wade in a suit should be illegal. I'm tempted to pounce on him, dignity be damned.

Thankfully, Florence pulled Libby from her thoughts by asking everyone to gather in the living room for a moment.

"Now, our guests will be arriving in less than three hours. I want to take this moment to share a few words with each of you." Florence looked lovingly at Libby, Paige, and Nathanial.

"Paige, from the moment I read your first romance novel, my life was forever changed. You made me laugh, cry, and most importantly, heal in a way I hadn't with the loss of Noah. It was a therapeutic experience seeing love through your eyes, and I want to thank you for that." Florence then focused her attention on Nathanial.

"To say you write fantasy doesn't accurately capture the profound nature of your first book. The world has been waiting for something like this, and I truly believe you will make waves throughout your career." Florence smiled and then faced Libby.

"And you, Libby. My mystery writer. From the first page, you had my complete attention. My mind danced between the joy of getting to know your characters, filling the space I was in with the detailed settings you described, and then of course, constantly trying to piece together the mystery that you laid out expertly. I am so proud of you for navigating the challenges you've experienced and I see a wonderfully successful future for you as an author." She spoke with such sincerity that Libby felt an even greater appreciation for her.

Florence waved in the waiter holding champagne, and everyone took a glass.

"To my three authors. To your bright futures, filling our world with epic novels. Cheers." Florence tapped her glass with Paige, Nathanial, and Libby.

Libby could feel the stare from her best friend, who was witnessing the fact that Libby had clearly not shared any of her concerns on being a full-time writer with Florence. As the two friends cheered, Libby mouthed, "I know, I know." The expression on Jane's face said it all. Sooner or later, Libby had to put the truth out there.

*   *   *

The party was glamorous, entertaining, and loud. An hour in, Libby had been introduced to dozens of influential people in the book industry. Florence had made most introductions and helped Libby navigate the conversations with ease. Libby's confidence in interacting with these strangers was growing, thanks to the immersion class the party provided. She was surprised how knowledgeable and positive everyone was about her first book. Part of her was still the woman who would look at her dismal sales with the feeling she would never get traction. It was a dramatic difference to be standing in this party with so many people regarding her as a great writer. She half-hoped the positive feedback would change her mind about her career in writing, but the fact still remained, the solitary experience of writing didn't fulfill her in the way she desired.

Florence seemed satisfied with the number of people Libby had met, and told her to go relax and enjoy the party before the readings. Libby was grateful for the time and knew exactly where she wanted to go. She told Florence she would be out back if anyone needed her. Grabbing her coat, she headed there to relax in the cool night air.

After a few minutes outside, Libby felt her shoulders drop as she concentrated on slowing her breaths. Crowded parties had never been her scene, and even though this was the nicest party she had ever attended, Libby felt out of place and drained.

"May I join you?" Wade's familiar voice filled the quiet outdoor space.

"Of course," Libby said, immediately drawn to looking in his eyes. Even in the darkness, they held a power over her.

Wade sat down next to Libby. "It's a lot, yes?" Wade asked, watching Libby closely.

"Very much so. I mean, your mom is incredible with this stuff. I'm so grateful to her, but I'd very much go for a quiet evening in front of a cozy fireplace rather than mingle with the 'who's who' of the book industry," Libby said, hoping she didn't come across as unappreciative.

"Dad and I used to joke that we were programmed without the party gene. Mom, Lake, and Brooke would go to every party possible; they love it." Wade paused, clearing his throat.

"I wish I could have met him," Libby simply said.

"Me too. I have a feeling he would have adored you. The three of us could have escaped this party an hour ago," Wade said, chuckling.

"Careful. If you say that near Nathanial, he'll be driving away before your next blink," Libby said, glancing through the windows at the party.

"I heard Viv got a lookalike for him. Rumor has it he's waiting outside in a car for her signal," Wade said.

"Amazing. I think he's going to get through it. He's a lot braver than he gives himself credit for and he's truly such an impressive guy," Libby said, smiling. She was so proud of Nathanial and knew he would succeed in the industry, regardless of how this evening went.

"Huh," Wade said, as an unexpected expression flashed on his face.

Before she could stop herself, Libby responded, "Don't tell me you're jealous of Nathanial."

Thankfully, Wade responded quickly, before Libby could chastise herself for assuming that's what his expression meant.

"I want to be the man that impresses you," Wade said, eyes locked again with Libby.

Before Libby could respond, she heard Brooke coming from the house.

"Libby, are you out here? We need you inside." As Brooke approached, she noticed her brother sitting outside with Libby.

"Shit. I ruined a moment. Don't say it; I did. I know I did. Crapity crap crap," Brooke said, in a panic.

Wade chuckled, stood up, and put his hand out to help Libby up.

"I'm sorry. So sorry," Brooke said, as she hurried back inside.

"Come on, the world is waiting." Wade smiled at Libby, sending a warmth throughout her body.

"For the record, you impress me constantly," Libby said, taking his hand and rising from her chair.

Wade's typical composure dropped for a moment as a sense of relief revealed itself on his face. They walked inside hand in hand, Libby feeling a combination of calm and excitement. The moment they passed through the door, Libby was swept away by Paige, saying they needed to get ready for the readings. Libby glanced back at Wade one last time, in disbelief of what had just happened.

I think I actually have a shot with the coffee-eyed god of my dreams.

Paige and Libby met Florence near the front door. They had decided on the front room for the readings, and a small podium had been set up on a platform there. The open floor plan of the residence provided an unobstructed view for most of the guests.

"Are you all ready?" Florence quietly asked the three, focusing most of her attention on Nathanial.

"Yes," they said in unison, some more confidently than others.

The plan was for Paige to go first, followed by Nathanial, and then Libby. Florence gracefully walked to the podium and, as usual, commanded the attention of the crowd with ease.

"I would like to take a moment to thank each one of you for taking time out of the busy holiday season to celebrate with us. Tonight, I am honoring three incredible authors that I have the honor of representing. You all will be the first to hear excerpts from their new novels being released in the spring. Please give a warm welcome to our first author, Paige Raine."

Paige made her way up elegantly, her long pink dress flowing behind her. As she read through her pages, Libby watched the crowd being enchanted by Paige's words. Libby placed her hand on Nathanial's arm as she noticed his hands shaking.

"Why did I agree to go after her?" Nathanial whispered.

"I believe in you," Libby whispered back, while Nathanial nodded nervously.

After Paige finished, the crowd clapped and cheered. The selection from her book was perfect, and Paige's delivery was done expertly.

Florence made her way back to the podium, confirming Nathanial was still in the room, and introduced him next. "Our fantasy writer will now read some pages from his new book. Now, Nathanial told me he chose to be a writer for the solitary nature, but I know this crowd will make him feel right at home. Join us, Nathanial Norris." Florence's introduction seemed to have relieved some of the pressure of being as dynamic as Paige, because Nathanial walked up to the stage steadily and with a smile.

"Thank you, Florence. I believe we can ask my stunt double to head home," Nathanial quipped, sending laughter throughout the crowd.

Libby was not alone in her shocked expression at Nathanial's ability to work the crowd. Ten minutes later, the crowd hollered with excitement, asking for more as he finished his reading. The look of pride on his face was one of the most beautiful things Libby had witnessed.

"Now for our last reading of the evening. My mystery writer that weaves a story with precision and joyful passion, Libby, please take the stage." Florence waved Libby forward.

Libby hadn't expected to feel the level of nervousness that she did in that moment. As she walked forward, she wondered if Nathanial's nerves had transferred to her instead. But as she made her way to the podium, she spotted Jane and Wade standing next to one another. Their confident expressions gave Libby a sense of calm.

Libby took a deep breath and slowly read through the pages. She had been so absorbed in her words that when she got to the end, she remembered to finally look up. Libby wished she could capture this moment, the look of pride and delight in the faces in front of her. Strangers and friends alike clapped and cheered as Libby stood frozen in time. After a few moments, she felt Florence's hand on her arm and heard her say, "Excellent job, Libby."

Libby walked back down from the podium as Florence said her final words.

"Incredible work, you three. As you can hear from the reactions tonight, we are highly anticipating the release of your next books. Thank you for the honor of trusting me in launching your careers as writers, though as we heard tonight, the talent each of you possess was meant to shine. Once again, thank you all for your attendance tonight, and before we get back to our party, my son Lake would like to share a few words." Florence finished her speech and gracefully came down from the stage, making way for Lake.

If Libby thought the crowd's excitement for the readings was a lot, the sounds that emerged from the crowd at Lake's appearance were ten times more enthusiastic.

"He's been here the whole time," Libby said, to no one in particular.

"Thank you, thank you. Now if I may, I have some thrilling news to share with you all tonight. In honor of my mother's new career as a book agent, I thought I would help, in the best way I know how, to launch the success of these authors. I am creating three new singles, inspired by their new books, that will be released along with the books in the spring." Lake threw his arms up as the crowd cheered loudly.

"Oh God," Libby said out loud. If she was worried before tonight about telling everyone her doubts in being a writer, the attention Lake would attract with this announcement was sure to make everything more complicated.

Lake practically skipped off the stage and came up to Libby.

"I know, I'm so generous. You're welcome. But you do know what this means?" Lake said, waiting for Libby to respond.

Internally, she thought, *I'm trapped and have no choice but to be a writer and give up on the hopes of a more fulfilling career.*

But of course, instead she said, "Um no, what's that?"

"That you need to let me read your book. Wherever it's at. How else will I craft an award-winning track inspired by the book?" Lake said.

"Oh, yeah, sure. Of course. I'll send it to you next week. And seriously, thanks." Despite the complications this announcement made for Libby, she was grateful for how much Lake wanted to help.

After Lake left to talk with Paige and Nathanial, Jane hurried over to Libby.

"You were incredible and wow, I can't believe what Lake is doing. That's going to complicate your secret." Jane said dramatically.

"That was wild," Libby said, still in shock from the announcement.

"Enough to make you change your mind about your future in writing?" Jane asked.

In that second, Wade came up from behind Jane, and it was obvious from his expression that he had heard every word.

Jane looked between Libby and Wade, trying to figure out how to salvage her words.

"I didn't want you to hear it like this," Libby said, looking at Wade.

"I'm so sorry," Jane said, looking at Libby.

"Does anyone else know?" Wade asked, his expression unreadable.

"No," they both responded.

"I'll give you two a moment." Jane mouthed "sorry" and hurried off.

Libby tried to explain while watching Wade's unreadable expression.

"I . . . I just . . . I haven't felt the way I had hoped." Libby felt overwhelmed as the words escaped her.

"In a moment, you're going to be swarmed with people wanting to talk to you. Tomorrow afternoon, my place. I'll cook and you share." Wade looked deeply into Libby's eyes and walked away into the crowd.

Libby's mind spun wildly. She had expected him to show some sort of emotion—frustration, annoyance, maybe shock—but he seemed so neutral. And then he asked her to come over? After the moment they'd had outside earlier that evening, Libby had hoped they could talk more, explore what they meant to one another, but now, it just felt awkward. Before she could think about it any longer, a few influencers she had been introduced to earlier came up, excited to hear more. Libby had no choice but to compartmentalize and focus on the people in front of her.

The rest of the evening passed quickly. Libby spent most of the time talking with people about her reading, selling herself as an author when most of her didn't believe it, or want it. Based on how swarmed Nathanial and Paige were, it was clear their readings made an impact as well. It was everything that Florence had described and more, but the moment she was back in her room, all she could think about was Wade hearing her secret. Jane had apologized more times than Libby could count, but she held no negative feelings toward her friend. She was the one that had waited so long to share, and it was bound to come out.

The morning after the party, Libby took Jane to the coffee shop for drinks and a small bite before Jane had to fly out. Despite the looming conversation she was going to have with Wade later that day, Libby was proud of herself for putting that aside and enjoying the brief time with her friend. As they said their goodbyes, Libby felt a mix of emotions. The time with Jane over the last twenty-four hours was bittersweet. Libby was grateful Jane was able to witness her book reading and meet so many people she now cherished, but with her secret out, Libby could no longer ignore her future.

When she got back to the inn after dropping Jane off at the airport, Libby texted with Wade to confirm the time to meet that afternoon and promptly decided to keep the information to herself. Thankfully, both Paige and Nathanial were still at Florence's house, so they weren't around to notice Libby's nervousness.

Unfortunately, Harrison was unusually perceptive that day.

"I'm surprised you aren't out celebrating on the town with how well last night went. You look so morose." Harrison watched Libby closely as he sipped his coffee.

"I am not morose. Just focused, thinking about the book I've got to finish." Libby made a note to fix her face before anyone else started prying. With Harrison, Libby knew exactly how to pivot the conversation.

"You look a little down yourself. I thought you'd be out celebrating, considering how well Nathanial did, thanks to all your help," Libby said.

"Ah, yes, I did brilliantly, didn't I? I think his spontaneous use of humor originated from the caroling. You should never question my methods. As for my slightly down demeanor, that's due to you all abandoning us for the holidays. I hate the holidays," Harrison said, with a full frown.

"Oh Harrison, I'm going to miss you too." Libby went over and gave Harrison a hug.

After the hug, Libby reminded Harrison, "We were willing to stay here and keep working, but Florence insisted we go home for the holidays so we could return refreshed in the new year. We'll be back before you know it."

Harrison's pouty expression remained.

Gani came into the room looking especially excited. "Speaking of the holidays, I have a small surprise."

"Surprise? From you? We both know that's my thing. Where is it?" Harrison said, anxiously waiting.

Gani smiled lovingly at his partner. "Well, we all know you've been down about everyone leaving for the holidays, so I thought I'd treat you to a vacation."

"Where? What? When? What do I pack?" Harrison looked overwhelmed with joy.

Gani chuckled as he handed Harrison a sheet of paper. "This is our itinerary. We leave in three days, and I just know you'll have the perfect outfits packed by then."

"Oh darling. I've always wanted to go to Maine in the winter. And an itinerary? You said you hate when I plan our time to the second," Harrison said.

"For you? I'd do anything. Including an itinerary," Gani said, as he embraced his partner.

After a moment, Harrison pulled away and frantically exclaimed, "I must go pack. Oh, I love the holidays!" and ran out of the room.

"You did good," Libby said to Gani, as he made himself a tea.

"Yes, well I might have had selfish intentions. If we stayed here, Harrison would probably have had me repaint all the bedrooms." He sat down next to Libby.

"So tell me, are you nervous to talk with Wade today about your future as a writer?" Gani took a sip casually, like he'd just asked about the weather.

"How do you know about my dilemma about the future and the fact I'm going to Wade's?" Libby said, shocked.

"I may have overheard a little something last night," Gani replied calmly. "And before you ask, I have not and will not say anything to anyone. Remember how I feel about secrets." Gani set his cup down lightly.

"I might have to ask Jane to apologize a few more hundred times," Libby said under her breath.

"I have to say, it's not a surprise. I could sense something was off with you," Gani replied.

"I'm quite mad at myself. I'm in my midthirties and I can't decide what I want to do with my life. I couldn't have a better setup, better connections, a clearer path to success as a writer, and I cannot believe I don't want it." Libby put her head in her hands.

"And I assume you aren't having second thoughts about going back to nursing?" Gani asked.

"Oh, absolutely not. I mean, I would write over nursing any day. But I thought I would go from the career that didn't fit to the perfect one when I came here. Now it just feels like I took a step in the right direction but it's not my path. I mean ugh, why can't this just be my path? I can do it. And well," Libby said.

"Just because you can do something, doesn't mean you should. Give yourself grace. You will find your calling, and when you do, you'll be proud of yourself for bravely searching, even when you were scared," Gani said with confidence.

"Thanks, Gani. I'm grateful for you."

"Yes, well, you make it easy to adore you. Now, I have to go help my husband pack before we're taking ten suitcases. I wish you well, talking with Wade. I hope you learn to trust him. He's quite a special person," Gani said.

"I don't know. I just hope he doesn't hate me for the trouble I will cause for Florence," Libby said, her voice full of concern.

"I wouldn't worry about that. I'm here if you want to talk later." And with that, Gani headed upstairs.

Libby made herself a tea, choosing the soothing blend that Gani always seemed to be drinking, in hopes she would emulate his more peaceful demeanor. She had two hours before she went to see Wade and was in desperate need to calm her nerves. Libby was glad that of all the people at that party, Gani had been the only other one to hear her secret.

She wondered if, after talking with Wade about her future, she would feel the same way about it, or the complete opposite.

*   *   *

When Libby arrived at Wade's house, it was like coming home to her treehouse. The serenity of the scenery, a small home hidden amongst the trees, struck a chord in her heart. She walked slowly to the house, not wanting to lose the peace that suddenly came over her.

Maybe there really is something to that calming tea.

She knocked lightly and took a deep breath as Wade opened the door. Libby immediately noticed the alluring smells coming from the kitchen. Taking off her coat, Libby carefully watched Wade's expression, noticing that he seemed happy and at ease. She told herself not to read into things, but her relief was immediate. The man in front of her didn't look an ounce annoyed or angry with her.

"I hope you're hungry. I've been trying a few recipes, hoping to narrow them down for the restaurant." Wade strolled back to the kitchen like he and Libby were old friends.

Libby followed behind and settled into the barstool Wade pulled out for her.

"I could eat. It smells heavenly in here. I thought after yesterday, you'd be more inclined to interrogate me than feed me." Libby couldn't help but point out the elephant in the room.

Wade laughed as he stirred something incredible in the pot on the stove.

"Well, I said I was feeding you, but I didn't promise not to poison you," Wade said, moving to the chopping board to mince garlic.

"I wouldn't blame you," Libby said, knowing she sounded dramatic.

"I'm glad you talked with Gani," Wade said, barely looking at the knife as he cut more garlic.

"How did you—" Libby started to say, shocked for the second time that day.

"Gani and I are good friends. We both had the pleasure of overhearing Jane, and we were worried about you." Wade placed the knife down, satisfied with the amount of garlic, and looked at Libby.

She shouldn't have been surprised, but the intensity of his brown eyes made her breath catch. "Can you just look away, please?" Libby hadn't intended to say that out loud.

Wade laughed, knowing the effect he had on her. He went back to cooking, sensing Libby had an easier time being honest when he was keeping himself busy.

Regaining her presence in the moment, Libby shared, "Worried was not the emotion I expected. Honestly, how can you stand there and cook food for me when I'm ruining your mother's reputation by backing out on a writing career because, for some ridiculous reason, I want more than what writing full-time can provide, which is absurd, obviously, because I thought I wanted this all my life." Libby took a breath, realizing how long she had spoken.

"I'm quite impressed you were able to write a book without so many run-on sentences," Wade responded, now dicing a bright-red tomato.

"You aren't the first person to say that…" Libby said, silently cursing her best friend for this awkward conversation.

"Are you still planning on finishing your second book?" Wade asked.

"Well, yes of course," Libby replied.

"Then you are in no way tarnishing my mother's reputation. What you do after the second book is written is up to you." Wade moved the diced tomato into the pot.

Libby sat in the chair, silent. On one hand, he sounded like a reasonable human being, but on the other, he was completely out of touch. Surely, Florence would be furious. She had invested time, money, and her heart into the three authors.

Wade spoke a minute later, bringing Libby back to the moment. "You disagree?"

"How well would you say you know your mom?" Libby asked, getting another laugh from Wade.

"I like to think I know her well. And I don't think you're giving her enough credit. Now Lake, he'll be a whole other story," Wade said with a smile.

"Yes, well his grand announcement didn't help things."

"Ah, well, he'll be alright. So, when are you going to tell everyone?" Wade asked, with a calm curiosity.

"I have no idea," Libby said, shuddering at the thought.

"When you're ready," Wade replied, turning his attention to prepping the garlic bread.

"I'm sorry, but what is happening here? I expected a little more upset coming from you. At least some pressure to tell everyone. This," Libby waved her hands up and down at Wade, "is tremendously easygoing and quite jarring. Between you and Gani, I feel like I'm in a parallel universe." Libby finished her rant while Wade's expression revealed a hint of amusement.

"Didn't have a lot of easygoing people in your life?" Wade asked, placing the garlic bread into the oven.

"Ha. You could say that. My dad was intense about everything: school, timing dinner perfectly, and moisture management in the house. It was a whole thing; you don't want to know. Then Mom had this limitless vibrant energy that she brought to every situation. Don't bring up the holiday decorations in our town or you will experience both energy and intensity from her. So, easygoing? No that wasn't a part of my upbringing," Libby said.

"My mom brought a similar passion and intensity for things in life. Dad was successful and hardworking, don't get me wrong, but he brought more of a calming presence. I loved that, so I've tried to emulate it," Wade said.

"Sounds nice. And completely unrealistic for me." Libby thought about herself as a calm person and almost laughed out loud.

"Don't sell yourself short. From what I see, you're working hard to find your way to peace. Now, let's get this plated so you can tell me again how good I am at cooking." Wade winked at Libby, causing her heart to skip.

Once they sat down, Libby and Wade transitioned to talking about his restaurant and consulting business. Libby learned that Wade had a big contract in Texas for the next few months that would keep him traveling more days than not. She felt a pang of sadness upon hearing he wouldn't be around, and she wondered if he felt anything similar.

After they finished eating and cleaning up, Libby made her way to the door to get her coat on.

"Thank you for..." Libby paused, unsure how to word it.

"My easygoing nature?" Wade asked.

"Yes, that and your cooking skills. I don't think I need to eat until after the holidays," Libby said, patting her stomach.

"Good, then I did my job." Wade helped Libby with her coat, but instead of letting go, he held her there, looking into her eyes.

"You have the most beautiful eyes," he said simply.

My eyes? Has he seen a mirror?

Libby couldn't find her words, so instead, she did the one thing she wanted the most in that moment, and kissed him. The kiss was like nothing she'd experienced with Thomas. It was intense and passionate, releasing Libby from any thoughts about her future, the book, or disappointing anyone. Her entire body, mind, and soul were there in that moment, kissing the man with the beautiful brown eyes.

Finally parting, Libby looked to Wade, wide-eyed. "That was … um …" She was at a loss for words.

"Perfect," Wade responded, confirming his experience matched hers.

"But I leave tomorrow. And then you're going away for work and I'm writing a book and then doing who knows what. This is terrible timing." Libby's mind had gone off to the future once again.

"Nothing about us feels terrible," Wade said, melting Libby's heart.

"Dinner in the New Year?" Wade asked, simplifying things once again.

"I would do every dinner with you next year," Libby said, with slight embarrassment at her confession.

Wade chuckled and whispered in her ear, "I hope to do more than dinners next year."

Libby's breath caught as she felt her entire body draw closer to Wade. Wade drew her in for another kiss, somehow surpassing the intensity of the first. After they released, Wade walked her to her car and opened the door. Libby got in, but before she closed the door, she felt the need to ask Wade, "We have remarkable kisses, yes? Or is this typical for you?" Libby blushed, realizing how ridiculous a question it was.

Wade smiled and kissed her once again, then said, "Remarkable. Yes, that's a good word for it. See you after the holidays, Libby Autumn."

*   *   *

When she arrived back at the inn, Gani was working out front, replacing some holiday bulbs that had gone out.

"I was going to ask how it went, but your face says it all." Gani smiled at Libby's glowing expression.

"That obvious?" Libby hadn't stopped grinning since she said goodbye to Wade.

Gani chuckled, nodding.

"Well, I have a book to write, a future to sort out, and a kiss to reminisce about," Libby said, as she drifted inside.

Gani watched Libby and said dreamily, almost to himself, "You look the same way I did when I met Harrison." And with that, he went back to his work on the decorations, humming a holiday song.

CHAPTER EIGHTEEN

The holidays seemed to fly by for Libby. She spent most of the time with her parents, the moments more precious now that she was living away from them. She was overly attached to her phone, thanks to the frequent flirtatious texts she exchanged with Wade. Libby had a calm confidence in her future with Wade, something she had never experienced with Thomas. It was clear that the intensity in feelings was mutual for Libby and Wade, which seemed to dissipate any remaining insecurities she had about their future.

While she was home, Libby made time every day possible to work from the library and visit with Miss Willa. It shocked her how, in a matter of months, she had found herself right back where she started, in the seat by the window at her hometown library. In some ways she felt like a completely different person, transformed by her time in Willowston and the revelations about her writing career and unknown future. But in other ways, she felt like the same girl, pouring herself into a novel created solely by her and whatever her imagination served up.

One morning had stuck with Libby while she was home for the holidays. She had arrived early at the library and was sitting in her chair and typing away at a scene when Miss Willa came up to her. It wasn't unusual for Miss Willa to spontaneously check in with Libby while she was working, similar to Pixie at Willowston. But this time, Miss Willa looked upset, which in itself was a rare sight. When Libby asked what was wrong, Miss Willa explained that a young woman had come in looking for a community program she could join. With their limited funding, most of the programs available focused on young children or teens, and the woman had left discouraged, despite Miss Willa's best efforts to engage her.

One specific statement Miss Willa made kept playing over and over in Libby's mind: "I wish I could have done more to help her feel part of this community." With Libby's work in Willowston, she felt a connection to that sentiment, but something more kept bothering her. The blinking cursor on her computer had brought Libby's focus back to her book, but the nagging feeling remained.

* * *

In early January when Libby headed back to Willowston, she was over halfway done with her book. Unfortunately, she hadn't made any progress on her future career plans or when she was going to tell Florence her true feelings on being a writer. All Libby knew was she wanted to have some sort of plan for her future before she said anything. Saying, "Eh, this writing thing isn't it, but I have no idea what is," felt wholly inadequate.

*   *   *

Libby, Paige, and Nathanial all arrived back in Willowston on the same day. Harrison and Gani had prepared an over-the-top spread in anticipation of their arrival. Catching up over food and drinks, everyone shared about their time at home. Harrison, true to his nature, had prepared a slideshow of photos and videos from their trip to Maine. Libby couldn't fathom how, but Harrison and Gani seemed even more in love following their trip.

Nathanial shocked everyone by sharing he had gone on three dates while he was home, all with different women. After Paige and Harrison grilled him with questions, it was clear Nathanial had made progress in his confidence around women but remained stuck on one barista.

Paige talked about the glamorous parties she attended in the city and the brief trip she and Diti took to the Caribbean. Based on her stories, Paige was living up to the "female version of Lake" title and had gained some valuable romance material for her future books. Libby was suddenly transported to the land of panic when she heard Paige talking casually about her next book.

Finally, it was Libby's turn to share.

"Well, this is quite a departure from Paige's holiday, but I spent most of mine at home with the parents and at the local library with my favorite retired teacher, now library director, Miss Willa," Libby said, suddenly feeling like the world's most boring person.

"Is Miss Willa the Pixie of your hometown?" Nathanial asked, impressing everyone with his insight.

Libby laughed. "Yes, I guess I tend to befriend a certain type. She was perfect to bounce ideas off while I was getting my writing done. One day, it was so out of character because she was upset about how a conversation went with a patron. It was this young woman that hoped to join a library program and meet some people, but with their funding limitations there wasn't anything that she resonated with. The look of disappointment on her face almost killed Miss Willa. I'm just grateful for the impact we're able to have here in Willowston."

Libby surprised herself that she shared that story about Willa. But no one seemed to notice, because the next question focused on her book. "I don't want to kill the vibe, but how's the book coming?" Paige's tone was kind but concerned.

"Over halfway done," Libby said, pretending to shine her nails on her shirt.

The reaction of the room was even more animated than Libby had thought it might be, but she appreciated every ounce of their excitement.

"That's our girl!" Harrison shouted, splashing his drink on his unsuspecting partner.

"Oh, thank God. The last thing Nathanial and I wanted was to put pressure on you, but we need you to finish this book and make it phenomenal, for the success of the launch." Paige looked more relieved than Libby had expected.

"She's right," Nathanial chimed in sheepishly. "We were really hoping you wouldn't mess this up for us."

If Libby hadn't known Paige and Nathanial better, she would have been devastated by their comments, but after months together, she had a good understanding of their personalities and how much the success of their book launch meant to them.

"I made a commitment, and I plan on delivering," Libby said confidently.

Libby noticed Gani watching her carefully as she shared more about her book and the direction it had taken. The room was enthusiastic, and it felt good to get the positive feedback.

"I can't wait to read it. I don't want to say for sure, but by the sounds of it, you've once again created a complex and satisfying murder." Harrison's use of reviewer-speak made Libby laugh.

"It's true. The story sounds great, and on behalf of everyone in this room, please never decide to murder us. I have a feeling you would get away with it," Nathanial said, looking genuinely terrified.

*   *   *

The next morning, Libby woke up early, determined to get back into her normal routine in Willowston. With both Florence and Wade out of town for the remainder of January, Libby wanted to make as much progress as possible on her novel. When she went downstairs for coffee, only Gani was in the kitchen, tending to some indoor plants.

"Your comments on Willa were interesting," Gani said, without looking up from the plant he was pruning.

"Morning, Gani. Based on the direction the conversation went, I was starting to question if I said that part aloud," Libby replied.

"Ah, well, this crowd has a vested interest in your future book, but me, I'm more interested in that story. Tell me more." Gani sat down on a barstool with his ever-present calming energy.

Libby took a breath and shared more details from the interaction and her thoughts following it. "I mean obviously, I hated to see Miss Willa sad, but the whole thing is gnawing at me, and I can't figure out why," Libby finally said, turning to Gani.

"Hmm," was his only reply.

"Can you please give me a little more than that?" Libby pleaded.

"I just find it fascinating how passionate you've been about how libraries can help community. How much you want people to find their way, connect with others, and feel a sense of happiness in this world."

"Well, of course. I mean, it feels so obvious. Books have such power with their ability to transport, and to me, libraries feel like the Grand Central Station of a community. A place that can take you to anywhere in the world, to learn about any topic you can think of, all while being surrounded by people doing the exact same thing," Libby said.

Gani smiled, adding, "You speak from experience?"

"The library at home was the first place I felt at peace. And now it's given me the chance to reconnect with Miss Willa, who's become one of the most important people in my life. I mean, all this"—Libby motioned to the room around her—"wouldn't have happened if it wasn't for that library, showing me I could have more out of life. Of course, the irony being it showed me the wrong path." Libby sighed defeatedly.

"Or maybe not," Gani replied and, with a chuckle, walked out of the room.

What is that man talking about?

Realizing she wasn't going to get anything more out of Gani, Libby got her journal out and went back to drafting thoughts for her next scene.

* * *

A few days later, Libby cheered joyfully from her seat in the Willowston library. The word count on her screen aligned with her timeline for completing the book by February, an accomplishment Libby of a few weeks ago wouldn't have thought possible.

"Aren't you a cheerful gal. Did the murderer get murdered? Oh, what a wonderful thing for Darcy that would be." Pixie sat down across from Libby as she passed her a cup of freshly brewed coffee.

"Thank you. And not exactly, but it appears this book will be completed right on time, barring any dramatic complications," Libby said, as her mind suddenly started drafting a few possibilities.

"Oh, stop it now. You were born for this," Pixie replied.

The kind but inaccurate words made Libby start to tear up.

"Oh my. Oh dear. What did I say? Did something happen to Darcy?" Pixie's constant concern for the fictional murder victim brought a small smile to Libby's face, despite her crying.

"Don't worry about our Darcy. She gets justice," Libby replied.

"Then what is it?" Pixie was full of concern.

"I don't want it. This writing career. I thought I did, but I find myself somehow more lost than when I started." Libby's tears fell faster.

"Ah," Pixie said, gently pressing a tissue into Libby's hands.

After the tears subsided, Pixie invited Libby to take a short walk outside. Once they had put on their coats and left the building, Pixie began to share a part of her past Libby had never heard before.

"Did you know I used to work in a perfume factory? At the time, I was so proud of myself. It felt like a dream. Help to bottle all these glamorous perfumes, come home smelling luxurious, and all while getting paid? I remember thinking this is all I could possibly want. Well, I probably don't need to tell you my dreams didn't live up to the reality. I left after two weeks, completely lost and permanently smelling like a chemical concoction of rose." Pixie's expression was moving as she reflected on that time.

"So what did you do?" Libby asked.

"The only logical thing. I went the opposite direction and started working on a dairy farm," Pixie said, laughing.

"And you loved it?"

"Oh no. It was dreadful. But I stuck it out for a while. Then one day, my friend suggested we go to a library a town over on one of my days off." Pixie's face lit up. "From the moment I walked in, I knew it's what I wanted."

"I'm so happy for you. You were lucky," Libby said, grateful her friend had found her way.

Pixie laughed, adding, "I'm sharing this story for a couple of reasons. One, I love to talk about myself, which you already know. And two, I've seen that expression of happiness in you, here at this library," Pixie said, reaching out and holding Libby's hands. "Sometimes the answer is closer than we think it is."

"I do wish people would stop talking in riddles today," Libby said, her frustration bubbling up. She let go of Pixie's hands and started walking again.

Pixie laughed once again. "What I'm saying is you should move to Ireland, take on a few Irish lovers, and work in a local library."

Libby burst out laughing and tripped on the pavement, just catching herself.

When Pixie confirmed Libby's body was intact, she said, "No need to fling yourself down on the ground. I'm just wanting you to learn from my own life."

Pixie sensed the need to transition to more practical advice. "I think you're going to figure it out sooner rather than later. When I see you helping people, explaining the workshop you developed, engaging with the patrons here, you look so happy. Maybe a future as a librarian isn't the worst idea?" Pixie said.

Pixie's words were the final puzzle piece. Libby turned hastily to her friend and said, "Pixie, can you show me a list of all the ongoing programs this library is offering and the numbers for enrollment of each?"

"Can a bird eat a worm? No wait, I have a better one. Can an Irishman be an amazing lover?" Pixie giggled while Libby gave her an exasperated expression. "Of course I can. Jeez, no one appreciates my creative use of the English language anymore." Pixie stood up and walked inside, with Libby closely following, busy in her thoughts.

*   *   *

Four hours later, Libby had piles of paper spread across the table in front of her, pages of notes in her journal, and a fire inside unlike any she'd experienced before. She had barely looked up in the hours since her idea blossomed, but she sensed Pixie watching from nearby. Finally, Libby stood up from her chair and called Pixie over.

"About time. I was wondering if I needed to call in reinforcements," Pixie said, trying to decipher what all the papers and notes on the table meant for Libby's future.

"Want to hear my idea?" Libby said excitedly.

"Very much so," Pixie said, settling down in the chair at the table.

The first time Libby heard her idea out loud, she felt even more confident. Pixie was engaged and helped Libby flesh out more of the details. The moment was reminiscent of the early times she shared her storylines with Jane and was able to refine and improve the novel in ways she never could alone. It felt all kinds of right and terrifying, and Libby had a lot more to work out.

* * *

For the next couple of weeks, Libby balanced making progress on her novel with fleshing out the details of her newly discovered idea. She only shared the details of what she was working on with a handful of people, including Jane, her mother, Wade, Gani, and Miss Willa, and they were all sworn to silence. The support was uncompromising and only contributed to Libby's motivation to make it work.

Libby had frequent meetings with Florence to discuss her novel and affirm she was sticking with her aggressive timeline. Florence was thrilled to see how much Libby had gotten done and had asked what her secret was to writing so many pages in a short time. Of course, Libby didn't say it out loud, but internally she knew the progress could be attributed to her side project, which was adding color and clarity to everything Libby did. She had never experienced the power of motivation to this level, but she was learning how understanding the purpose and why of something she did could make all the tasks simpler.

* * *

By the end of January, Libby was only a couple of chapters away from completing her second novel and, as Pixie frequently reminded her, "providing justice for our beloved Darcy." Libby was slightly concerned that Pixie was too emotionally attached to her fictional murder victim, but she appreciated the enthusiasm.

With Florence coming back to Willowston the next day, Paige, Nathanial, and Libby decided to spend the day together taking a well-deserved break from their writing. All three were on track to having their books written and edited by the February deadline. It felt surreal that their time in Willowston was winding down. Their official checkout day—or doomsday, as Harrison called it—was only two months away.

The three authors went into the coffee shop, a favorite spot they all shared. Nathanial's whole body tensed as he approached the counter first, Grace smiling broadly. The connection between the two was obvious, but neither had made a move over the last months, leading to a predictable and awkwardly charming interaction.

"Hi Nathanial. How is your book coming along?" Grace said, her face luminous.

"I finished the last chapter late last night," Nathanial said, shyly.

Libby and Paige exchanged looks, both hearing this for the first time.

"That's incredible. Oh Nathanial, I cannot wait to read it," Grace said, her smile somehow getting bigger.

"You see how much she says his name? That's another clue she likes him. Course, with these two, we'll never make it past the coffee order," Paige whispered to Libby.

"Thank you. Just the usual, please," Nathanial said, as his hands shakily reached for his wallet.

"Absolutely not. My favorite author does not pay for his coffee on the day he finished his next novel," Grace said sweetly, as she started on his drink.

Paige, unable to resist, shoved Nathanial from behind, hoping she could knock some courage into him.

"Thanks. That's very kind," he said simply, putting his wallet away.

After Grace finished his mocha, she handed it to him, saying, "I really am so proud of you for getting your book written. It's an accomplishment to be celebrated."

Nathanial reached for the coffee, his fingers touching Grace's for a moment. The two stood there staring at one another, the entire coffee shop and thirsty Paige and Libby forgotten. Finally, Grace slowly took her hand away, moving to take the next orders. Suddenly, Nathanial choked out the word, "Wait."

"Did he just say, 'Kate'?" Libby whispered to Paige.

"I believe he said 'Wait.' Holy, freaking..." Paige said, watching as Grace faced Nathanial.

"Yes? Is something wrong with your mocha?" Grace said.

"Will you do me the honor of dinner at your earliest convenience?" Nathanial said, nervously but clearly.

"Weird way to ask, but damn, he did it," Paige whispered, as Libby held her breath to hear Grace's response.

"I would love that," Grace replied, her eyes glowing.

Libby finally took a breath and cheered as subtly as she could with Paige a few feet away.

"If this was my next romance, it'd be 2000 pages before the couple gets some momentum. But wow, I'm proud of him," Paige said, as they watched the two schedule their dinner date.

▪ CHAPTER NINETEEN ▪

Florence had asked that all three authors meet her at the library by 8 a.m. the next morning. The request was easy for Libby to achieve, with her established early-morning routine, but getting Nathanial and Paige out of the inn in time was like assembling a bunch of toddlers. Finally, a few seconds before 8, the three authors made their way to one of the small conference rooms in the back.

"Well, if it isn't my three writing stars," Florence said, wearing an immaculate teal-blue suit and looking full of energy.

By Florence's side was Brooke, grinning widely, her newly dyed hair matching Florence's suit perfectly.

"I cannot wait to tell them. Tell them. Tell them!" Brooke said to her mom.

"Tell us what?" Libby asked, as Paige and Nathanial seemed at a loss for words, the energetic scene conflicting with their grogginess.

In that moment, Libby thought about the profound difference in her feelings compared to her fellow authors' with whatever news Florence would share. Libby hoped that whatever Florence was going to say didn't further complicate her confession about no longer wanting a writing career. But for Nathanial and Paige, this news could mean a dramatic difference in their future success as writers.

"Let's all take a seat," Florence said calmly, encouraging her daughter to sit down.

"First of all, may I say how proud I am of all three of you. To get your books written on this short timeline was an accomplishment by itself. But based on everything I've seen, you all managed to write something even better than your first books, and we all know how much we loved them," Florence said, indicating Brooke and herself.

"The news, Mom!" Brooke said impatiently, creating more anticipation in the room.

"Right, yes. Lake had hoped he could be here to share this, but he had a scheduling conflict. He asked we record your reactions with a camera crew, but I reminded him that not everyone is as comfortable with a camera in their face as he is," Florence said.

"Oh, I don't mind. I love capturing my reactions. I've been told my facial expressions are enchanting," Paige said, getting a playful eye roll from both Libby and Nathanial.

"*Mom*," Brooke said, motioning for her to share.

"After this, we are getting you to the inn so Gani can make you his calming tea," Florence said to her daughter, and then refocused on the authors. "Now, as you know, the official launch party for your new books is scheduled in April. This, we hope, will make a big splash in sales. But Lake, my promotion genius, had another idea to help grow interest in your books and in you as authors. The three of you will be joining Lake on the United States portion of his rap tour, starting in May." Florence paused as Brooke stood up, cheering.

Libby took a moment to turn to Paige and Nathanial to gauge their reactions. Paige's entire face lit up as she processed the news. *Dang, her face is enchanting.*

Next, Libby saw Nathanial's eyes growing bigger and bigger. He looked shocked and may have stopped breathing.

Libby wondered for a moment what expression her face wore as she looked over at Florence and caught her watching curiously. Libby tried to hide the panic rising inside of her by mimicking Miss Enchanting's face next to her, but sensed she was failing, as her eye couldn't stop twitching.

Brooke enthusiastically launched into details on the tour—the cities they were visiting, and how they would set up book signings in each of the cities and make announcements during the concerts. Brooke explained that Lake's creation of songs for each author would make the perfect avenue to promote the books.

She squealed with excitement, talking about how amazing it would be to come out on the stage during his concert, all the screaming fans and bright lights.

After Brooke finished squealing and sharing, Florence spoke. "Now, we know this is a lot of information to process, so please go take some time. We'll talk through any concerns you have when we meet for our regular check-ins tomorrow afternoon." Florence had looked directly at Libby when she said "concerns."

"Concerns? Florence, this whole thing is perfection. The publicity we'll get from this idea alone can propel our careers to heights we only dreamed of," Paige said, waving her hands excitedly.

"Don't love the idea of going out on the stage, the crowds, loud noise, or bright lights, but I know it'll be huge for us. I assume there'll be a lot of rap music?" Recognizing that was an odd question and receiving nods of concern but confirmation, Nathanial went on, "Thanks, Florence and Brooke. For looking out for us and pushing us well past our comfort zones. So far past..." Nathanial said, trailing off.

"Ooh. I won't mention that you called Lake's music 'loud noise,'" Brooke said, with a giggle.

Libby smiled politely as they finished the meeting and left the room. To her best ability, Libby avoided looking Florence in the eyes, knowing she was perceptive and would detect something was off. Libby was aware she couldn't put off her news for much longer, but there was no way she could go on that rap tour.

* * *

Libby was grateful for the distraction both her book and her new idea provided for the rest of the day. She worked diligently and was mostly successful at avoiding any thoughts related to her future as a writer. At 5 p.m., she had begun to gather her things and head back to the inn when she got a text. Every time she saw Wade's name pop up on her phone, her stomach did a somersault. This message in particular launched a thousand somersaults.

Wade: Surprise. I'm home. Care to join me for dinner tonight? My place, 7 p.m.?

Libby hadn't expected to see Wade for a least another week. She squealed with excitement, getting a fake-stern look from Pixie for her outburst. After texting him back an enthusiastic yes, she walked over to Pixie to say goodbye.

"What, you have a hot date or something?" Pixie asked, looking closely at Libby.

"In fact, I do," Libby responded. She hadn't told anyone other than Jane and her mom about her growing connection with Wade, but with her level of joy, she couldn't help herself.

"I hope he's Irish," Pixie said with a straight face.

"I'm saving all of them for you," Libby said with a wink, and she headed to the front.

"You better give details tomorrow," Pixie shouted, resulting in a shush from her fellow librarian.

Libby smiled and heard her friend say, "That was a justified shush, but I still didn't like it."

* * *

Libby knew she'd have to give her housemates a reasonable excuse for leaving that evening. Per usual, Gani already knew what was happening before Libby said anything to him. She had a feeling Gani and Wade texted as much as she and Jane did, which made her incredibly happy. After getting ready in one of her favorite sweaters and buttery soft fitted jeans, Libby headed downstairs.

"What's going on?" Harrison motioned to Libby's outfit.

"What?" Libby asked innocently.

"Usually when you get home from a day of writing, you put on those comfortable clothes that, let's be honest, do nothing for your figure. But this, you look all dolled up. Are you, Nathanial, and Paige going out to dinner without me again?" Harrison said, bringing up the rare occasion that the three authors would go out to eat without him.

"No, we don't have any plans," Paige said, walking into the room wearing her lounge clothes that always managed to look better than most of Libby's best daywear.

"I have plans," Nathanial said, drawing everyone's attention away from Libby and over to him as he strolled into the room.

"Everyone stop. Is tonight official 'make a move on a barista' night? How did you not tell us until this moment?" Harrison said, hurrying over to Nathanial to pull and tuck his shirt like he was his personal stylist.

"It is," Nathanial said proudly.

"Is Libby your chaperone?" Harrison asked, bringing the focus back on her.

"No, but it looks like she's going out on a date too," Nathanial said, purely based on observation.

"I am," Libby admitted. With so many things being hidden from these people she had come to adore, she couldn't stand to keep her relationship with Wade a secret another moment.

"Who?" the room said in unison—minus Gani, who looked at Libby with raised eyebrows.

"Wade," Libby said, more nervous than she expected to be. But any hesitation she had in telling them was immediately wiped away with the celebration and kindness that erupted in the room.

"What a beautiful couple you two make. I want all the details," Paige said.

"Oh, my. How did we not know? How did WE not know?" Harrison said, focusing on his partner.

"Truly a surprise, but I'm happy for you both," Gani said, with the stealth of a CIA agent.

"I'm actually a bit jealous we aren't focusing on me right now," Nathanial said, making everyone burst into laughter.

Libby spent the next five minutes giving a summary of her relationship with Wade. She fully admitted the timeline and was happy that no one was offended she took so long to share, especially after their involvement in the application of Nathanial's "Do I Have a Shot" formula. Libby felt a moment of hope that when she shared the news about her writing career, she would receive the same level of support.

* * *

Arriving at Wade's house, Libby felt full of warmth and peace. One thing she knew without a doubt was this entire experience was worth it, because she was able to meet the man in that house. Wade opened the door before Libby knocked.

"Hey," he said, drawing her in for a kiss.

The intensity of the kiss had Libby melting into his arms.

"I missed you," she said, not wanting to separate from the embrace.

"Yeah, but if we weren't apart, we wouldn't have discovered the potential of our text exchanges. You're an author, so I should have known you had a way with words, but I'm starting to think you're writing in the wrong genre," Wade said, smiling down at Libby.

Libby immediately blushed as her mind flashed to the steamy texts she'd been sending him. But it was only a moment until the reality of Florence's news came rearing its head.

"Did you hear? About the tour?" Libby asked.

"Brooke called this afternoon and told me," Wade said, offering Libby a spoonful of the sauce she was now staring at.

After Libby took the bite, she sat, eyes closed, enjoying the flavors that burst across her tongue.

"I'm going to have to tell Pixie that Irishmen are great and all, but she really needs to shift her focus to a chef," Libby said. Wade looked confused, but Libby continued on.

"I have to tell Florence and Lake and Brooke about my new idea. Like, yesterday. Oh, and Harrison, Paige, and Nathanial know about us," Libby said, nervous to see Wade's reaction.

Wade raised his eyebrows. "Sounds like good news to me. Keeping my hands off you in public was really getting challenging."

"Oh God. Your family. We haven't told them about us! They can't hear about it from someone else."

Wade chuckled. "Not the reaction I thought you'd have when I said I can't keep my hands off you, but I have no doubt my family will be nothing but thrilled for us. And let's be honest, no one's going to be surprised."

Libby's shoulders dropped. It was true, Lake had all but pushed Libby toward Wade, Brooke loved all things Libby, and Florence was so perceptive, she probably already knew.

A smile spread across Libby's face. "Tell me more about your hands."

* * *

The rest of the evening was perfect. Libby and Wade's connection was growing in intensity, and despite all the unknowns in her life, she felt a profound sense of rightness being with him. Libby had confidence that whatever happened with her future career, Wade would be a supportive presence. That alone was more than most people could find in their entire lives, and Libby felt grateful for it.

When Libby got home, well after midnight, Harrison and Gani were waiting like a pair of protective parents.

"Are you two seriously waiting up for me?" Libby said, laughing at Harrison's look of impatience.

"*He* is. I'm merely keeping him company," Gani said, looking up from his book.

"Tell me everything. Did you kiss? What did he make you for dinner? Did you bring leftovers?" Harrison asked.

Libby smiled and handed him the box of leftovers Wade insisted she bring home. Wade was aware of

Harrison's love for his cooking and had correctly predicted the need to provide some for Libby to bring home.

After they talked about their evenings, Libby asked about Nathanial.

"He's not home yet," Harrison said, full of drama.

"What?" Libby was shocked.

"Our brave boy is achieving new heights tonight," Harrison said, full of innuendo.

"Okay, time to get you to bed," Gani said, helping Harrison up out of his seat.

"Goodnight, Libby. We're happy for you," Gani said, winking at Libby as he guided his partner out of the room.

* * *

The next morning, Libby went downstairs and was surprised to see a sheepish-looking Nathanial at the bar. Gani and Harrison were out of the house, as they had plans to meet with a top travel blogger to discuss a feature on their inn. Florence had connected them, knowing the impact this blogger could have on the bookings at the inn after the authors left.

"Long night, huh?" Libby said, smiling at Nathanial.

"I can't believe they were waiting up for us," Nathanial said, putting his head in his hands.

Libby laughed. "It's true. Harrison always loves to be the first to hear how things went. I'm sure he's devastated he couldn't talk to you this morning."

"Oh, I've received about a hundred texts from Harrison since last night. When do you think harassment has been reached and I can talk to the police?" Nathanial joked.

Libby laughed and poured herself a coffee. "So, tell me, how was it?" Libby asked, taking a seat next to Nathanial.

"Magical. She's incredible, Libby. The way she sees the world, and honestly, the way she sees me, makes me feel like a different, better version of myself. And she's so pretty." Nathanial looked happy.

"I'm glad you enjoyed it. The whole *long* night together," Libby said, sounding like Harrison.

"It was innocent. I swear. We fell asleep on her couch after watching a dozen episodes of *Schitt's Creek*. This morning when I woke up and saw the endless texts from Harrison, I knew I'd be in trouble. It took me a century to ask her out. I'm estimating at least two years before I get the guts to kiss her," Nathanial said, throwing his arms in the air.

Libby chuckled. "I think you'll find your way much quicker than two years. I'm proud of you for asking her out. Did you tell her about the big rap tour you'll be attending?"

"I did. Honestly, part of me thought she'd just say forget it then and there, but you know what? She just said life has a funny way of working out, and that we enjoy the moments where we can. She was so chill about the whole thing. You think that means she doesn't like me that much?"

"I think Grace is an incredibly mature person who wants the best for you and your writing career. Based on everything I've seen, she likes you very much," Libby said encouragingly.

"I suppose you're right. She gets that twinkle in her eyes when we look at each other. Twinkling eyes lead to twinkling hearts," Nathanial said, looking off into the distance.

Libby spit out her coffee, hearing Nathanial's words combined with the wistful look on his face.

"Nathanial, never stop being yourself. You are truly amazing," Libby finally said, after cleaning herself and the counter off.

"What? What'd I say?" Nathanial said, full of confusion.

· CHAPTER TWENTY ·

Two weeks passed by in an instant. Libby managed to pretend nothing was amiss during her routine meetings with Florence and even feigned dramatic interest in Lake's tour proposal. But behind the scenes, Libby continued to work on her idea. With each passing day, she was more confident that she could turn this idea into a lifelong career path, which was both terrifying and magnificent. Libby talked to Miss Willa and Pixie daily, bouncing ideas off them and getting advice based on their extensive knowledge of the library system and its offerings. The two librarians even connected Libby with librarian friends across the country to get more feedback.

One morning, Libby had just returned inside the library after having a clandestine call with Miss Willa, outside by a tree, to discuss funding streams for her idea, when Pixie spotted her.

"I can only assume with the eighteen layers of clothing you are wearing, you were talking to"—Pixie altered her voice into a barely detectable whisper—"Miss Willa about your new, secret idea, outside amongst your trees," Pixie said, raising her eyebrows like it was their secret code.

As Libby began taking off her layers, she smiled at her friend. "Yes, you would be correct. I can't risk anyone hearing me at the inn or in this library. Unrelated, you have an impressive whisper voice: quiet yet crisp. Viv could take lessons."

Pixie continued whispering. "Ah, one of my lovers can be thanked for that. He was sensitive to sound, so we used to talk dirty in whispers. His favorite was when I would say—"

Libby quickly chimed in, "Uh, another time, maybe? I still have a lot to do." As much as Libby loved listening to Pixie's stories, she was not in the headspace to hear about another one of Pixie's lovers, especially with the level of detail Pixie insisted on providing.

Pixie returned to speaking at her regular volume. "Fair enough. But you look ridiculous, and I think you're scaring some of our patrons away. Plus, you'll be no good to anyone if you die of frostbite," Pixie said, helping Libby take off the next coat.

"I just don't understand. I thought North Carolina was in the south. It's freezing out there," Libby said shakily.

"Look, I know you're still working on getting your bravery badge and sharing your future plans with everyone, but why don't you just work from my office for the time being?" Pixie suggested.

"Really? Oh, that'd save me so much packing every morning," Libby said, grateful.

"Also, I was thinking, you should set up a meeting with Miss Willa and me together. I feel like I've heard everything about her, and it'd be helpful to brainstorm all together," Pixie suggested.

"That's a great idea. Let me see if she is around this afternoon for a quick call." Libby headed back to her favorite spot in the library to continue working.

*   *   *

That afternoon, five minutes into the call with Miss Willa and Pixie, Libby regretted meeting with the two of them together. She had gotten all of three words in before the two went off talking about everything but her idea. After another fifteen minutes of the back and forth, Libby interrupted.

"Hello? Can I just interject for one moment here?" Libby gave Pixie a stern expression when Pixie kept talking.

"Yes, yes, sorry dear. I had no idea you were keeping my very best friend away from me all these months," Miss Willa said from the other line.

After refocusing, the three spent the next hour going through the details of Libby's proposal, talking through the best grants to apply for and other potential funding avenues.

"I really appreciate this. I can't believe how much we got done. This might work," Libby said in near-disbelief.

"Of course it'll work. It's brilliant, and you have two of the world's greatest librarians on your side," Pixie said.

"Pixie, well said. We are fabulous. And so is this idea. Libby, I'm so incredibly proud," Miss Willa added.

"Thank you. Both of you. Well, I'm off to review more edits on my book. Talk to you soon, Miss Willa," Libby said, about to hang up.

"Oh, don't you dare," Pixie said, taking Libby's hand away from the phone. "Miss Willa hasn't heard my Ireland stories, and you know how important they are as a foundation of friendship for me."

"Got it. Well, you two enjoy, and don't cause too much trouble," Libby said as she stood up and walked out, hearing the start of Pixie's great tales of Irish men.

*   *   *

That evening when Libby got back to the inn, she knew right away that something was amiss. The usual calm evening routine of the house was replaced by an unusual level of energy and excitement.

"Finally. We've been wondering when you'd get home. We didn't see you at your usual spot in the library. We've got to get to Florence's in an hour. She said she's got another surprise," Paige said, pulling Libby into the house.

"Oh, okay," Libby said, trying not to lose her balance. "These surprises are getting a little old..." she said to herself.

"What are you mumbling?" Paige asked.

"Nothing, nothing. So uh, what do you know about *this* surprise?" Libby asked.

"Just that we should dress up a bit and be there by 6:30. So come on, we can do much better than this," Paige said, indicating Libby's overly layered outfit.

"I was a little cold today," Libby said defensively.

* * *

An hour later, Libby, Paige, and Nathanial arrived at Florence's house. Before they stepped inside, Lake burst out from the front door, yelling, "Surprise! The writing-career-launching king has arrived."

"Uh oh," Libby said, not liking where this was going.

"He's the surprise?" Nathanial said, slightly disappointed.

"Yeah, you are!" Paige said, running over to give him a hug.

From behind him, Viv came out and said, "Lake, what did we talk about? No referring to yourself as a king. It's unbecoming."

Libby was so excited to see Viv. It'd been weeks since she was in town, and as Paige and Nathanial greeted Lake, Libby went immediately to hug Viv.

"I missed you too, kid," Viv said, hugging her tightly back.

*　*　*

Once everyone was inside, Lake told them he'd finished the first drafts of their songs. Libby's heart sank, as her hopes that he wouldn't work on them for another month and waste his time, crashed and burned.

"Now, I'm open to feedback, but the lyrics are perfect. I made sure to capture the essence of who you are as creative artists while, of course, highlighting the best of me. We haven't recorded them yet, but I'm thinking in the next few weeks I'll have time in the studio. I need to make sure they're ready to go before the tour, in case I decide to whip them out at one of my shows," Lake said, sipping from his glass.

I've never disliked the word "tour" so much.

Florence waved hello as she walked into the room, watching Lake with pride.

"I read them all and I must say, you did an amazing job with these. I think you three will be thrilled.

Now before we get into that, let's have some dinner," Florence said.

"Eat? I can't eat without seeing the lyrics," Paige said loudly.

"That's my girl," Lake said, saluting her.

"I could eat," Libby said, getting an annoyed look from Lake in return.

"Come now, dinner is ready, and I promise the lyrics will be worth the wait," Florence said, drawing the attention away from Libby, whose attempt at being swallowed by the floor was failing.

*   *   *

Throughout the whole dinner, Libby kept thinking how she needed to come clean. She had written the book, the revisions with the editor were right on track, and she'd fleshed out her future career idea as much as she possibly could. She wished Wade were here for moral support, but he'd been called back to Austin for the restaurant he was consulting with.

After dinner was finished, Lake handed them the sheets with their lyrics and told them to take some time to really process the brilliance. Libby chose a quiet corner by the fireplace and read through the words Lake had put together.

She knew the path she'd taken wasn't right
Working late shifts that kept her up all night

Filling her sunlight space with words in between
Writing yet another passionate scene
How do you step away from the only thing
  you've known
When you know it's not right but the right one's
  not shown
The story plays out all typed on her computer
  screen
A master of mystery, the world's secret queen

Her path illuminates, will she take it or choose
  to stay
Keep counting down her life in uninspired days
She knows which way she's got to go
But without the bravery she just can't grow

A loser dude there right by her side
Telling her lies to break her stride
She's seen the way it all plays out
Examples of lost souls with lifelong drought
I'm here watching her falling deeper down the
  hole
The entirety of her life she knows must unroll
Potential requires an endless persistence
Without achieving it she ends up with a sad
  existence

Her path illuminates, will she take it or choose
  to stay

> Keep counting down her life in uninspired days
> She knows which way she's got to go
> But without the bravery she just can't grow

Libby rereads the words a few times over, her mind spinning as she realized he wrote the song about her and not her book. On her fifth reread, Lake came over.

"Perfect, right?" Lake stood proudly rapping the lyrics to himself.

Libby interrupted him. "Um, Lake, quick question. I thought you were writing about the book, my characters, like maybe more murder-focused?" Libby understood the urge for murder in that moment. The last thing she wanted was to be the focus of a famous rapper's new song talking about her inability to grow.

"Thought yours needed something different," Lake replied, oblivious to Libby's hesitation.

"It's just not what I was expecting," Libby finally said, unsure how else to respond.

"That sounds like success to me. My fans are going to love it. The struggle you've had to find your way to being a writer is relatable. I mean, how many people spend their days doing work they hate and dream of finding a way out of that?"

"Oh God. I can't keep this up," Libby said, standing up as her breath got faster and shallower.

"Everything alright?" Florence said, walking over to Libby and Lake, full of concern.

"This is not how I wanted to do this. I'm hot, anyone else feel ungodly hot?" Libby said, the panic rising in her body.

"Do what?" Viv said, drawing the attention of Paige and Nathanial from the other room.

"Why don't you take a moment to breathe, Libby. We aren't going anywhere." Florence walked up to Libby and helped her take a seat on the soft couch away from the heat of the fireplace.

"My words are truly powerful. The effects can be profound," Lake said, to no one in particular.

Everyone gathered around Libby as she attempted to slow her breathing, sipping from the ice water Viv had brought.

"You can tell us anything," Florence said.

"She's dying. I can't believe it, our girl's dying!" Viv said, throwing her hands in the air.

"How? Oh my God, what do you have? Have you investigated all the possible treatment options?" Paige said, before Libby could speak.

"It's always the best ones," Nathanial said sadly.

"I'm not dying. Viv? Where do you get this information?" Libby said, as she watched the room's shoulders drop in unison.

I guess that's a great place to start this conversation from. Only up from dead.

"I've changed my mind about being a full-time writer." Libby looked down on the ground, not wanting to watch anyone's disappointed expressions.

"You *what*?" Lake asked, the shock coming through his voice.

Still looking down, Libby began to explain. "I thought it was all I ever wanted, and this opportunity was a dream come true. But my doubts started early and piled on until it was obvious this wasn't meant for me." Libby finally looked up at Paige and Nathanial. "Not the way it's meant for the two of you. I mean, the way you talk about your futures and writing every moment you can, it's just not the same for me. It's not my path."

Paige and Nathanial wore similar expressions of surprise, but they also looked sympathetic, recognizing the toll this secret had taken on their friend.

Before Libby could say more, Lake stood up, the words pouring out of him.

"This is so predictable, it's ridiculous. It's just like I wrote in that song about you. It takes bravery to walk a new path and you don't have it. You wasted our time." With that, Lake stormed out of the room before anyone could stop him.

Paige was the first to speak, hung up by what Lake had said. "What does he mean by the song he wrote about *you*?"

Libby handed her pages over to Paige, and Nathanial hovered from above, reading through them.

When Libby finally found the courage to look at Florence, she received a polite smile and then Florence got up and left the room.

Viv spoke up. "Damn, Libs. That was unexpected. Throws a wrench in some plans, but are you sure about this? You want to go back to nursing?"

"No, no, not at all. I am not doing that. I have another plan that I wanted to share, but the way this played out, I'm not sure anyone will want to hear it."

"We do," Paige and Nathanial said, coming to sit by Libby.

"I mean, once I process my jealousy that Lake wrote the song about you and not a character in your book," Paige added, smiling.

"Yeah, this is nothing like what he wrote for us. Seems more personal, which I'm guessing contributed to that . . . reaction," Nathanial said, struggling to find the right word to describe the outburst.

Libby appreciated the support from her fellow writers but waited to see how Viv would respond. After the months of getting to know her, Libby had a lot of respect and admiration for the woman and was terrified of losing the relationship.

Viv sat down next to Libby on the couch. "Well, I'm impressed. Lake has you all wrong. You're even more brave than I thought. I mean, this book deal is career gold, and for you to walk away from it and pursue some other path, that's badass and obviously important to you. I've got your back."

"Thank you," Libby said, as tears filled her eyes.

The moment, the emotion, was all so overwhelming that Libby herself needed some space.

"Come on, let's get you home. Give Florence and Lake some time to process." Viv quietly talked to Nathanial and Paige, telling them to get her back to the inn.

* * *

By the time they got there, Libby had dozens of texts from Wade, Brooke, Jane, and her mother. Libby wasn't sure who was responsible for notifying all these people, but the words of support in the texts felt soothing. When they walked inside, a curious Gani and Harrison were waiting.

"They'll explain. I need the bathroom ceiling," Libby said, heading upstairs.

"Careful with your back," Paige yelled after her.

Libby heard Paige start to explain what happened and couldn't help but smile at the dramatic gasps coming out of Harrison.

I've created quite the mess, but at least he's enjoying it.

Libby grabbed the blanket and pillow off her bed and headed to the bathroom floor. She settled in and closed her eyes, focusing on her breath and trying to allow the events of the evening to drift away.

* * *

The next morning, Libby came downstairs, feeling all kinds of guilty. She hadn't received any messages from Florence or Lake and wondered if they were ever going to forgive her for this.

Despite the early hour, Nathanial, Paige, Harrison, and Gani were all gathered in the kitchen. Without saying a word, they signaled for Libby to take a seat and poured her some coffee. Paige hugged her from behind and Nathanial gave his signature thumbs up.

Gani was the first to speak. "We all gathered here because we want you to know, all of us in this room support you no matter what decisions you make on your future.

"And for the record, that doesn't mean those *not* present are unsupportive of your decisions," Gani added, seeing the hesitation on Libby's face.

"Thank you, all. I'm sorry I kept this from you," Libby said.

"That's two things in a short period of time! Any other deep, dark secrets you care to reveal?" Harrison said.

"Ignore my partner here, he's just frustrated at himself for not figuring out your secrets on his own," Gani said, knowingly.

"Well, yes," Harrison said. "That and the fact that I missed the big reveal last night. Oh, it sounded grand. The glowing fireplace in the background, emotions exploding like stars in the night sky, and our lead heroine revealing the secrets in her heart." Harrison danced around the kitchen as he spoke the words.

"Wow, what an interesting description. Maybe you can write a book and replace Libby as the third author," Nathanial said, getting a laugh out of the room.

"I promise, no more secrets," Libby said, realizing for the first time the weight that was off her for having everything in the open.

"You mentioned last night that you had another idea for your future. So, we"—Paige gestured to everyone in the room—"coordinated with Viv and set up a meeting with you and Florence for this afternoon to talk."

"She's willing to talk?" Libby said, full of hope.

"Yes, she's agreed to meet with you," Paige said.

"If I may," Gani interrupted. "It sounds like Florence's reaction was out of character for her. This may have more to do with something other than you not wanting to be an author. She absolutely wants to talk with you."

Libby hadn't thought of that. She figured Florence would be surprised and disappointed, but it was true that her walking out of the room without a word was unlike her.

"What can we do to help you prep for this afternoon?" Nathanial asked.

"Are you all willing to hear my idea? Wouldn't hurt to run it through with some more people," Libby said.

"More? Good Lord, child, what else don't we know?" Harrison said, throwing his arms in the air.

Libby quickly said, "Miss Willa and Pixie may be in on the idea. To be fair, I needed their input with their experience as librarians."

"Intriguing," Paige said.

"Let's hear it," Gani said.

"Alright, give me a moment to grab my things," Libby said, hurrying upstairs to get her computer and the papers she'd prepared.

At 3 p.m. on the dot, Libby arrived at Florence's house. She was grateful for the practice session she'd had, presenting her idea that morning to everyone in the house, but as she stood at the door waiting for someone to answer, the nerves were overwhelming.

The expression Florence wore when she opened the door surprised Libby. Rather than the professional or friendly expressions Libby had come to know, this one was sad, and her eyes looked red like she'd been crying.

"Thank you for coming. Let's take a seat. I have some explaining to do," Florence said.

Hello, parallel universe. Aren't I supposed to be the one doing the explaining?

Libby settled into a soft armchair by the window and Florence took the seat next to her, her entire body looking drained.

"I'm sorry for walking away last night," Florence said kindly.

"You had every right. I disappointed you and I'm ever so sorry, Florence. Everything that you've done for me has meant the world. I wish so badly that this path of being a writer was what I wanted, but it's just not." Libby spoke the words softly but with confidence that she was doing the right thing.

"I want what's best for you. If this isn't it, then that's okay. Truly, I mean that," Florence said.

Continuing on, she said, "When you shared last night, my mind went elsewhere. I haven't told anyone this, and I would greatly appreciate you keeping this between the two of us." Florence looked around, confirming they were alone.

"Of course," Libby said, shocked at the direction this conversation had gone.

"When you were talking about not wanting this opportunity I'd created for you, it brought me back to a moment I've tried to avoid for the past few years. As you know, Noah passed away suddenly after a terrible car accident. Well, the night before the accident, we'd gotten into an argument. And it was just awful.

"He'd told me that he wanted to move to Willowston full-time, open a small diner, and create this whole new life. It caught me completely off guard, him saying he wasn't happy with the life we were living and that he wanted *a different path*.

"With everything going on with Lake and his career, I hadn't even sensed Noah was unhappy. We both said horrible things. I told him he was being

selfish, and I was the ultimate definition of unsupportive." Florence started to cry, her head falling into her
hands.

Libby stood up, grabbed the nearby tissues, and
kneeled in front of Florence, giving her a moment to
cry.

After a while, when Florence's tears started to
subside, Libby spoke tenderly to her. "I'm so sorry
you went through that. And I'm even more sorry you
never got the chance to talk through this potential
huge change with Noah. I know without a doubt, if
life had given you two more time, you would have
found a way to come to a mutual decision and find
happiness for you both."

Florence squeezed Libby's hand. "I suppose you're
right."

Libby thought for a moment and added, "So does
Lake know about that conversation? Is that why he
was so upset?"

Florence chuckled. "No, he just hates when he
doesn't get his way. Just give him a bit of time and
he'll come around. Might draft a brutal song about
your betrayal in the meantime, though."

Libby and Florence laughed together, and Libby
could have collapsed on the floor from the relief.

"Now, I heard you have a new idea on your future.
If you're willing, I'd love to hear it."

Libby sat up proudly and began to explain. "Well,
thanks to the inspiration the new library provided, I

think I may have found a passion project that I'd like to pursue."

Florence raised her eyebrows, listening closely.

Libby took a deep breath and delivered her idea with all her heart. "As you know, the Willowston library is offering more programs in the community than libraries in most larger cities. With these programs, we've gotten a large portion of the community into the library. Because of the loneliness epidemic we are experiencing in this country, getting people into the library and building community and relationships is paramount. I'd like to work with libraries throughout the country to expand their community programs, tailoring them to the needs and interests in each community." Libby took out some papers and handed them over to Florence.

"Now, one place I suggest we start is with adult reading programs. My two favorite librarians, Miss Willa and Pixie, have connected me with dozens of librarians across the country. After speaking with them, it's clear they are struggling to get funding and opportunities for young adults and older adults. The children's programs are where most of their funding is going, which excludes a huge portion of the community. These are just some examples of adult reading programs." Libby showed Florence the various lists she'd created.

"As you can see, I've outlined reading programs for people interested in psychology, environmental sciences, romance, history, functional medicine, and, of course, mysteries." Libby watched Florence process the information.

"So," Florence said, "these are like book clubs in a way, but you've outlined speaker series, linked ongoing community events, and drafted potential local activities related to each topic. Libby, this is great work. You create these programs, engaging the community starting at the library, and then you provide avenues for local groups and events that are ongoing." Florence continued looking through the example programs Libby drafted.

Libby felt relief at Florence's immediate understanding of her idea. "Exactly. The library can be thought of as the hub for the community, and then we leverage all the amazing efforts that the community is already doing and just connect people from there. And this is just a start. I created these example programs based on the library in my hometown, but my idea is that I would work with local librarians and community-engagement specialists in different cities to tailor the programs that create the largest impact."

"This makes a lot of sense, but I know libraries across the country are struggling with funding as is. How are you going to support these efforts?" Florence asked.

"I've identified a dozen grants that could fund a framework like this. I've started the application process for them. Here, take a look." Libby handed

Florence the draft budget and funding sources she'd put together.

"When did you do all of this? Please tell me you didn't get a ghostwriter, or worse, use an artificial intelligence chatbot to write the rest of your book," Florence said, full of worry.

Libby laughed. "No, no, that was all me. Remember, I wrote my last book while balancing my nursing career. This whole idea just gave me a boost to work harder. In fact, I think this may be part of the reason I was able to get the book written."

Florence laughed. "And there I was thinking I was helping you when I lightened your library workload."

Libby's expression became quite serious. "Florence, you've done nothing but help me. If it wasn't for your opportunity, I wouldn't have discovered this idea."

"Well, in that case, good job to me." Florence playfully patted herself on the back. Then, her smile fading, she asked, "Do you still want to write?"

"Actually, I do. I love writing, but not under a strict timeline or as my sole job. I have a couple of ideas, and I see myself writing more books in the future, but nowhere near as many as my friends," Libby said.

"Will you make me a promise?" Florence asked.

"Most likely yes because it's you, but I'd like to hear it first," Libby said.

"Promise me whenever you write a book, you'll let me help you publish it. There's an authenticity with which you write that creates this hopefulness and joy that remains long after I finish your story. I want more people to experience that." Florence spoke with sincerity.

"Really? Of course. Yes!" Libby said, allowing the positive words to soak into her brain.

Take that, bad reviews.

"Deal. Now, is there anything else you'd like to share? Perhaps regarding one of my children?" Florence said, with a subtle smirk on her lips.

"Yes, well, all your children are wonderful, as you obviously know," Libby said, not starting off strongly.

Florence chuckled. "Yes, they are all quite special."

"Right, um, so Wade and I are especially fond of one another." Libby had no idea why she was being so awkward.

"Oh Libby, spit it out already," Florence said.

"We're dating, exclusively, and I adore him," Libby said quickly.

"Ah." Florence leaned back in her seat. "Well, Libby. It sounds like despite your change in career, you and I will continue to see lots of each other, and for that, I'm grateful. Now, tell me more about this idea."

* * *

A few hours later, Libby drove back to the inn, feeling a thousand pounds lighter. Florence was more supportive and encouraging than Libby had expected, and she was grateful Florence had opened up to her about Noah. Libby could only imagine how heavy the burden Florence was carrying because of their argument before he passed.

Harrison burst out the door with Paige, Nathanial, and Gani closely following. "Was it horrible? Does she hold a forever grudge against you? Do we need to pack your bags and send you on your way?" Harrison said dramatically.

"Harrison, for goodness sakes. Give the girl a moment," Gani said, jogging to Libby.

"Come on, let's take a walk," Gani said, guiding Libby to the gardens in the backyard.

Harrison shouted at them, "Really? Not even a hint?" as Paige and Nathanial nudged him back inside.

For a few minutes, Libby and Gani walked side by side, silently taking in the landscape. It reminded Libby of a walking meditation class she'd taken once at a local park back home. After they settled at a bench by the back of the garden, Gani finally spoke.

"Sorry about Harrison's enthusiasm. He's just worried about the conflict. Despite his love of drama, he hates conflict within his close circle. Now tell me, how are you doing?" Gani asked.

"She accepted me," Libby found herself saying, as a few tears escaped her eyes.

"Feels quite nice to be accepted for who we are, doesn't it?" Gani said.

"Yes, it does," Libby replied, as they sat on the bench looking at the gardens.

"Take a few minutes, and then when you're ready, come share the news with everyone." Gani patted Libby on her shoulder and headed inside.

Libby was grateful for the time to sit by herself outside. Gani knew what he was doing when he pulled her away. She was excited to tell everyone the good news, but it felt like she hadn't taken the time to truly process on her own. After a while, Libby took the deepest breath she had in days and made her way inside.

"Finally. Now tell us," Harrison immediately said when Libby walked through the door.

Libby shared all the details of her conversation with Florence, minus the part about Florence and Noah's final conversation. Libby lost track of the number of gasps that came out of Harrison but appreciated the enthusiasm and support of her friends.

Afterward, Libby called Jane and her mother to share the good news. Libby thought she had been anxious about keeping this secret from Florence, but the relief in her mother's and Jane's voices made it clear they were just as worried. She asked her mother to keep the details from her father for now. Libby knew without specific details on the funding, John Autumn would have a meltdown upon hearing his daughter once again wanted a career change and that she was never going back to nursing.

After she got off the phone, Libby knew there was one person left that she needed to talk to.

Libby: I don't know if you're still around Willowston, but I'd love a conversation when you're ready.

Lake: Fine. I'll have my driver pick you up in 30. We're talking in the car, where I do my best thinking, and if I deem necessary, will drop you off in the middle of the road with no service.

Libby sighed. *Not the most mature response,* she thought, *but at least he's willing to talk.*

* * *

Thirty minutes later, Libby climbed into the black SUV to see Lake scowling at her. Libby had to bite her tongue to not start laughing. It wasn't that she didn't take Lake seriously, but knowing that she had the support of Florence, Viv, Brooke, and Wade gave her the courage to take the situation with grace and slight amusement.

"I'm sorry for disappointing you," Libby started off.

Lake crossed his arms like an angry toddler. Libby bit her tongue some more.

"I appreciate every bit of support you've given me, Lake. I just need to listen to my heart on what's right. Because without bravery, I can't grow." Libby knew quoting lyrics from Lake himself would soften him.

"It sounds to me like you're running away. You finally got the chance to be something big, a famous writer, a huge following, and you just want to discard it. How is that brave?" Lake said, maintaining his angry exterior.

"I want to impact people but in a different way than just through my writing," and Libby dove into the details of her tailored reading programs. Lake listened carefully, not interrupting Libby at any point, which itself was alarming. When she finished her explanation, she watched as Lake was deep in thought.

Finally he spoke. "Driver, please pull over."

Uh oh. He's following through with his threat.

Once the driver stopped the car, Lake got out and motioned for Libby to follow. Considering they were nowhere near any building, Libby couldn't understand where Lake was walking with such determination. Finally, he stopped and sat down under a tall tree.

"You made me realize something," Lake said, looking up at the tree.

Libby sat down on the ground next to Lake. "Yeah? What's that?"

"I need more perspective. Need to take a moment and look at things from a different lens. Take this tree. Look how tall it is." Lake pointed up, causing Libby to laugh.

She covered her mouth, attempting to stifle her laugh. "I'm so sorry, but this is the second time we've sat under a tree, and you've been shocked at how tall trees can be."

Lake let out a small laugh. "Yeah, I guess you're right."

After a few moments of silence Lake added, "My dad's accident, he lost control of his car and hit a tree. They think the impact is what killed him. I've hated trees since then . . ." His voice trailed off.

Libby had never known those details of Noah's accident. "Lake, I am ever so sorry. And I've been going on and on about how much I love them." Libby felt the guilt creeping in as she remembered how many conversations she'd had with the Sterling family members about how much she loved trees.

After a moment, Lake replied, "It's okay. Like I said, I needed a new perspective. I'm finding some peace now. In fact, as we sit here, I have no desire to chop this tree down," Lake said, proud of himself.

"That sounds like progress," Libby said kindly.

"Your idea sounds good. I think Dad would have loved it, which is good enough for me. You have my support," Lake said, standing up and reaching his hand out to help Libby.

"Does this mean you'll drive me back to the inn?" Libby said, smiling.

"I couldn't have left you out here, or Wade would've killed me," Lake replied, walking back to the SUV.

When they got to the inn, Wade was outside in the gardens with Gani. As soon as Wade saw the car pull up, he trotted over to help Libby out and immediately drew her into his arms for a kiss. Lake chuckled from his seat and said, "Better not change your idea about that one, Libs, or I'll do a whole album on your idiocy."

CHAPTER TWENTY-TWO

Two months later, on a picturesque spring day, Libby woke up filled with excitement for the official launch of her, Paige's, and Nathanial's second books. After much debate, Florence decided to hold the event at the hotel Libby had first stayed at in Philadelphia. The large suites and luxurious treatment were incredible, but it was nothing like the Mountain Steam Inn that they had come to love back in Willowston. Thankfully, Gani and Harrison were in Philadelphia to attend the party, along with five large suitcases to accommodate all the potential party outfits Harrison was still debating between.

Florence encouraged the three authors to invite as many family members and friends as they wanted, since they had plenty of room thanks to the enormous event space at the hotel. Viv was responsible for helping with travel arrangements, which was how she and Libby's mom became close friends. Libby wasn't sure if she loved this for her mom or if it completely terrified her. However, she was keeping a close eye out for any mysterious tattoos that appeared on her mom's body.

Libby looked out her window at the view of Philadelphia and couldn't believe how much her life had changed in a matter of months. She authored a second book, one she was incredibly proud of; she found who she believed to be the love of her life; and she was pursuing a new path that filled her with passion and energy. Turning back to her room, she marveled at the elegant red gown that she and Brooke had found, now hanging in the closet.

Tonight will be a night to remember.

Libby joined her parents and Jane for breakfast, finding much entertainment at her father's reaction to the luxurious and over-the-top hotel. It was a known fact that John Autumn was conservative when it came to money, and people that were flashy with their wealth were "irresponsible." Betty often joked that was why the universe wasn't sending much money their way, because John would refuse to use it: "Those light fixtures are worth more than our house." "Careful, Betty, if you break that centerpiece vase, we'll have to liquidate all our investments." "Where do these servers keep emerging from and how did they know what you drink? And how much *is* that drink?"

Libby still hadn't told her dad about her proposed plans. Whenever it came up, which was basically during every conversation with him, Libby would deflect, talking about the marketing plan for her two books, or saying she had just renewed her nursing license so she was well-positioned to apply back at the local hospital. Of course, Libby knew being well-positioned and going back to nursing were two completely different things.

When they were finishing up with breakfast, Wade came over to greet everyone, as he'd just flown in from his current consulting gig. Libby had shared her relationship with Wade with her family and even did a weekend trip home with him so they could all meet. The way her parents and Jane connected with Wade made Libby fall even harder for him.

After Wade had said his hellos, he took a seat next to Libby and gave her a look that she always dreamed she would get from a man one day. Filled with love, desire, and hope. Libby looked at his gorgeous brown eyes and for a moment forgot everyone else was there. A not-so-subtle cough from Jane brought Libby back to reality.

"Right, hi," Libby said to no one in particular.

Coming back to the present moment, Libby excitedly said, "Wade, don't you have something you'd like to share with everyone?"

Wade chuckled. "Yes, in fact I do. I have some very good news to share."

Libby glanced at her mother and immediately regretted not telling Wade to be more specific. Betty looked overly excited and stared at her daughter's ring finger. Catching the gaze on her finger, Libby subtly shook her head no, to defuse her mom before things got overly awkward.

Wade cleared his throat. "Well, my restaurant will be officially open for business next month in Willowston, and I would like to extend an invitation for opening night to you all."

"Oh. Not quite where I thought that was going . . ." Betty said, again looking at Libby's ring finger.

Wade smiled, realizing what Betty had been hoping for.

John chimed in, oblivious to the self-perpetuated emotional roller coaster his wife was on. "That's a great accomplishment. Sounds like you've been working hard." Per usual, John resonated with the productivity in others.

John continued, "This means we get a free meal, yes?"

"Dad!" Libby said, horrified.

"Yes, yes, of course. Your dinner is on the house," Wade said, rubbing Libby's back to reassure her he was not offended.

Jane, keeping a completely neutral expression, said, "That's so generous of you, considering it's about $500 for three courses."

John choked for a moment on the water he was drinking. When he finally cleared his throat, he said, "What kind of place is this? Do I need to rent a tux?"

Libby shook her head. "She's messing with you, Dad."

Betty laughed. "Good one, dear. Our Jane is just the absolute funniest." Betty always did like to pretend Jane was her second daughter.

"Now let's get some mimosas to toast to this incredible news. I've heard good news can come in waves," Betty said, a hopeful expression back on her face.

Jane leaned back in her chair laughing, while John looked confused. Libby made a mental note to avoid saying anything about good news to her mom when it came to anything Wade-related.

*   *   *

That evening, Libby walked into the ballroom confident, proud, and beautiful. The gorgeous red gown that elegantly slipped down her shoulders and hugged every curve helped, but the recognition that she'd found a path that resonated for her future is what made her love herself in a way she never did before.

For the next hour, Libby flowed from conversation to conversation, talking to influencers in the book industry, friends old and new, and her favorite two authors, Paige and Nathanial. The excitement they all shared was palpable, and even though Libby wasn't going on Lake's tour, she knew they shared a connection no one else could possibly understand.

After the cocktail hour, Florence walked to the podium to officially announce the release of the three books. Her speech was engaging, sprinkled with humor and emotion, and personalized to each author. Just when Libby thought Florence was finished, she transitioned to talking about the next steps for promotion.

"I am pleased to share that two of our authors will be accompanying my son Lake on the US portion of his tour to promote their books and potentially inspire more music. But one of our authors here today, Libby Autumn, I'm proud to say will be pursuing another path." Florence lifted her hand, directing the attention to Libby, who did her best to maintain steady breathing.

What, what, WHAT? She's doing this now? Here?

The murmuring in the crowd, including some gasps—one of which was Harrison enjoying the drama—demonstrated how surprising and unexpected the news was.

"Now before we have any panicking, Libby Autumn, our talented mystery writer, has promised me she will not give up her writing. But for now, she would like to dedicate her time to improving community strength by enhancing reading programs at local libraries throughout the country. As many of you know, we recently opened a new library in Willowston, North Carolina, in honor of my late husband, Noah Sterling. The success of the various programs in engaging a diverse and substantial portion of the local community inspired Libby to come up with this brilliant idea. Now, I know many of you here tonight are strong proponents of local libraries, and I'm sure our Libby would be happy to talk in more detail about her proposal with any of you tonight that are interested." Florence smiled effortlessly at the crowd as the heads nodded in agreement.

"Better get ready." Libby hadn't realized Lake had come up behind her.

"What do you mean?" Libby whispered, as Florence went on with her speech.

"Mom knows what she's doing, and I have a feeling you'll be pretty busy for the remainder of the evening." Lake winked at Libby and made his way back through the crowd.

After Florence finished her speech and the clapping subsided, Libby looked around for her parents, knowing her dad would have questions. But before she could find them, she was inundated with questions about her library program idea. For the next hour, Libby talked with dozens of people in the publishing industry about her plans for the tailored library reading program. It all started to make sense, the conversations she and Florence had over the past two months regarding her proposal. Libby was prepared for every question and opinion that was posed to her. The feedback was overwhelmingly positive, and to Libby's disbelief, many of them said they were interested in assisting in the funding of her project. With the grant applications only recently submitted, Libby hadn't yet secured any funding, although she felt hopeful about her chances.

When Libby finally had a gap from talking to people about her idea, Florence came over with a knowing smile.

"You looked busy," Florence said.

"You knew all along they would be interested in helping me, didn't you?" Libby said, still in shock.

Florence smiled innocently. "I may have had an inkling. Most of the corporations that these folks work in fund countless community programs, and this brilliant idea of yours fits perfectly with their mission. Now, I don't want you to think I didn't believe in you with those grants, but I figured a little extra funding might help."

"Thank you," Libby said, as her eyes misted.

"I think *we* should all thank *you*. You're going to do a lot of good with that program. Ah, now I see a couple of people dying to talk with you." Florence waved Libby's parents over.

"Oh, my, Libby we are so proud of you!" Betty came over and wrapped Libby into a big hug, bursting with excitement.

"Hard to get a moment with you after that announcement," John said, as Libby tried to decipher his expression.

"Thank you for all you've done for our daughter," Betty said, surprising Florence with a strong hug.

Libby continued to watch her dad, who seemed deep in thought.

"I have to admit, I'm quite surprised. Although, I am happy you aren't going on that rap tour. I can just imagine how rowdy those get," John said, mortifying both Betty and Libby.

Florence kept a friendly expression. "Lake does bring out a lot of passion in the crowds."

Betty laughed awkwardly as she smacked John lightly from behind.

Changing the subject, Betty said, "You know, Florence, I've been wondering, how did you come across my talented daughter's book in the first place?"

Libby was surprised by her mother's question, as she'd never brought it up to Libby before. Libby had never asked the question herself, just assuming Florence had found it with an online search serendipitously.

"It was incredibly random, actually, since *someone* had zero social media or marketing to promote that gem of a novel," Florence said, smiling at Libby as she continued.

"I was on vacation in Tacoma and one morning decided to play pickleball."

As was always the case, John's interest was piqued the moment the word "pickleball" was spoken.

"The friend I was traveling with refused to join me, so the hotel matched me with another group of guests.

They were quite entertaining, the most competitive group of strangers I've ever come across." Florence chuckled, remembering.

"Did you win?" John interrupted, receiving another playful smack from Betty.

Florence smiled. "I did indeed. The person I teamed with was very talented, so it wasn't me alone. Anyway, afterward, we were just talking about what we do, and I brought up my new career as a book agent. The one gentleman, Mr. Simpson, I believe, started talking about his friend's daughter that wrote a mystery book. The man's wife said she just finished it that morning and had it in her gym bag. She asked if I'd want it and I said yes."

Florence went on, as realization came across John's and Betty's faces. "I read it that morning in one sitting and knew immediately I wanted to represent her."

"I'm sorry," Betty said, grinning widely, "but are you saying my husband is the reason you discovered Libby's talent as a writer?" Betty looked like a kid on Christmas morning.

"Oh my God," John said, shaking his head.

"Yes, I believe that's the case." Florence kept a calm demeanor, but it was clear she was enjoying the moment.

"Damn Simpson," John said, still shaking his head. "Libby would still be a nurse living ten minutes from us if it wasn't for his big mouth."

Betty added, "What he means to say is, we have to thank Simpson and his wife for changing our daughter's life in the direction *she* wanted."

Libby took her dad's hand and looked directly in his eyes, more confident than she ever had been when speaking to him.

"I'm grateful for everything you've done to support me and mold me into the independent, strong woman I am today. But Mom's right, I'm happy, and this is what I want to do with my life." Libby saw her dad's eyes start to tear.

"Well…" John coughed, trying to regain his composure.

"Then in that case, I support you," he said, adding, "but not financially. You're on your own for that."

Ah, there he is.

"I know, Dad," Libby said, smiling with relief.

John turned to Florence and said, "For the record, I have much more talent than Simpson when it comes to pickleball."

Florence, with a neutral face, replied, "Oh, I don't doubt it."

With that, she waved a waiter over to pass out glasses of champagne.

Once everyone had a glass, Florence lifted hers and proposed a toast.

"To our Libby, to her future, and to the power of an unexpected connection."

THE END

▪ ABOUT THE AUTHOR ▪

The Unexpected Connection is Catherine Gupta's second novel. The novel was inspired by her passion for community, love of music, and continued journey to find a life that aligns with her heart. Prior to becoming an author, Catherine earned her PhD in pharmaceutical sciences and worked as a researcher, publishing less-entertaining manuscripts. Today, you can find Catherine reading with her daughter, teaching yoga at the local library, and escaping to the nearest nook to write her next novel.